Praise for *California Drean*

"A splendid debut novel—confessional, engaging, honest. I very much look forward to reading more from this writer."

—Lynn Freed, author of *The Romance of Elsewhere*

"In this tender debut novel, Noa Silver takes the reader back in time to one of those magical eras in Berkeley when young people, powered by their own idealism and multigenerational dreams, believed they could change the world. Fast-moving and unflaggingly engaging, *California Dreaming* tells a coming-of-age story that we need more than ever to hold close to our hearts."

—Barbara Quick, author of *What Disappears*

"*California Dreaming* is a spectacular debut, shot through with wit, pathos, and wisdom and teeming with sentences so alive they seem to be reaching out to grab the reader by the lapel. At once a page-turning bildungsroman and an insightful commentary on the Bay Area in the twenty-first century, this book heralds the arrival of a talented writer whose work we're bound to see on our shelves again and again. To read this book is to love it."

—Molly Antopol, author of *The UnAmericans*

"A rich, insightful story about an East Coast transplant attempting to make a life within her own personal myth of California. Full of bittersweet longing, hard-won wisdom, and a pursuit for connection amidst personal and social change, *California Dreaming* is a pitch-perfect portrait of the Bay Area in the midst of the last tech boom."

—Michael David Lukas, author of *The Last Watchman of Old Cairo*

CALIFORNIA DREAMING

CALIFORNIA DREAMING

A Novel

Noa Silver

SHE WRITES PRESS

Published 2024
Printed in the United States of America
Print ISBN: 978-1-64742-660-6
E-ISBN: 978-1-64742-661-3
Library of Congress Control Number: 2023919355

For information, address:
She Writes Press
1569 Solano Ave #546
Berkeley, CA 94707

Interior Design by Kiran Spees

She Writes Press is a division of SparkPoint Studio, LLC.

For my parents

And for Jack

PART 1

Chapter 1

I always imagined the Bay Area as a gathering place for dreamers. Free speech and free love, long hair and long skirts, that place on the map where all those who were running and all those who were searching would stop—one last holdout for those of us who believed that even though the universe was random and moving ever closer toward chaos, something like meaning might still exist. I grew up on the words of Ginsberg and Ferlinghetti, on the tie-dyed memories of tripping acid on Mount Tam, on the aging and graying nostalgia of generations before.

When I got to the Bay in 2011, my mom's copy of Kahlil Gibran's *The Prophet* in my backpack, I started taking the bus around the East Bay. As I rode around Berkeley, I saw signs advertising quick routes to nirvana: LEARN TO MEDITATE! WANT INNER PEACE? JOIN THIS 10-SESSION COURSE. ONLY $1,425. There were yoga studios a dime a dozen, with drop-in prices that ranged from $18 to $25, and countless little shops that all seemed to be named some rendition of "Little Tibet." Buddha statues and prayer flags hung in the windows; batik-patterned dresses sold for $45 each; volumes published by Shambhala Publications stood on the bookshelves. Singing bowls and meditation cushions were on offer everywhere—all the accoutrements needed for your very own meditation room.

Near the university, I'd sit in People's Café, sip Mexican hot chocolate, and read the slogans on the bumper stickers they sold by the counter: SAVE TIBET, FREE PALESTINE, IF YOUR HEART IS IN THE RIGHT PLACE, IT'S ON THE LEFT, I ♥ AHIMSA, and ABOLISH CORPORATE PERSONHOOD. In and out of the café swished Cal students in yoga pants and big, round glasses (the kind I suffered through middle school wearing until my mom finally let me get contact lenses), interviewing for tutoring jobs and grabbing a vegan, gluten-free, cacao nut bar after their most recent donation-based Yoga to the People class.

Early on, I spent one blustery weekend morning going on a walking tour in San Francisco. The tour had a literary bent and began at City Lights Bookstore, mecca for the Beats-inclined. We paused in front of the apartment where Allen Ginsberg had lived, and my fellow tourists and I snapped photos of quotes by Maya Angelou and John Steinbeck painted on the wall outside Vesuvio Café.

Our tour guide pointed out that San Francisco was the perfect place for the literary and cultural revolution inspired by the Beat poets—the San Francisco Poetry Renaissance. The same buildings in which *Howl* was composed and Jack Kerouac and Neal Cassady drank and dreamed up a new vision of literary America, a hundred years earlier had housed brothels and speakeasies to entertain the gold rushers, traders, and merchants from across the seas. There was a certain lawlessness that characterized San Francisco, a lawlessness that was connected to vision, to imagination, to the desire—and the tenacity—to live outside the constraints of the times.

"Think of this city in terms of layers," said our guide, "of one generation after another living and dreaming and drinking on top of the other in these same apartments, these same cafés, these same streets. Each layer sets the stage for the next. The current example of San

Francisco's revolutionary vision is Silicon Valley," he said. "Aren't we in a kind of modern-day gold rush? A technological renaissance? Our generation's attempts to refashion, remodel, re-envision what is possible?"

At the time, I mostly paid attention to the points about the Beat generation. I roamed through City Lights at the end of the tour, flipping open Kerouac's *On the Road* and Frank O'Hara's *Lunch Poems*; I copied down inspirational quotes in my notebook, circling and starring my favorites from Kerouac a dozen times.

Chapter 2

I came to the Bay as a Teach for America (TFA) teacher, and in those last days of summer after the TFA boot camp had ended and before the first day of school, I'd hole up in the back of People's and read Audre Lorde and think about biomythography, about the ways that writers blend myth and history in narrative. In between chapters, I'd flip through the book of Adrienne Rich poems I'd bought (*A Wild Patience Has Taken Me This Far*) and dream up lesson plans for English language arts that would help students understand the way words could mimic the sound of a bell chiming. Words like "*cer*tainty," or "*lov*ingly," where the emphasis is on the first syllable, and the second two syllables reverberate, and then drift off into quiet.

My TFA placement was at a middle school in Fruitvale. Bright pastels painted the sidewalks; street vendors stood at the corners selling fruit and vegetables, little bags of popcorn, and spice-crusted nuts. The houses seemed to shrink into themselves: the roofs and walls sagged slightly, as though there had been too much rain and the houses had started to slouch over. Although, when I started teaching in 2011, California was in the midst of a drought that has continued for most of the years I've lived here. Signs were in Spanish and English, or just in Spanish, and at the middle school where I taught for two years—Bright Star Academy (BSA)—96 percent of the student body was Latino, many of them first-generation American, and others immigrants themselves. The other 4 percent was either Black or from the Pacific Islands. The only white people were among the teachers—a fact that took me years to recognize as problematic.

BSA is a charter school with a mission to prepare first-generation and immigrant students, most of whom did not speak English at home, to succeed, and even excel, in high school and beyond. The year I started teaching, the first professional development training scheduled was on how to incorporate the principles of restorative justice into the classroom. I had a feeling of *Yes, this was why I came to the Bay.* To be around vegetarians and teachers, yoga practitioners and abortion advocates; to be where people built their careers around mission statements rather than bank statements; to get to teach poetry in the way that I believed in it—as a lifeline.

A couple of weeks before school started, the teachers went on an overnight trip together. We drove up to Ukiah, a few hours north of Berkeley, into the golden grasses of the California hills, and bunked down in a rented farmhouse. On the drive, the principal, Jay, asked me what books I'd been reading to prepare for my first year of teaching, and I told him about Parker Palmer's *The Courage to Teach*, and Frank McCourt's *Teacher Man*, and Paulo Freire's *Pedagogy of the Oppressed*. They were books rich in ideas, in stories, in the pursuit of a grand ideal, and I was giddy on theory, on sentiment, on the notion of teaching as a calling.

Jay nodded and someone in the back of the car coughed, and then he said, "Write this down. These are the things you need to read: *Teach Like a Champion, Understanding by Design*, and *Why Are All the Black Kids Sitting Together in the Cafeteria?* Got it? These books will teach you how to make lesson plans, how to structure your classroom, how to set expectations. They'll make you think about the realities of the day-to-day, and how to understand your own positionality."

I wrote the names of the books down, but I got lost somewhere between setting expectations and positionality—a concept I had never heard of before.

We all gathered around the campfire that evening, holding plates piled high with spaghetti and tomato sauce seasoned heavily with garlic. There were maybe twenty of us, not counting a few others who hadn't been able to come on the trip. We crouched together on haystacks that had been haphazardly thrown together in a circle around the firepit. While we had spent the afternoon setting up the space, assigning teams to cook and clean—I was on dish duty that evening—and meeting in small groups based on the subjects we'd be teaching, this was the first time we were all gathered together. I imagine this was why Jay asked us to take a few minutes to introduce ourselves. The prompt, though, was unlike any name game I'd ever played, and I was caught off guard when Jay asked us, "Which of your tattoos is your favorite, and why?"

Nobody else seemed fazed by this, though there were a few titters around the fire, and I saw at least one of my fellow teachers pull her shirt away from her chest and look down with a smile. It didn't seem like there was even an option to be sans tattoo, but after the snickers had subsided, Jay offered, as an afterthought, "And if you don't have a tattoo, why not?"

We started going around the circle, each one saying their name and where they were from, what subject they taught, how long they'd been teaching, and then, of course, their favorite tattoo. I had been sure that someone else would also be tattoo-free, but by the time the metaphoric conch shell arrived at me, there hadn't been a single one.

"I'm Elena, Elena Berg," I said, and wondered if there was any tomato sauce on my chin or around my lips. "Uh, so I'm a TFA teacher, and I'll be teaching seventh- and eighth-grade ELA. Um, I'm from the East Coast, from New England. And this'll be my first year teaching."

It was time to disclose both the fact of and the reason for my being tattoo-less, and as I looked around the circle at the faces glowing gold in the firelight, I thought about my grandparents back in Brooklyn. My grandfather, Nathan, and my grandmother, Sadie, both tiny in stature, with white curls haloing their crinkled red faces, sometimes looked more like brother and sister than husband and wife. They, apart from my mom, were my only family. They'd had no other children besides my mom and each of them was the only surviving member of their immediate families. I wanted them to do one of those genetic testing programs like 23andMe to find out if there were cousins or second cousins or second cousins once removed who had survived, maybe emigrated. I had visions of an entire shtetl's worth of family waiting for us out there, but my grandparents would just chuck me under the chin and say, "You and your mama are all we need, *bubbeleh*."

I thought about the blue numbers tattooed onto their arms, on the underside of their wrists, and how even as the years had brought on new wrinkles and folds of fat, the numbers themselves had not faded or disappeared. I thought about telling these glowing faces— my new teacher colleagues—about the weight that tattoos have in my family, how not even my mom, in her rebellious years of getting high and having threesomes, had ventured to mark her skin. I thought about adding that cremation was also out of the question for me, even though I thought it was more ecologically sound than being buried in the ground. I thought about saying that I wasn't religious, never had been, that my grandparents weren't either, but that we had turned our trauma into something sacred, and to go against it would feel sacrilegious.

But I didn't say any of that. Instead, I said, while staring down at my plate of spaghetti growing cold, "Yeah, so I don't have a tattoo. I guess just because I haven't found the right one yet, you know?"

Later that evening, while washing dishes alongside Henrietta, a social studies teacher with fifteen years of experience under her belt, I started talking about my mother, how she had come out to California in the sixties and was now a professor of history.

"When did your mom start teaching?" Henrietta asked.

"After she left California," I said. "She was political, protesting, but left when things got a little . . . hot. She was disillusioned; things weren't working out here."

"She went back to school?"

"Yeah. Studied history. She had some revelation about the fact that only certain stories get taught, that whole other narratives are silenced."

"Is that why you want to teach, too?"

I slid a soap-sudded plate into a plastic basin of warm, gray water, rinsing off the remnants of spaghetti sauce.

"I guess so," I said. "I want to teach kids that their voices—and stories—are important."

Henrietta nodded.

"What about you?" I asked.

She laughed. "Well, some days it can feel like you spend most of the time telling them to take out their headphones and actually open their books."

"I remember this one time in kindergarten I got in trouble for using the wrong color crayon," I said.

"What do you mean, the wrong color?"

"We were supposed to make 'realistic art,' or something like that," I said. "So, I drew a family—you know, parents, kids, the sun in the corner."

"House in the background with the chimney poking up?"

"Probably a flower or two, as well."

"Weird. How did your drawing get on my refrigerator?" Henrietta said with a smile, sponging the last remaining camping mugs.

"So, I pulled out a crayon that I thought was black and started coloring in the people's faces."

"You got in trouble for using a black crayon?"

"No, no," I said, "it turned out that the crayon wasn't black at all; it was purple."

"No purple people allowed."

"Exactly. I got in trouble."

"Oh dear."

"When I went home that day and told my mom, though, she was livid. She wrote a letter to the school."

"What did it say?"

"She went on and on about how we use color in expressions to describe our emotions—you know, 'tickled pink' and 'green with envy' and 'seeing red.'"

"Nice."

"She said realism was overrated."

"She sounds like a force to be reckoned with."

"And she said it was a teacher's job to encourage creativity in students, not to criticize them for artistic exploration."

"And is that what you're hoping to achieve?" Henrietta asked. "You want them to be creative? To explore?"

"I want them to be transformed, you know? The way I feel when I read great poetry."

"And do you have a sense of how you want to create your classroom norms? How to set up a dynamic between you and the students to really allow for transformation?"

"You mean like what rules I want to establish? Needing to ask to go the bathroom or whatever? I'm not really into that. I believe that if they think that the rules are wrong, for example, then they shouldn't follow them."

My fellow TFAers and I had spent the summer repeating these ideas over cheap cups of coffee late at night, as we scrambled to write lesson plans for the following day's mock classroom run.

Henrietta nodded and looked at me, her hands red from dishwashing. "Here's the question, though," she said. "How do you expect to actually get through to them, to encourage transformation and exploration, if they don't, for example, want to read the poems you choose? How are you going to get them to buy in to your vision?"

Chapter 3

"I want to work in women's health," said Monica, a friend of a friend from back home. When Monica and I met for the first time, we walked along the Berkeley Marina. By the end of that walk, we decided to sign a lease together. When I met her, Monica had shoulder-length, dark, wavy hair that (over the course of the year living together) would gradually disappear into a tightly cropped pixie. A surprising number of freckles dotted the pale skin over her cheekbones and sharp nose.

"I watched this documentary in college, *Jane: An Abortion Service*, about this underground collective that would set up abortions for women in Chicago. You know, before it was legal? But then I started reading about how even though technically it *is* legal today, actually the states can—and do—make all these extra types of restrictions around getting one *and* that Planned Parenthood might lose government funding. Anyway, what are you going to do here?"

"I'm a teacher," I said, and realized it was the first time I'd said I *am* a teacher, rather than I *want* to be, or I'm *going* to be. I would be the third-generation teacher in my family—my mom and her father had both been teachers. My grandfather grew up in Eastern Europe, the first son of a tailor, and became a teacher when he and my grandmother moved to New York after the war.

"I'm doing TFA and I'm going to be teaching English to seventh and eighth graders," I continued. "I want them to be able to write well, you know? To have their voices heard. And I want them to read things that will blow their minds open."

"Yes!" Monica said, grabbing my arm. "This is exactly why I wanted to move out here. To be around people who want to do things like this. Not like all my I-banking and consulting friends back home."

I had those friends too, and so I laughed and nodded, and we linked arms as we watched the sun start to set over the bay. The light dipped, glinting off the houseboats and yachts that lived permanently in the marina. Cyclists started to turn for home, and parents corralled their children into the back seats, their little faces sticky from ice cream and popsicles. Frisbees and kites were collected and stuffed into the trunks of cars. While Berkeley's families packed up for the night, Monica and I made plans to stock our future kitchen with huge mason jars filled with grains and dried beans, every different kind of nondairy milk—to find the one we liked the most—and a compost bin (it would take me several years of living in the Bay to finally figure out that the best place for compost—if you don't want a plague of fruit flies—is in the freezer).

Monica and I moved into our apartment the Saturday before the first day of school. The apartment had orange walls and gray carpet, south-facing windows, and a washer and dryer. I paid $700 a month for my room, and we could pick as many Meyer lemons as we could carry from the tree in the backyard.

We spent the weekend hauling suitcases up the stairs and navigating the tight corners as we tried to wedge an old couch Monica had inherited into the living room. We drove to Urban Ore—a warehouse one step up from a junkyard—and wandered between the stacks of unhinged doors and rickety upright pianos and Persian rug knockoffs that had seen better days. We contemplated buying one of the doors and laying it across bricks or cinder blocks to create a makeshift coffee table. I found a matching bookshelf and dresser and we decided to buy a round, chestnut-brown table and six mismatched chairs for our kitchen, reasoning that the lack of uniformity among the chairs was itself a type of style, one that we, still in our early twenties, could certainly get away with. I bought a $99 mattress on sale at Mattress Firm, hyperventilating at the price (having never purchased a mattress before), and then went with Monica to Earthsake, an organic mattress store on Fourth Street, where she bought a queen mattress with a bed frame. We set up a shopping rotation, a weekly budget, and a list of items we should always have—coconut oil, Himalayan salt, avocados (no matter the season), organic yogurt, almond butter. I took the room in the back, overlooking the garden, while Monica took the room in the front, overlooking the street, but with the bigger windows. We agreed to use only environmentally friendly cleaning products.

I spent the night before the first day of school sprawled on the living room floor, construction paper and scissors and stickers and string and the books of poetry from my college seminars strewn around me. The first day would be mostly administrative, Jay had told me, with students writing their names on binders and notebooks and getting their seat assignments, but I should plan some kind of get-to-know-you activity for each of my classes, he advised. I'd be teaching two seventh- and two eighth-grade ELA classes, along with supervising a homeroom and a study hall.

"So, what are you going to do with them tomorrow?" Monica asked from the couch, sipping the rooibos chai tea her mother had sent us in bulk as a housewarming gift.

"This is going to be great," I said, as I carefully copied out lines from my favorite poems onto red, yellow, and green sheets of construction paper. "I'm going to put all these lines and stanzas on desks and around the classroom and have the kids walk around until they find one they resonate with, and then they can sit down. Then we'll go around, and everyone can say their name, you know, and then read the line and talk about why they chose it."

"Oh, that's awesome! What lines do you have so far?"

"'The Brain—is wider than the Sky—,' 'Things fall apart; the centre cannot hold;' 'Do I dare / Disturb the universe?' 'Tell me, what is it you plan to do with your one wild and precious life?'"

"I love that last one."

"It's Mary Oliver."

In the morning I showered and took BART from Ashby to Fruitvale. I didn't eat breakfast. I hadn't eaten breakfast for most of high school or college because—other than freshman year when I stupidly signed up for Intermediate Spanish, which met five days a week from 9:00 to 10:00 a.m.—I hadn't been awake early enough for breakfast. I did, however, pack a lunch of quinoa, sautéed kale, and nutritional yeast, three things I'd never heard of before moving to the Bay.

The walls of the school's hallways were still lined with the posters and student work from the previous year. Along brightly colored, construction-papered walls, book reports on *The House on Mango Street* were stapled next to biographies of Cesar Chavez and Rosa Parks. This was nothing like the public middle school I had attended back East, where we read *The Hobbit* in sixth grade and *The Pearl* in seventh, and were taught that racism, along with slavery, had ended well over a century ago.

We were supposed to meet the kids in the cafeteria and then take them to our classrooms. The cafeteria, it turned out, was sort of a catchall Room of Requirement. There was a whiteboard on the wall, a photocopier in the corner, boxes of old textbooks and gray plastic tables with attached stools folded upright against the back wall, ready to be pulled down for the lunchtime rush. There was a reception desk with two teachers sitting behind it, greeting students as they walked in and sending them off to their designated homeroom corners.

I could tell what grades the kids were in because the sixth-grade boys were all about eye level to my chest and many of the eighth-grade boys stood a head or two above me. Some had the beginnings of stubble on their chins and the shadow of a moustache playing above their mouths. The girls smelled of hairspray and chewing gum. Some—the gangly ones in big glasses with skinned knees standing off to the side with just one friend or two, or with their noses in a book—reminded me of myself in middle school: all limbs and four eyes and not a hint of breasts. Others seemed to have newly launched into puberty over the summer, and quite a few had arrived at school with thickly mascaraed lashes and painted lips.

I was directed over to my homeroom corner of seventh graders. They barely looked up as I approached, and as I tried to come up with something cool and witty and profound to say, something that would immediately inspire both respect and camaraderie between us all, I saw some of the other teachers organizing their classes into neat, quiet lines. At the time I thought to myself, *How antiquated, how disciplinarian.* It called to mind the lines I had stood in, in the cold New England winters on the playground when I was in kindergarten and first grade. That wasn't the type of teacher I wanted to be for these kids. I wanted to create a classroom culture based on personal connection and a deep love of learning—not rules and consequences.

Jay found me in the cafeteria.

"How're you feeling, Ms. Berg? Or, Elena? What do you want the kids to call you?"

"Oh," I said, "I'm fine. I'm good! I'm excited," although I could already feel the sweat pooling in my armpits, "and, Elena, I think. Right?"

"Well, Elena, I'm afraid we've had a bit of a snafu, here."

"What do you mean?"

"I thought we were going to have this figured out by today, but unfortunately it seems as though we don't have a classroom for you yet."

"I'm sorry, what?"

"Many of our teachers share classrooms, actually, and we make do, you know, with a rotation schedule, which mostly works out just fine."

"Mostly?"

"But it seems we haven't—we weren't quite able to figure it out so that you'd be in the rotation schedule—at least not for the first quarter, though I hope by the next, or at least by midyear, we'll have this all sorted out."

"So, wait, what am I supposed to do now? Where am I going to teach?"

"Yes, yes. Well, I've thought about that, and I've come up with something. It's not perfect, but I think it'll do. You can set up here, in the cafeteria. It might get a bit confusing during the lunch blocks—you know, the kids have lunch at different times—but it's a big enough space that you can hold your classes in the corner, I think, and it won't be too rowdy. Now then, how does that sound?"

"Well, okay, I mean, I guess, sure. But where can I put all my stuff? All my supplies and things?"

"Not to worry," Jay said, patting me on the shoulder. "We'll get you a cart!"

The thing about standing in front of twenty-five twelve- and thirteen-year-olds is that you start to realize that just because you're excited about the way that "The Love Song of J. Alfred Prufrock" begins with a simile that juxtaposes the expansiveness of the "sky" with the limits of a "table," linking both infinity and finitude in a single phrase—which is just what a human being is, you believe: infinite potential contained within a finite being—doesn't automatically mean that your students will be.

By the end of that first day, my glittered and stickered lines of poetry had been ripped and crumpled, accidentally tossed in the trash, and stained from sticky fingers and lunchtime spills. My get-to-know-you exercise had been duly acted out by the kids, mostly politely, though with some resistance along the way, and to my great surprise and disappointment had elicited no visible soul movement. I had met almost 150 individual students and, in a group, found that my voice didn't project as much as it needed to. I figured I had an approximately one-week grace period to learn all their names, and in the meantime I needed to come up with fifty-five minutes' worth of activities several times over for tomorrow. And the next day.

At the sound of the final bell, I ducked out along with the students and dragged myself home. I felt the way I used to feel at the end of a school day when I was in middle school or high school—utterly spent and totally uninterested in doing any of the work I had been assigned. At home I crawled straight into bed, ignoring Monica's cry of "How was it?" from her bedroom.

Chapter 4

When I was ten, my mom took me on a road trip to upstate New York to meet a friend of hers she hadn't seen in thirty-odd years, someone she'd known back in California in the late sixties. As we drove up the endless highway, tuning the radio station to the "Golden Oldies," my mom took a look at me and, I guess, decided I was ready to inherit her mythologies. She started telling me the stories of her twenties, that unmoored, tripped-out decade between childhood and adulthood, after she'd finished being the kid I'd heard about—the one who spent hours practicing how to draw horses—and before she'd become the adult I knew—the slightly awkward history professor who read thousand-page books and could make only one thing for dinner: tacos.

My mom graduated from high school in the late 1960s. In the years afterward she was living in Manhattan, working in a record store on Second Avenue and getting deeper into the drug scene of the times. Crowded basements filled with bodies sprawled over sofa backs, unsettled hands reaching out to the hallucinations wandering before their eyes. She was doing all kinds of things—pot, hashish, cocaine, LSD, mescaline, opium. The only time she put a needle into her veins was when she took amphetamines. Anything to soar, body and mind, away from the confines of the stilted, embarrassed interactions most people were having with each other and into the fierce, defiant openness where colors and gravity merged.

In 1969 she hooked up with a couple of guys who'd bought a van and intended to drive it out to California. They took turns driving day and night until the transmission went out somewhere along the detour they took up in Washington. They stopped to work for a while picking apples and then hitched the rest of the way to Berkeley.

Back then, my mom told me, Berkeley really was a town that had opened its doors to the misfits, the seekers, those craving love and finding weed, rich and poor alike, all dressing up as believers and holding out for something greater. Maybe because Berkeley was so close to the Pacific Ocean, it had the feel of being at the end of a long, winding trail, a collecting point for all those too tired to keep walking. My mom stumbled into the foggy streets and pretty quickly linked up with an old friend from New York. He was living in the Weathermen collective, so she ended up there too. It wasn't much more complicated than that, though it got plenty complicated later on. She didn't have anywhere else to go, and those guys offered a bed, food, and a creed she didn't have to think too much about to take hold of. It fed right into her lonely, raw anger, and pretty soon she was about as deep in as you can get.

Weathermen, though, didn't exactly sound like the sweetest deal you could ask for. Its whole mission was to eliminate anything that smacked of bourgeois sensibilities, and that included things like classical music and monogamy. My mom would sometimes sneak off to the library to listen to recordings of the classical music of her childhood. Strands of melodies still tugged at her through the haze of antiwar politics and the drug-clouded nights of hallucinations that bridged the gap between waking and dreaming. If she had been caught, she would have had to go through a "reeducation process" not unlike those of the Soviet Union—intensive interrogations with no sleep for days. They used to post weekly charts on the wall assigning each of them sex partners throughout the week, to ensure that nobody would be monogamous.

She walked into a supermarket once, starving and broke, and stuck a whole chicken down her pants. As she was heading out the door, she grabbed a bottle of Coke as an afterthought and shoved it under her ragged T-shirt. She didn't get more than a hairbreadth outside before a burly and bleary-eyed security guard stopped her. He didn't say anything, just put his hand out as she handed over the bottle of Coke. He shook his head at her like she had disappointed him deeply and said, "All that, kid, for a bottle of Coke?" She murmured an apology and slipped out; the chicken was still squeezed somewhere beneath her left butt cheek.

By this point, she told me, her sense of anything real and meaningful had shrunk down to the size of a peanut, and whether it was wedged somewhere deep inside or not, she just didn't seem to care much about her loneliness and the nagging ache that sat with her at all times unless she got really high. And she did that plenty. But even that wasn't doing it for her quite the way it had been, and making love had all sorts of hidden pains to it, so she turned herself outward, toward everyone else's sorrows, and took up their fights like some goddamned martyr.

Many of the collectives around the country were planning small bomb blasts, set to go off in the middle of the night in banks and military induction centers. Soon, they were all scrambling around with bomb parts trying to fashion something that would make the country sit up and listen to them. On the day itself everyone had different assignments. Some were putting bombs in place, while others were spray-painting "Purple Star Gang" on sidewalks and brick walls.

My mom was sitting on the corner making out with someone. She was the "lookout." In the end, though the bombs didn't go off at all, my mom was still tear-gassed and cuffed along with the rest of the ragtag group of lonely twentysomethings turned domestic terrorists.

Chapter 5

After school started, I went back to People's Café on the weekends to grade student work and plan my lessons, and so in early September, it was from People's that I watched the Occupy movement begin. Tents popped up along the street corners and outside the Bank of America; clumps of people huddled together along the sidewalk. I read *New York Times* articles about the Arab Spring and scrolled through my Facebook feed looking at pictures of young Tel Avivians camping out on Rothschild Boulevard and the thousands of protesters taking over New York's Zuccotti Park. Though I wasn't quite bold enough to take a tent myself and pitch it on the sidewalk, the fact of it happening around me was thrilling. *Finally, I get to be part of something*, I thought, some social justice movement that involved marching and singing and sign-holding.

In college I danced in the streets along with everyone else when Obama won. We did the Electric Slide, took shots, and got the cars to honk right along with us all through the night. And the next day I went back to class with a general feeling of *job well done, the world has righted, progress is real*. I read articles lauding my generation for its brand of political activism—going to the polls, convincing our parents to vote—and generally claiming that the era of Woodstock and Weatherman was well and truly over. I resigned myself to the idea that I had missed out on the time when "fighting for a cause" meant "taking to the streets."

But when I saw the tents on Shattuck and the handwritten signs in blue Sharpie saying, WE ARE THE 99%, I thought maybe my time had come. On a Saturday that fall I joined up with one of the big marches headed toward downtown Oakland and city hall; I wondered briefly what would happen if my students saw me pumping my fist and chanting out slogans but relaxed when I saw most of my fellow teachers marching in the crowd. We ambled our way down Broadway and called out "Banks got bailed out! We got sold out!" over and over again. I looked around and saw kids sitting on shoulders, people posing for selfies with their signs, a man wearing an orange wig and walking on stilts. Public libraries and green-juice sellers had set up tables and stands all along the route and were handing out flyers and sign-up sheets and little cups of liquefied grass.

It was at that march that I met Kyle. He was tall and lanky with loose red curls. Kyle and I ended up walking in step with each other for most of the rest of the march. That day he was wearing a light blue T-shirt under a checkered flannel shirt, and reddish-blond stubble lined his jaw. A green backpack with a silver water bottle poking up out of the corner pocket was slung over his left shoulder, and instead of a watch, a few bracelets of multicolored thread hung loosely on his wrists.

He carried a sign that read INVEST IN THE EARTH, NOT WALL STREET! We jostled into each other early on.

"Sorry," I said.

"Nothing for you to be sorry about," he said, and we smiled, then continued on our way, chanting and clapping as we went.

But somehow, every few steps or so, we'd be back in pace with each other.

"You again," he said, as I bumped into him while we were rounding Lake Merritt.

"Sorry," I said again, shading my eyes.

He laughed and I was caught somewhere in between the freckles and the crystal-blue eyes.

"Seems like we're in this thing together," he said. "Grab a corner."

He offered me a side of his sign and I took hold of the white butcher paper with my clammy hands as we wandered the rest of the way to the steps of city hall. Every now and again I'd turn my head sideways and up to look at Kyle's profile and would wish I had worn my hair down, instead of pulled up and back into a messy—and, if we're honest, greasy—bun. We didn't speak that much for the rest of the march, except to point out signs and slogans we saw in the crowd.

"Look at that one over there: IF ONLY THE WAR ON POVERTY WAS A REAL WAR, THEN WE WOULD ACTUALLY BE PUTTING MONEY INTO IT."

"Or how about that one? LOST MY JOB, FOUND AN OCCUPATION."

"See that little girl on that guy's shoulders over there? Hers says: SORRY FOR THE INCONVENIENCE; WE ARE TRYING TO CHANGE THE WORLD."

"Or that one! THIS SIGN WOULD BE MORE CREATIVE BUT YOU'VE STOPPED FUNDING THE ARTS."

By the time we'd reached city hall, the hot autumn sun of the Bay was blazing down, and we were almost at the back of the crowd. We arrived in the middle of the speeches and rallying cries and stood jammed together between other sweaty and hoarse protesters. Kyle pulled out his water bottle and offered it to me.

"Thanks," I said, taking a swig.

"Protest rookie?" he asked, smiling, as I returned the bottle.

"Is it that obvious?" I said, and then, with some hesitation, continued, "I'm Elena, by the way."

"Kyle," he said, and we shook hands for a second or two longer than might have been expected. "Nice to meet you. Nice to march with you."

"Yeah."

The speeches and calls to action were lost in the maze of marchers ready for lunch and coffee and the plans rumbling around us to go play basketball or skip out now to beat the rush on BART. There's an awkward moment at the end of a march when the momentum no longer has anywhere to go, when it has arrived at the steps or the artificial endpoint, and for those not camping out, a type of restless aimlessness settles in. We start shifting our feet, turning our heads to see if anything else is going to happen, or perhaps to see if we might recognize someone. At that first march of mine, the awkwardness came upon me in a rush, and I was torn by my desire to come up with more to say to Kyle, something to draw out the moment, and the already familiar anxiety that would sneak up on me halfway through the weekend when I realized that Monday was coming and I needed a lesson plan, needed a SWBAT ("Students-Will-Be-Able-To") statement.

We stood in place for a few minutes, each of us glancing around through the crowd. Finally, I coughed, made a few "um" sounds, and then mumbled, "Well, I guess I gotta go, uh, plan my lessons."

"Oh yeah? All right. Are you a teacher?"

"Yeah. Yeah. First year. Don't really know what I'm doing."

I let go of my corner of Kyle's sign and shifted my bag to the other shoulder. "Anyway, so, yeah. Thanks for the, I mean, nice to, you know, march together."

Kyle laughed again, and I think I smiled too, and just as I was about to push my way through the throng, silently berating myself for not having the guts to ask him for his number, or at least his full name so I could stalk him on Facebook, Kyle said, "Well, hey, are you going back that way? To BART? Me too. I locked my bike up there. I'll walk with you."

"Oh, sure, yeah, great."

"Since we seem to be good at walking together and all."

We made our way back along the route we'd just walked, marchers and protesters transforming back into their regular selves, texting on phones, filling their kids' mouths with Cheerios and cheesy puffs.

"So, you're a teacher, then?" Kyle asked. "What do you teach? And where?"

"ELA," I said, "I mean, English. And to middle schoolers in Fruitvale."

"Teach for America?"

"Yeah," I said, "how'd you know?"

Kyle shrugged and laughed. "First-year teacher in Oakland? High probability."

"All right, then. What about you? What do you do?"

"I work at a community urban farm in West Oakland."

"Hence the sign," I said, pointing at the now rolled-up sign under his arm.

"Yeah," he said, "exactly."

At the Twelfth Street BART station, we stood at the steps and again shifted slightly on our feet, a different type of awkwardness having come over us now. But just as I started to say goodbye, turning toward the underground, Kyle took out his phone and handed it to me, saying, "Maybe you can give me your number? You know, just in case I ever have any questions about grammar or something."

Chapter 6

O n the day of our first date, San Francisco was experiencing one of its blue-skied, warm afternoons in late September, and the narrow, multicolored, pointy-roofed homes were drenched in a gentle glow. I walked toward the water; we were meeting at the Ferry Building and then making our way to a hole-in-the-wall Chinese restaurant that Kyle knew. Although now my association with Market Street is equal parts bougieness and homelessness, I remember that day in the late afternoon that San Francisco was in fine form.

The trees that lined the streets were still in full bloom and the tram lines hinted at bygone days. The promise of the ocean is always in the air in San Francisco, and with it comes the glory of a port city—tightly packed, people in every corner and square, lining up outside Blue Bottle Coffee, kids with painted faces and crowds gathered around street drummers and dancers and saxophone players. Amazon had not yet killed off every small bookstore, and there were books lined up on racks or piled inside boxes with hastily drawn signs that read 3 FOR $2 outside storefronts. Even when, as on most days, you can't see the bridges or the hills of Marin because of the fog, there's the idea of mountains, and distance, and the feeling of being at the edge of it all. That day, an unofficial street market had sprung up in front of the Ferry Building—twisted silver necklaces and green beads and red and orange threads woven together were displayed on folding tables and chairs and blankets laid out on the ground. Skaters were whizzing around the plaza in front of the Ferry Building, and artists had laid their sketches and paintings out in full view. Inside I sampled Cowgirl Creamery cheese and slices of ripe plums.

That day, I didn't see the needles on the ground or the sleeping bags stretched out in doorways and in the BART station. I am still trying to figure out whether it is San Francisco or me that has changed the most in the years since. The BART station, I have come to understand, turns into something quite different at night—a hostel, a bathroom, a sick house, a drug den. In the mornings, we sometimes see the ghosts of the nighttime inhabitants of BART—the men curled up into the fetal position on the floor, wrapped in dirty duvets, beards untended, belts unbuckled; or the women in long, colorful skirts, babies hung in a sling around their midsection, nursing at the breast, holding a cardboard sign that reads: No Job, Two Kids, Please Help. There are others, too, more shocking, or more sad: women with no shoes or trousers; men with no socks or coat; couples with sagging cheeks and blank stares; older white men with wrinkles carved into their faces like marble veining; younger Black and Brown women talking to the air, the universe, God, shouting frantically, moving their limbs unwittingly and unknowingly. We walk by them, as though through their living rooms, on our way to our offices, to Starbucks, hands and eyes glued to our phones.

That day in San Francisco, though, when I was sampling cheese in my pre-date glow, waiting for Kyle to arrive at the Ferry Building, I knew nothing of the transformation of BART stations at night; I did not pay attention to those on the outskirts of my walk along Market Street. Instead, I aired out my armpits, shook my hair down from its ponytail, and wandered between the circles of tourists that had gathered around the drummers, skaters, and break-dancers.

I soon felt a hand at my elbow, and there was Kyle leading me away from the spectacles, away from the performers holding out their hats.

"Hey," he said, extricating me from the crowd.

"Hi," I said, my sweat marks unimportant, suddenly forgotten.

"Ready?" he asked, with that green backpack from the march slung over his left shoulder.

I nodded.

"Come on, then," he said, "let's go. I'm starving."

We ordered fried rice, noodles with broccoli, and egg rolls; and as I chased grains of rice around my plate with chopsticks, Kyle slipped me a spoon out of sight of the waiter.

"So, how was your first protest experience?" Kyle asked.

"It was fine," I said.

Kyle laughed. "Fine?"

"Well, I guess it wasn't quite what I had been picturing."

"Oh yeah?"

"I really want be part of a movement, you know, to feel that things are breaking loose, but . . ."

"But the 'march' wasn't much more than a shuffle, a mass of people ambling down Broadway?"

"Exactly! Most of the chitchat happening beside me was about where to go for lunch afterward."

Kyle laughed. "Still people, even if they're protesting."

"I don't know, I could hardly hear the speakers, even through their megaphones."

"Yeah," said Kyle, "to be honest, I've been wondering if what they—we—were actually saying was, *Dear 1%, please be nicer to us.*"

"Maybe they'll surprise us," I said.

"Yeah, maybe," Kyle said.

We sat quietly for a while, and I tried not to get broccoli stuck between my teeth. I was struck by a kind of stillness Kyle had to him, a calm unhurriedness, like he was totally at ease where he was. There was nothing frenetic in him.

"So, are you from here?" I asked.

"No," he said. "No, not at all. I'm from Western Mass."

"Oh yeah? I'm from New England, too."

"I miss it," Kyle said, "I miss the woods. I feel most at home deep in the woods."

"But you came to do urban farming?"

"I know," he said, "it's a bit of a disconnect. But I also believe in it. So many parts of Oakland are a literal food desert. I kind of feel like my mission in life is to get fresh produce to as many people as possible. But it's hard."

"Yeah, it's funny. I mean, I'm here teaching because I love books, you know? I love poetry. If I could spend all day reading, that's what I'd do. And I also want to do something with that feeling—share it, if I can, I guess."

"Did you graduate in the spring?"

"No," I said. "No, I took some time off and traveled. Southeast Asia mostly."

"Oh, amazing," he said, "I did that too—spent time in Costa Rica exploring ecovillages."

"Wow," I said. "So cool."

"Was it hard to come back?"

"Kind of," I said. "I mean, I've wanted to travel my whole life—I grew up in this little town and I just couldn't wait to get out, to college but also really out."

"I hear you. Traveling gives such perspective."

"So many different ways of living, different ways of being in the world."

"Yes," Kyle said, "that's exactly what I always say."

We paused, looking at each other.

"But, yeah," I said, "coming back. It wasn't too bad, since I knew I was coming out here, out to the Bay."

"And why did you pick here?" Kyle asked. "Why California?"

"My mom spent time out here in the sixties and I grew up on all these stories of hers, of the magic and wildness out here. It just always seemed that this was the place where anything was possible."

"I'm with you on that one. Plus," he said, "it's starting to seem like that might be true."

At the end of the meal, we cracked open fortune cookies and read the silly lines out loud. I blushed at Kyle's, which read: *Beauty is right in front of you.* When we finally stood to leave, I slipped the discarded piece of paper into my bag and kept it there for many weeks.

Chapter 7

My first fall living in the Bay was spent texting Kyle late into the night and meeting for glasses of cheap beer on the early side of happy hour, when I'd leave school along with the students and swear to myself that I'd do my grading the next day or over the weekend. We met at bars that had board games and played Scrabble and made out in booths of cracked leather and scratched wood. In the evenings I'd climb into bed with Monica and go over each text message line by line, analyze each look Kyle gave me during our dates, obsess over the things not yet said.

By the winter we had stopped going out and instead started staying in, and I stopped worrying about whether there would be a next date. I loved his discipline then, in a vaguely reverential way, hoping that it might rub off on me, that maybe I'd pick up Spanish again after all and learn to play the guitar. "I don't eat processed sugar," he said, and so I stopped, too. He went running in the mornings and ran the makeshift stand at his urban farm in the afternoons. I gave him *One Hundred Years of Solitude* to read. He drove me into the Berkeley Hills, and we walked through Tilden Park at dusk, spotting a coyote, a blue heron, a banana slug.

I stopped going to People's on the weekends and started going to his apartment, where we watched reruns of *The Office* in bed on

Saturday mornings. Then, while he'd spend the afternoon reviewing soil charts, I'd grade the haphazard assignments my students turned in that showed me I was neither encouraging them to engage with literature in a way that would enliven their souls, nor properly teaching them the fundamentals of academic writing. Throughout the day we'd drink mug after mug of Good Earth's Sweet and Spicy tea, and in the evening, we'd curl up on Kyle's bed and watch action movies and burn the brown rice we were boiling on the stove before we wised up and got a rice cooker. I introduced him to *Casablanca*, and he took me to the Thai Temple Sunday brunch in Berkeley and the farmers' market in Jack London Square.

I set up Skype dates with friends from college and with a German girl I'd met while traveling in Southeast Asia the previous winter and spring, whom I'd traveled with for a month in Thailand. In Koh Phangan, we had spent a night painting our bodies in glow-in-the-dark greens and yellows, drinking buckets filled with Red Bull and vodka, and ogling the idiots who tried to jump the famed "fire rope," swung by two silent Thai boys sitting atop lifeguard seats at the Full Moon Party. My college friends told me about their jobs as paralegals and executive assistants. Most had stayed on the East Coast; they sent photos of that winter's snowstorms, and of the every-other-week get-together a bunch of them had started having at a bar in New York, where one of our friends was regularly singing at an open mic.

My college roommate, Amelia, was in London taking acting classes and attending plays almost every evening. We wrote long, rambling, and rapturous emails to each other about our unfolding post-college lives.

To: Amelia Carr
From: Elena Berg

Subject: Apple Butter

Ame,

Recently, I was reading about the origins of nostalgia. The term was coined first by a young doctor in the late eighteenth century, meant to describe the terrible homesickness that Swiss mercenaries felt while fighting far from home. The malady was considered to be so dangerous and debilitating— possibly even fatal—that the Swiss boys were forbidden from singing their songs from home. It was these songs, the doctors thought, that triggered the symptoms of nostalgia: a kind of wasting away; deep sighs; a terrible longing that manifested in physical pains. The fear of music became so pronounced that punishments were devised to keep the Swiss mercenaries from listening to these melodies of the Alps.

Yesterday, Kyle came back from a run with a crate of apples. The fog sat low and the jasmine outside Kyle's window was shrouded in white mist. I was on the couch, wearing those woolen socks of yours, a mug of cold tea perched on the armrest, when Kyle came home. There was a whole stack of them, he said, on a corner of a street in the Berkeley hills. A big "FREE APPLES" sign in front.

The apples were in an old wine crate, wooden and slightly soggy, stained purple in the corners, and they smelled like home. Like when my mom and I used to make apple butter in the late fall. I used to love the way the smell of simmering apples would take over the kitchen, a syrupy sweetness unlike any other. You could taste the stickiness in the air. My mom would peel each apple in one continuous strip of skin, letting the peels pile up on the kitchen table in their perfect spirals. When I was little, I would sit, still as I could, by my mother's side the whole time she peeled those apples. Sometimes she would hum one of her old hippie tunes—"The river is flowing / Flowing and growing / The river is flowing / Back to the sea." Sometimes, it could almost seem as though she was praying with her hands, praying through peeling those apples. In the winter, the first snow would often remind me of those falling apple peel spirals—the snowflakes would fall to the same tempo, piling up slowly, silently.

Yesterday while Kyle and I sat at his kitchen table peeling apples, I was overcome by nostalgia, and I thought about the Swiss boys in the mountains, and how they were forbidden to sing their songs. And then I taught Kyle my mom's old hippie tune, and we sang it together to the rhythm of the falling apple peels—"Mother carry me / Your child I will always be / Mother carry me / Back to the sea."

Yours ever,

Elena

To: Elena Berg

From: Amelia Carr

Subject: Re: Apple Butter

Mi Amor,

Re: Nostalgia. I have heard that sometimes, when there is a particular type of weather in the air, the atmosphere becomes like a reflecting pool for that which lies beyond the horizon. In these instances, the sun can appear where it is not. Ghost ships have been sighted. Islands mapped where no land lies. Mirages in the sky. Shimmers in the cool air that hint at a different world. I wonder if this is how nostalgia works. Something is struck in just the right light, the right wind, and then home is suddenly reflected back to us, although it is not there. We are both seeing and not seeing. We can imagine, can envision something, but it shimmers. It is shaky, and the image is ghostlike. We cannot touch or hold on to it.

You sent me down a nostalgia-inspired Wikipedia rabbit hole, which led me to this:

Hiraeth *(Welsh pronunciation: [hɪraɨθ, hiːrai̯θ]) is a Welsh word for longing or nostalgia, an earnest longing or desire, or a sense of regret. The feeling of longing for a home that no longer exists or never was. A deep and irrational bond felt with a time, era, place, or person.*

Isn't that marvelous?

There is a small used bookstore at the end of my road that I've started to visit. Harry, the slightly hunched, white-haired owner, and I have become great friends over the last few weeks. That is, in a manner of speaking. Harry doesn't do much talking, but he knows books. And he knows where they all are in his jumbled-up store. I actually think the disarray might be a ploy to get his customers talking. You simply have to ask Harry for the book you're looking for, or you'll never find it. He wanders through the shelves and piles for several minutes, muttering under his breath, and then reappears, book in hand.

Come visit me! I'll take you there. You'll love it.

Yours, with Hiraeth,

Amelia

My German travel friend had kept traveling and we Skyped—or tried to—from internet cafés in Phnom Penh and Yangon. She was planning to go to Nepal, to do the Annapurna trek, and then maybe down into India, to Dharamsala where the Dalai Lama lived, or to Auroville, where, so she'd heard from some Israelis, she could stay awhile. She talked to me about her chakras, about healing with crystals, about astrology. I told her to come visit me in Berkeley, that she'd fit right in.

I talked to my mom on my commute, and she advised me not to tell my grandparents that Kyle wasn't Jewish.

"At least not yet," she said. "Wait and see."

"Why does it matter?" I retorted. "Since when is that a thing?"

My mother just sighed.

All through that winter I went to bed early and got up early. I began to recognize others whose schedules aligned with mine. The gorgeous, dreadlocked woman perfectly decked out in a long linen skirt and black boots with low heels, who also got on at Ashby and off at Fruitvale; the ruddy-cheeked man with perfect curls who was always wearing a Patagonia windbreaker and reading on his Kindle; the short, balding Asian man whom I would find reading the paper while hovering next to the garbage can when we changed trains at MacArthur; the tall Black guitar player who stood in front of the broken-down escalator and sang Ray Charles and Christina Aguilera at nine o'clock in the morning, case open for the buck or two someone might toss in on their way up to the street. I would imagine the movie of my life, in which viewers followed each of these characters through their days and weeks and months and years, all with the assumption, the implicit understanding between audience and filmmaker, that disparate points do collide, and that there is more to living than mere randomness.

I wanted to start practicing yoga—I'd taken a few classes while traveling, and though I wasn't totally sure that it was for me, I really wanted it to be. I started making the rounds at studios, taking them up on their new student deals: $25 for two weeks of unlimited yoga; first class free; first week free. I was intimidated by the super-bendy girls who could stand on one leg and lean back while lifting the other leg up behind them to meet their heads, and the super-strong ones who could do handstands without missing a beat and whose Chaturangas did not flop down to the floor, elbows shaking and splayed. I was turned off by the *om*-ing and the chanting but gradually convinced by the suggestion that would come, often while in chair pose or attempting to do Warrior III, that though it was difficult, though my legs may be shaking and my breath shallow, though I believed I could not stay one second longer, why not, in fact, try to do just that? Stay in the pose just one second longer. And then two. And only then, when I saw that I *could* stay, would the instruction come to inhale one last time, then to exhale and straighten the legs, bring both feet to the floor, forward-fold at the top of the mat, and sway slowly, side to side.

Chapter 8

After aimless weeks that turned into months, Monica was finally able to get her dream job with Planned Parenthood at the beginning of the new year, and she started commuting out to Walnut Creek every day. We found each other in the mornings and evenings, sometimes on lazy winter Sunday afternoons, when we'd bump into each other in the kitchen, me cutting up carrots and celery sticks and placing them into five little baggies in the fridge, one for each day of the week, she making something more elaborate, like coconut-cream lemon pie or flourless brownies.

By the spring, Monica was also in a relationship, and we were each splitting our time between our apartment and those of our partners. It seemed a given that when our lease was up at the end of the summer, we wouldn't renew it. Monica had started seeing a woman she'd met through one of her colleagues. Rae had light brown skin, long, straight, dark brown hair, and green eyes. She was tall, and somehow softer than Monica's sharp edges. She had tattoos in Sanskrit on the underside of her wrist and the back of her neck, and she wore earrings in the shape of dream catchers that just grazed the top of her shoulders. She, like the rest of us, was a transplant to the Bay. She worked odd jobs at odd hours, now a nanny for two toddler twins, now a barista at a hip new café. She didn't seem to stick with one thing for very long, and I wondered if that was true in relationships as well.

Occasionally the four of us would end up in our apartment together for an evening, and then we'd combine forces in the kitchen, share the pot of spaghetti I had made or the bottle of wine Rae had brought. Rae would smoke a joint while sitting on the couch, window open, and Monica would curl around her legs like a cat and talk to Kyle about the gender equality cases that Ruth Bader Ginsburg had argued in front of the Supreme Court in the seventies.

It was Rae who was able to check Kyle when he dwelled too deeply in his issues. "You sound like a talking head on late-night TV," she'd say, laughing. And it was true: Kyle did regularly spew terrifying facts about rising sea levels and the need for federal policies against fracking. He—not I—would bemoan the fact that my seventh- and eighth-grade students were reading at a fourth- and fifth-grade level, and how would they ever be ready for high school, never mind college? I never figured out how to laugh at him during those tirades. How to make fun of him in such a way that he'd come down off his high horse and return to me. But Rae somehow could. It was Rae who said to him, "Cut it out, not everything needs to be a political issue." And he would. He wouldn't turn red or start to lecture her. He'd just throw his head back and laugh, slurp spaghetti into his mouth, hold out his wineglass and say, "You're right, pour me another."

Rae had come to the Bay for music festivals and Burning Man, for sunshine and good vibes—definitely *not* for activism—but still it was Rae who made the first comment at the community Passover seder I dragged all four of us to that spring. It was because of my grandparents that I thought to go at all. The only time I ever celebrated Jewish holidays growing up was when we visited my grandparents, and of all of them, Passover was my favorite. Though both my grandparents had been raised in observant homes, they did not bring my mom up to be religious. I had always felt uncomfortable whenever we would go to their house on Friday nights and suddenly my grandfather would don a yarmulke and start intoning prayers in his Yiddish-accented Hebrew about God and Creation. I couldn't reconcile that image with my otherwise secular, intellectual grandparents and my rebel-turned-history-professor mother.

But Passover was a night for storytelling, and that I could get behind. We followed the Haggadah loosely (but took seriously the suggestion to drink four full cups of wine) and spent the evening drinking and eating and telling tales. My grandparents would tell stories of the old country, my mother would tell stories of the new country, and by the second cup I'd have managed to switch out grape juice for wine and would feel my face turning red as my grandmother started to giggle and my grandfather sang songs about goats and slipped me $20 for finding the *afikomen*, the broken piece of matzah he hid at the beginning of the meal. He always hid it in the same places, either behind the picture of my grandparents on their wedding day or inside the piano.

When I was in college, I'd take the train up to New York for the seders—it was more just an excuse to get away right before exams, and a settled time to visit my grandparents, than any kind of religious need—but it meant that I hadn't missed a seder since the seventh grade, when I had strep throat in the spring. I was surprised, that first year living in the Bay, to find that as April approached, I felt sad not to be going to a seder that year. It had never occurred to me—neither in college, where I only once stepped foot in Hillel, nor in the Bay—to seek out any kind of organized Jewish community. My Jewishness was so wrapped up in my grandparents, so connected to their dining room table, to my grandmother's latkes and sweet breads, I'd never needed it outside of their home and so had no idea where or how to go searching for it.

It was Monica who said to me one evening in March—while I sat on her bed and complained about the fact that I wouldn't be able to go back East in April, that the seders were on weeknights, and anyway a trip across the country was expensive—that there must be a community seder somewhere around here, that weren't there JCCs or synagogues that offer such things? She was right, of course, and a quick Google search directed me to half a dozen community seders around the Bay, or services promising to match seder-seekers with hosts. With the offer of free food and wine, I convinced them all— Kyle, Monica, and Rae—to come with me.

We arrived at a nondescript building on a tree-lined street, guarded by a sleepy-eyed Black man who nodded his head and said, "Happy holidays," as we walked inside. Inside, we were greeted by an overweight, redheaded, red-cheeked woman, who checked our names off a list and made sure we had registered online. We walked down a hallway plastered with children's drawings of the Ten Plagues, handmade seder plates constructed out of cardboard and glitter paint, labeled with each component and its significance: "*Charoset*: Paste of Dates and Nuts and Wine → This symbolizes the mortar the Israelites placed between the stones of the pyramids when they were slaves in Egypt."

The seder was being held in an auditorium-like space. Round tables were packed into a square room, each covered in blue-and-white paper tablecloths, set with compostable plates and cutlery, adorned with mason jars filled with wildflowers and stacks of yellow Maxwell House Haggadot next to stapled pamphlets printed with the speeches of Martin Luther King Jr. and the lyrics to "Go Down, Moses." Harried-looking parents stood at their tables watching their children run around the hall, crawl underneath tables and chairs, get sugar-high on the chocolate frogs that had been passed out to represent the second plague, and fight over the costumes for the biblical-drama moment of the evening, when the kids would reenact the Exodus and the splitting of the Red Sea.

We found a table that still had room for four; our seder companions were an older couple, Harold and Larry, each of whom was wearing a Maccabi Games zip-up sweater over their button-down shirts and slacks, and whose yarmulkes were definitely party favors from bar mitzvahs of the nineties—large, shiny, and pink. A microphoned rabbi welcomed us and led the blessings over handwashing, while preteens walked around with bowls and pitchers of water to pour over our hands. We dipped parsley into salt water and broke the matzah in half, and everything seemed to be going fine until we got to *"Avadim Hayinu,"* or the section beginning with the words, "Our fathers were slaves." The rituals complete for a while, the next chunk of the seder was all the slave narrative. The rabbi directed us to our supplementary packets and asked the students in his bar and bat mitzvah prep class to read aloud. It was at this moment that Rae spoke up.

"It's kind of strange to be reading Martin Luther King Jr. speeches, isn't it?"

"Why is that strange?" said Harold.

"I don't know, it feels sort of like, appropriating maybe?"

"I think it's cool," said Monica. "It shows how this narrative is still relevant."

"Sure," said Rae, "but doesn't it feel a little forced? Like it's *trying* to be relevant by hopping on to another culture's more recent experience?"

"We share a common history. It's not 'hopping on,' as you say. It's connecting our cultural heritage to others," said Larry.

"A biblical story about slavery isn't the same thing as actually having been slaves in America. And besides, the present-day realities are pretty different."

"What do you mean?" said Monica.

"Well, I mean, it seems to me that being Black in America right now is a lot harder than being Jewish."

"Maybe you'd be surprised to hear that there's still rampant antisemitism in this country," said Harold. "Why do you think there's a guard outside the JCC here?"

"Maybe," said Rae, "but for the most part, Jews in America seem to be doing fine, you know, as a whole. I mean, Jews are—mostly—white. And being white in America gives you a lot of privilege."

"Not to mention," Kyle piped up, looking at me and winking, "it's not only in America where there's disparity, you know, between Jews and others."

I glared at him and sent him the most intense *shut up, shut up* stare I could manage. Harold and Larry looked both amused and tired, as though they'd heard all this before. I knew vaguely how most people my age in the Bay felt about Israel. I had tried to steer clear of the issue for much of my life. My grandparents were of the generation that believed it was practically treason to speak ill of Israel "outside the home," as they said. I had witnessed so many of the fights my mother had had with them over the years as she tried to convince them that being critical of policies was not the same thing as denying Israel's right to exist, was not contributing to "their" desire to "push all the Jews into the sea."

I had sat still and silent during those outbursts, not recognizing my usually jovial grandfather as he pounded the table and reminded my mother that not so very long ago the entire world had turned its back, had shrugged its shoulders, while the "enlightened" West sought to systematically wipe out every last Jew on earth. Why did my mother think things were so different now? Did she really believe that antisemitism had simply vanished in a fit of "progress"? Did she not understand that by speaking out against Israel among the goyim, she was justifying the media's obsession with undermining Israel's very existence?

"When we are broken and downtrodden and close to death, then the world is sympathetic to us," he would yell. "It is because we have become powerful that they cannot stand it. It is not our place in the world's order."

I had learned over the years not to touch the subject, that it was like a pressure valve that could explode at any moment, that if only we could all skirt around it in conversation, we might have a pleasant evening together. There were trigger words and trigger ideas. My grandmother and I would meet each other's eyes across the table when either my mother or my grandfather started to come too close, and we would try to tug them away, steer them to safer shores, sweeter, more loving topics of conversation. I knew what Kyle was going to say and I felt my stomach tighten with an old anxiety, an old pain. Except at this table, I had no ally to help me. At this table, there would be no way to avoid it.

"I mean," Kyle continued, "it is pretty ironic to read about slavery and being oppressed and then look at what's going on in Israel right now. You know, with the occupation and everything."

As I saw Harold and Larry prepare to launch, to strike back, and Kyle lean in to engage, I buried my head in my hands, turned the pages of my Maxwell House Haggadah, bit into a piece of matzah, and tried to drown everything out—except the crunch of the dry cracker and my grandfather's melody to the song about goats, which I started to hum quietly to myself.

* *

"You had to go there," I said to Kyle later that night, long after Harold and Larry had excused themselves from our table and drawn chairs over to another, more crowded table when the meal was served; after we'd dropped Monica and Rae off at home and they had skipped and stumbled their way upstairs to our apartment, Rae's discomfort with the use of MLK's speeches not impeding her ability to embrace the free wine; when Kyle and I were finally in bed, heads buzzing, cheeks flushed.

"Oh, Elena," Kyle said, "it's like Thanksgiving, right? What's the fun of it without a little politics?"

"It's not fun for me," I said. "Besides, there's more to it; it's not such a black-and-white issue."

"Well, why didn't you say anything?"

"You don't know what it was like, with my grandparents and my mom."

"Okay, but you weren't with them tonight, you were with us, with me."

"Why couldn't you have just let it alone?"

"Why are you so afraid of speaking your mind? Of actually going there?"

"I'm not afraid."

"You are, you don't engage. I know you have opinions about all these things, but you don't voice them."

"There's value in being quiet, you know," I said. "To actually listening to what people are saying instead of steamrolling over them with self-righteousness. You might want to try it sometime."

We lay side by side, not touching, the buzz from the wine now a dull ache in my head.

"I can never bring you home with me, you know," I said, rolling onto my side and turning my back to him.

Kyle laughed and wrapped his arms and legs around me, spooning me so that, despite myself, I melted into his chest.

"Then I guess you can't ever go home," he said, his mouth on my neck.

Chapter 9

My grandmother, Sadie, was born in Berlin, the youngest daughter of a concert pianist, and was herself a promising young singer. She grew up skipping through performance halls, fidgeting through her father's rehearsals, dozing off to the same musical phrase played over and over again and later falling asleep to the sounds of tequila shots and the suck of limes taken in the living room after the concert was over, the nerves subsided, the reviews not yet published. As a young girl, my grandmother was thin, with eyes too big for the rest of her face. Her eyes were dark, almost violet-colored, and they stood out starkly against the pale white of her skin. Her brown hair hung straight down her back. Sometimes she lost control of her long fingers. They would fly up in front of her, unbidden, and twist and shake and wave about, some unknown energy shooting through her arms and imbuing her wrists and hands and fingers with a kind of autonomous agency.

She was supposed to be on a *Kindertransport* train out of Germany to London in the summer of 1940, but she woke up that day with a fever and her mother kept her home. My grandmother's two younger cousins were on that train and made it to the English countryside by autumn, but the trains stopped running soon thereafter. By the time my grandmother's fever had subsided, there were no more opportunities to leave. Instead, in 1943, she and her family went to Terezin, the death camp reserved for musicians and artists, and she sang in the children's choir while her father, emaciated and starving, performed for the Red Cross and the Nazi guards.

My grandmother has always said that her childhood home was full of jumbled-up secrets. Piles of memories scattered through the living room and the kitchen and the hallway. They lived together, not just her and her siblings and parents, but with the older generation too. Her grandmother and great-aunt lived with them, and they carried with them all sorts of hidden tales, love affairs and bitter deals, bits of old-world trauma that crept in through the genes. Sadie's great-aunt Esty moved in with them when her mind began to wander. Esty would catch sight of herself in the mirror and not recognize the image as a reflection. Instead, she saw another version of herself. The "other Esty," she called her. She would speak to this other Esty and beg her to leave her alone, implore her to go away. At night, she would leave a coat, hat, and scarf hanging by the door. An invitation to the other Esty to please leave, to take her things and go. At some point, without discussing it with anyone, my grandmother's parents took down the mirrors that hung in the hallway and the bathrooms. But they couldn't replace every piece of glassware, or the piano top, or the window on a foggy morning. The other Esty found her way in, even without the mirrors, and my grandmother and her sisters would slip in between the real and the reflected Esty, not knowing whether to laugh or cry at the sight of them each yelling and gesticulating at each other.

Of course, it wasn't a secret that Esty was troubled—her suffering happened out loud and in front of everyone—and yet somehow it remained something of an open secret, one that was never spoken about. Some form of taboo was in place, a belief in the magical power of assigning words to terrible things. That doing so would make it real and therefore permanent. Something that had to be dealt with. Whereas, when it was tacitly ignored, it could be contained. Esty's pain could be kept in check. It was as though the family's silence was what was holding them all together, keeping everything from collapsing, crumbling out in the open.

My grandparents met in a displacement camp when the war was over, the concentration camps liberated but the ashes not yet swept away. He heard her singing—a Yiddish lullaby she had learned from a bunkmate, a young woman who did not survive—and approached her, hat in hand.

"My mother used to sing that to me," he said.

They were an unlikely match. My grandfather, Nathan, was from a small town outside of Lviv—Kamionka-Strumilowa—and the eldest son of a tailor. Once, during the Great War, a section of the Soviet army put out a call for bids from local tailors. It was winter; the soldiers needed warm clothes and boots. The army was desperate—they were even willing to accept bids from Jewish tailors. My grandfather's father put forth the lowest bid, lower by far than any of the competing tailors. The army selected him to make the additional uniforms required. But it was only after he signed on that he realized he had made the offer at cost, that the payment he would receive would only cover the price of the fabric, that there would be no profit. It almost ruined him.

When my grandfather would talk about Kamionka-Strumilowa, his voice would take on a singsong quality. The Jews of Kamionka-Strumilowa, he would say, much like the Jews of elsewhere, relied heavily on their history. The stories of their collective and individual pasts were essential to maintaining their sense of existential rootedness. For what other reason did they read and reread the ancient texts year after year, reminding themselves again and again of the creation of the world and the creation of themselves? With each telling of a story they constructed and reconstructed themselves, shaping themselves, as sculptors would create a figure out of shapeless clay each morning, so that only by nightfall had they become fully formed and could rest easily. In the evenings as they lay down to sleep, they prayed that they would not die in the night, that they would return to wakefulness the next day and begin again the process of forming themselves anew. Children were taught the stories from the time they could speak, and the people of Kamionka-Strumilowa walked around muttering them constantly under their breath, almost as if they believed that if they stopped telling the stories for even a minute, they would cease to be. The clay would crumble, and they would disappear into the earth.

As history continued on, the culmination of stories eventually became overwhelming, so that a person would have had to mutter continuously, and at a highly uncomfortable speed, from before dawn until after dusk, to get through the entire history of the world. It became essential to share the responsibility of storytelling among the people of Kamionka-Strumilowa. Between the townspeople, therefore, there were those responsible for the early stories of the creation of the world, those responsible for the creation of the Jews, and those responsible for the creation of the town itself. Among families, the responsibility for the family history was divided too so that, generally, the women and children became the bearers of the individual family history, while the men were responsible for the collective history. Each person, then, was dependent on their neighbor to ensure his own survival.

My grandparents were married—"unofficially," my grandfather always said, with a wink—in the camp, and "officially" several years later, once they arrived in New York. My grandmother wanted to pursue her singing career, but my mother was conceived, and so instead my grandmother sang lullabies and songs to wake up to, songs to clean the dishes and sweep the floors to. My grandfather was hired as a teacher—"What subject do you teach?" they asked him; "What subject do you need?" he responded—and ended up teaching geography to middle-schoolers for decades. I am convinced there are generations of New Yorkers who know absolutely nothing about land formation or soil composition but could tell you the history of Irish soda bread and how many stones were used to build the Great Wall of China (100 million tons of stone, bricks, and mud). My grandfather's stories were wide-ranging, and his ability to spin a single question into a class-long tale—a legacy from growing up in Kamionka-Strumilowa—legendary.

Chapter 10

The year I turned twenty, my college boyfriend and I spent our winter break in Salzburg, Austria. His parents had friends who were living there for the year on sabbatical, and they were vacating their apartment for ten days around New Year's. We took advantage of the offer of free lodging and the dream of European romance.

We argued on the way from the airport to the center of town. He was reading a book about four friends growing up in the Midwest, where he was from. He was nostalgic, he said, for the antics of boys, the rivers, the open skies, the miles and miles of grass.

"I want to move back home after graduation," he said. "Promise me you'll come too, when you graduate."

"I can't promise," I said. "How can I know that's what I'll want?"

Later, our argument on pause, we walked through the old town of Salzburg, across a bridge covered with snow, beside horse-drawn carriages, next to a life-size chess game set up in the square. *It was like being inside a Hans Christian Andersen fairy tale*, I wrote to Amelia. We ate roasted chestnuts scooped into a paper bag, burning our fingers, and went to see Mozart's opera *The Magic Flute* one evening.

We drove to Munich to spend New Year's with the apartment owners, my boyfriend's family friends. We slowed down in the middle of the highway through the Alps and took pictures through the dirty window of the rental car. The pictures of the mountains came out splattered with dust and specks of dirt. In Munich we went to a New Year's Eve party at the home of professor friends of the apartment owners. We were the youngest people there by fifteen years, and everyone seemed to be either involved in the arts in some way or a professional intellectual. We played a game where we melted down metal figurines and then shone a flashlight onto them to project a shadow on the wall. The shape of the shadow was then used to tell our fortunes for the upcoming year. My shadow looked like a discarded Jackson Pollock painting, but the Germans were convinced it was a voluptuous woman with long flowing hair. I don't remember what that foretold. At midnight we went down to the street and set off firecrackers, still clutching our champagne glasses, trying to seem older than we were.

When we returned to Salzburg, my boyfriend flew home a day before me, and I spent my last hours retracing our steps through the snow. For most of the afternoon I sat inside a stone church. With high ceilings and stained-glass windows depicting scenes from the Bible, the church managed to be both silent and loud at the same time. The afternoon stretched out before me, time suspended in a swirl of snow and green- and red- and yellow-tinted light, and I thought of the Borges story about a playwright who is also a revolutionary. The revolutionary has been apprehended, condemned to be executed by firing squad. Just at the moment when he stands in front of the guns, back to a wall, he prays to God for reprieve. He has left behind an unfinished play, and now he begs for time to complete it. And God—or whoever—hears him and grants him this time. Time stops—the soldiers and the playwright all frozen in place—for an entire year. A year in which, in the playwright's mind, he completes his play. At the moment when he places the final period on the final sentence, time starts up again, and the condemned man is battered by bullets and falls dead.

This was the feeling that reading poetry often called up in me. The word *stanza* in Italian means "room," and reading a poem—made up of stanzas—was like entering into a room suspended in time. Often, the room I entered was that church in Salzburg. It was a room of quiet, a quiet that resounded against the wooden benches, a quiet so full and exalted that it seemed as though a choir were singing, as though a symphony were being performed all around me.

Chapter 11

In the fall of my first year of teaching, I assigned my students to read novels, chapter by chapter; by the winter, after they had complained enough, I assigned them short stories; and by the spring, it was just paragraph-long excerpts from longer texts. I assigned them to write essays and response papers and spent months handing out pink and green and blue highlighters so they could practice peer editing. Pink for the topic sentence, green for the evidence, blue for the reasoning. We wrote paragraph after paragraph using this model and I gave them A's on exams when they highlighted a sample paragraph correctly.

I chickened out on teaching poetry for most of the year after my unsuccessful get-to-know-you exercise and instead handed out vocabulary lists. For a while I tried to incorporate spelling bees on Fridays and brought in candy for bribes and rewards to pass out when words were spelled correctly. But after a few of the kids stole the big bag of Jolly Ranchers from my cart one Friday afternoon, I switched to silent tests and implored them not to cheat.

My decision to have the students call me Elena turned out to be a bad one. While I thought it would make me more personable, break the boundaries in this false hierarchy of teacher and student, instead it seemed to make the students think I was . . . exactly what

I was: young, totally inexperienced, barely older than their older siblings, and not much taller than most of them. Especially because none of the other teachers in the school went by their first names, the decision isolated me even more from the rest of my colleagues. In the end, while I had wanted to be a kind of friend-teacher, I managed to gain neither their confidences as a friend nor their respect as a teacher.

Toward the end of my first year, I decided to give it one more go and try to teach a class on my favorite poem. I had studied Elizabeth Bishop's poem "The Fish" in a seminar my junior year of college and had fallen in love with both the professor and his read on the poem. Poetry seminars were, at one point in my life, one of my greatest sources of delight. Eight to twelve students sitting around a table, each with a poetry anthology—those Norton ones with the silky, thin pages—perched open on the table in front of us. A single poem could take an entire three-hour session to discuss. Line by line, metaphor by metaphor, rhythmic choice by rhythmic choice, we'd talk about how the poet was transforming the sonnet, challenging the poets who had come before. My advanced poetry seminars in college didn't linger much on iambs or trochees, but we talked about the music of language nonetheless.

I thought I would try to mimic the feel of a seminar with my eighth graders, rearrange the tables in the cafeteria into a U-shape, rather than in rows and pods, so that we could have cross-circle conversation.

"Now, Esme, why don't you start. Read the first few lines, and then Jorge can take over, and so on. Okay?"

"I caught a tremendous fish / and held him beside the boat / half out of water, with my hook / fast in a corner of his mouth."

"Why'd she stick a hook in its mouth?"

"How else are you gonna get fish to eat, huh? Someone's gotta catch it."

"My uncle used to catch fish, he says. So nasty."

"He didn't fight. / He hadn't fought at all."

"Pussy."

"What did you say?" I interjected.

"That fish is dumb. I would've fought her."

"Don't use that kind of language," I chided.

". . . battered and venera- ven- venera . . ."

"Venerable."

"What's that mean? Man, I can't read this."

". . . and infested / with tiny white sea-lice—"

"Ew! So gross."

"Just like Maria, no?"

"Shut up, Javier!"

"Yeah, everybody knows Maria has lice. That's why she's always scratching her head."

"I do not!"

"Enough!" I shouted. "Keep reading."

"—the frightening gills / fresh and crisp with blood, / that can cut so badly—"

"I bet this lady poet don't know anything about blood."

"My brother said he saw two guys in a knife fight behind the grocery store—"

". . . the dramatic reds and blacks / of his shiny entrails . . ."

"What's 'entrails'?"

"That's the inside bits, idiot."

"Language!"

"That's the best part to eat."

"No way, you don't eat those parts."

"Yeah, you do."

"I stared and stared . . ."

"What does she wanna stare at it for? She should cook it already!"

"This poem's too long."

"—until everything / was rainbow, rainbow, rainbow!"

"Gay."

"So fucking gay."

"Quiet!" I yelled. "Nick, go and stand in the hallway and wait for me there when the bell rings. You cannot use that kind of language in my classroom."

"And I let the fish go."

"Aw, what?!"

"She let it go, Elena?"

"After that whole poem she didn't even eat that old fish?"

"That's so dumb."

"Man, this was stupid."

"What a waste."

My great poetry lesson failure. We had barely been able to read the entire poem during class, never mind get to the heart of it. I had wanted to show them the way the narrator begins as an oppressive force, hooking the fish on her line and noticing only the fish's lack of fight, the ugliness of the fish. We would have lingered on the turn, when the narrator "looked into his eyes" and sees that they are "far larger than mine." How after this moment the language becomes admiring, and venerating. How the narrator starts to see the fish not as a barnacled sea creature, not as "the Other," but a being with eyes and lips and a face, designations normally reserved for human beings. We would have talked about the transformation that occurs in the narrator, how by deeply looking at the fish she develops empathy and respect for him, how letting the fish go signifies the narrator's understanding that she and the fish are equals, that their lives are of equal value. It would have been an opening to talk about how we can do this in our own lives, how we carry around prejudice with us, and how it colors the way we look at each other. How the balance of power is uneven, but how, when we learn to see each other as full, complete beings, worthy of admiration and respect, we tip the scales a little more toward justice.

But instead, the bell rang, and all twenty-plus students flung themselves up from their chairs, sneakers scraping the sticky cafeteria floor, papers flying, pencils dropped, cell phones whipped out of the pockets of backpacks with broken zippers. In the fray, most of my students left the photocopied versions of their poems on the table or crumpled and dropped to the floor. I picked them up slowly before heading outside to chastise Nick, who spent our entire conversation with his eyes on the ground, his foot scuffing the floor, murmuring affirmation while I tried to gently but firmly explain to him the harmful impact of using "gay" as a derogatory term.

Chapter 12

My placement at a charter school meant that I was assigned a coach who was supposed to regularly observe me teaching, be available for lesson plan consultation, and provide general mentorship. In my first year, my coach was Sylvia, an administrator who'd taught English for thirty years in the Oakland public schools, retired at sixty, taken the trip of a lifetime on an Alaskan cruise with her husband, and promptly gone back to work when they returned to the Bay. "Ms. Sylvia," her kids had called her; there were teachers at BSA who had had her as a teacher when they were in middle school and still referred to her as such.

Ms. Sylvia popped into the cafeteria-cum-classroom every now and again throughout my first year, usually with a Tupperware filled with oatmeal raisin cookies, which she distributed liberally among students and teachers alike.

"Oh, honey," she said, the first time she came into the cafeteria, taking in the students eating lunch, the finicky photocopier, and my attempts at a reading comprehension lesson amid the chaos. "This just won't do."

She took me out to dinner a couple of times during the year to her favorite hole-in-the-wall Vietnamese restaurant up by Mills College, and she told me about the generations of students she was reconnecting with now that she was on Facebook. She had a raspy voice—they said she had only one working vocal cord—and cheeks that were laced with spidery red veins. One of the most useful pieces of advice she gave me was when she told me, "Now, honey, you have to stop asking them if they want to do things."

"What do you mean?"

"I keep hearing you say things like, 'Do you want to help me clean up?' or 'Do you want to take out your books?'"

"Okay, what's wrong with that?"

"Well, you don't really mean it as a question, do you? When you're telling them to do something, just tell them. Say, 'Please take out your books.' Otherwise, you're not being clear. What's going to happen when one day one of them decides to say, 'No, I don't want to'?"

"Huh," I said, "I never thought about that."

"It's cultural, dear."

"Cultural?"

"Sure. It's a pretty common way of talking among white and middle-class folks. You probably grew up with it at home and in your classrooms."

"I guess so."

"But your students aren't white or middle-class, are they?"

"No," I said. "No, I guess not."

For the most part, Sylvia just told me to teach "from your heart, dear," and the rest would come. But when I came to her after my attempt at teaching "The Fish," disheartened and confused, she told me to go sit in another teacher's classroom and observe a lesson.

"Take notes, dear," she said, "and find someone who's been doing this awhile, so you can see what they're doing, and what you can do differently."

I went to Henrietta, the social studies teacher I had washed dishes with back in Ukiah before the school year had started, and asked if I could slip into one of her classes and sit in the back. I went during one of my off periods and found myself sitting alongside my eighth graders, in a classroom set up in pods of four or five desks. They were studying the creation of the transcontinental railroad, reading accounts of the thousands of Chinese immigrants who built the tracks. Henrietta perched on the front of her desk, flicked through slides on a projector showing pictures of the railroad, of the stark working conditions, the blazing sun, and the unforgiving rock.

The students sat quiet and still during the slideshow, and then raised their hands eagerly to answer questions about the night's homework reading, the first-person narrative of a young immigrant working for the railroad. I was stunned to see Nick—the same Nick who had said that the poem we were reading was "fucking gay"— raise his hand again and again to offer insights and ask questions. I watched Jorge, who in my classroom had accused Maria of having lice, take notes in his notebook and trace the direction of the railroad across a photocopied map of the continental United States. The very same kids I could barely corral to read a text during my lessons were, in Henrietta's classroom, active participants.

Later, when the class was over, I stayed to talk things over with Henrietta.

"I just can't seem to get through to them," I said. "I feel like I'm making it all up every day—and I think they can tell. Honestly, I feel totally out of my depth."

Henrietta nodded. "The first year is hard. For everyone."

"But how do you get them so engaged?"

"Well," she said, "for one thing, I know a fair amount about each student. Nick, for example, loves trains, building projects, wants to know about how things work. So, he's into the engineering aspect of this unit, the sheer magnitude of the project. And Jorge and many of the others are themselves immigrants, or their parents are. So, I want them to know how important immigrants are to the foundations of this country—without sugarcoating all the ways in which they have struggled."

"So, it's relevant to them."

"Right. You have to make whatever you're teaching, whatever you're offering, relevant. You want to teach poetry, right?"

"Yeah."

"And do you know what kind of poetry your students are into? Are excited about?"

"I . . . no—"

"You see them with their headphones on—what do you think they're listening to? Music is poetry, right?"

"Yes, I guess that's true. I just—"

"I know, you want to teach them the things that blew *you* open, the poems *you* love."

"Yeah."

"Which is okay! But don't assume they don't have their own poetic interests. Why not show them that they are already into poetry, that it's already in their lives?"

"Right. It makes so much sense. I just, I don't know."

"You had a vision," Henrietta said, wiping down the whiteboard, "I get it. But now you also have students. And you need to adapt your vision, your ideas, to who you're actually teaching."

When, a few weeks later, the bell rang for the final time that year, I emptied my cart's worth of pencils and never-graded quizzes into a Trader Joe's canvas shopping bag to take home with me. The books that Jay had recommended to me on that camping trip to Ukiah back in August sat at the bottom of the cart, underneath papers ripped from notebooks, pencil sharpeners, and photocopies of poems, unopened and unread. I placed them in the shopping bag as well and silently promised myself that I would read them over the summer, that indeed I would spend the entire summer preparing for the following year. That I'd have units and assessments ready by mid-July; I'd ask the students to call me Ms. Berg; I'd establish classroom norms right away and design my lessons with my particular students in mind; that, all in all, I would be better, surely, next year.

Chapter 13

On the Saturday after school ended, we threw our backpacks into the trunk of Kyle's car, stuffed in a hammock, a jar of peanut butter, some apples, and a ready-made trail mix from the bulk section of Berkeley Bowl, and drove down the coast until we got to Big Sur. The highway wound its way around the mountains, ocean to our right, signs for SEAL WATCHING jutting out of the coastline. It was Rae, of course, who directed us to Sykes Hot Springs, and who slipped us the fair-trade chocolate hearts laced with psilocybin.

We parked in an overnight lot, rubbed sunscreen into our shoulders, the tops of our ears, and my long, jutting nose, and headed onto the trail. We were not alone; Sykes Hot Springs may have been a Big Sur secret at some point, but in 2012, it had long been a renowned pilgrimage for those of us in the Bay Area who prided ourselves on being hot springs aficionados and hiking mavens—so, basically, everyone. Still, while an empty trail to ourselves might have afforded slightly more romance, the presence of our trekking companions could not detract from the glory that is the redwood tree.

Soft and sturdy, still and rooted, the trees exude ancientness, and wisdom, and something gentle and kind. A redwood forest always has the same kind of soil underfoot, silky, with scraps of bark scattered throughout. And the light. The light filters through a redwood forest in streaks, dappling the ground, the trees, the leaves, with dashes of sparkle; the undersides of leaves are lit up a brilliant, bright green, contrasting the darker, more muted green above. If you are quiet, you can hear the wind coming before you see or feel it, and as the tall—endlessly tall—trees begin to bend and wave, it feels as though a spirit is drawing near.

Kyle and I took our time among the redwood and oak forests, huffing slightly on our uphill climb, and taking a long, leisurely lunch break on the rocks beside running water where we found ourselves in the middle of the day. Over apples and peanut butter, we fantasized about our plan to move in together at the end of the summer, when my lease with Monica was up.

"Instead of having a couch or something, let's string up hammocks in the living room," I said.

"And we can have a whole section of the living room filled with instruments, like drums and your ukulele and a guitar, so when people come over, we can jam," Kyle said.

"Let's never do any dishes—"

"And we'll never make the bed—"

"It's going to be amazing."

"It sure is," Kyle said, as he kissed the peanut butter off the side of my mouth.

"Gross," I said, swatting him away.

It took us seven hours to reach the Edenic valley that Saturday afternoon. After miles of hiking up, we suddenly had a sharp descent down, scrambling over rocks, butt-first sometimes, until we arrived at a warm, flowing stream. Above us, perched in the trees and on the branches, were hidden birds warbling, and not-so-hidden Santa Cruz hippies, all of whom were completely naked, with long, blond dreadlocks flowing down their backs. They called out to us as though they were the archangels guarding the gates of Eden.

"Hey there, sweeties! Welcome! Take off your clothes! What are you waiting for?"

We did not wait long for our turn in the boulder-rimmed pool, and as we sank our aching legs down into the hot water, dusk began to settle on the valley, and the first glittering star shimmered into view. We didn't speak in the hot springs, but Kyle's fingers found mine, and I lay my head back on the cool rocks and felt the heat soothe the tension from the hike—and the entire school year—out of me. We slept in the hammock that night, strung up between two trees, our heads at either end and our legs scissored together. We tucked our one sleeping bag around us both, cocooning ourselves into the hammock and each other. A deep sleep descended upon me for a full fourteen hours, cradled as I was between the trees, the hot springs, the Santa Cruz hippies, and Kyle.

In the morning we woke with the light, packed our backpacks, brushed our teeth, and spat the toothpaste out onto the grass shoots that rose up between the rocks by the river. We walked deeper into the valley, found our way to a secluded patch of ground, set up a blanket, and made sure our water bottles were full. Neither of us had done shrooms before, or any psychedelic in fact. When I was packing to move out to the Bay, my mother came and sat on my bed and said, "Want to know my favorite place to trip acid out there? Mount Tam. You've gotta go to Mount Tam; there's no place like it." Sykes wasn't Mount Tam, nor shrooms acid, but then again I also wasn't—and am not—my mother.

The chocolates were shaped like hearts and wrapped in pink foil; for the first thirty minutes or so after we had eaten them, I couldn't feel anything happening and wondered just how reliable Rae's connection was. But soon the waves of nausea started coming over me and I felt myself come slightly unhinged from my body. I was not wholly removed, not floating away, but there was space between my feet and me, my hands and me, as though I had just released the clasps that were pinning me to my physical self. And then, just as the nausea passed, I opened my eyes and saw that the trees in front of me, which just a little while earlier had been blowing gently in the wind, had now suddenly turned into sea anemones, opening and closing their tentacles in breaths of inky black and deep green. When I pointed this out to Kyle, he nodded seriously and then puckered his lips and blew kisses toward the tree-anemones. We looked at each other and started to giggle, stomachs and chests heaving. We pitched our bodies to the ground, grasped hold of each other and reached out toward the breathing, sighing, laughing universe in front of us.

Before me there had been a hill, which over the course of our four-hour trip turned into a great mother, rocking a child in her arms. The valley breathed and I could see the breath sweep across the water, the grasses, the treetops. I started to match my breath to that of the valley. The earth kaleidoscoped before me; great swaths of neon color brushed through the trees; the land swirled in technicolor whirlpools; and at the center there was a pulsing, beating heart, and I felt as though I were sitting in the Sahara, in the midst of a great herd of walking elephants. I knew that they had always been walking, these elephants, and that they would continue walking for a long time to come. I knew, too, that even as they walked, as they moved, they remained still. I turned to Kyle and told him, "God is elephant legs," and he smiled, eyes closed, leaning into bliss, into certainty, into that beating heart of love that is at the center of all things.

Chapter 14

I spent much of the days and weeks that summer poring over Craigslist ads and dragging Kyle to apartments and in-law units and cottages all around the East Bay that were outside of our budget. One evening, we met outside an apartment complex in downtown Berkeley, stood in a line with fifteen other couples, and held our noses as we walked through the tiny, box-like apartment lined wall to wall with stained blue carpet and featuring white plastic blinds that needed to be coaxed and pleaded with to open or close.

On another Saturday afternoon we knocked on the door of a house in North Berkeley, on a tree-lined street where fathers walked behind their five-year-olds as they learned to bicycle up and down the sidewalk.

"This is the one," I said to Kyle, as we both caught sight of the dozen miniature dachshund garden statues placed strategically around the front lawn.

"Sure about that?" Kyle asked.

"One-bedroom cottage in-law unit in North Berkeley for $1,350? Yes," I said, "this is definitely it."

"Okay. I guess we'll see."

"It's quirky. We like quirky."

The door opened to reveal a short, older woman with graying

hair wearing a long pink cardigan. Around her, yapping at her ankles, were five, ten, then twelve, altogether seventeen dachshunds, she told us through pinched lips. Throughout the living room and corridor that led from the entryway through to the kitchen were arranged small dog beds in various shades of purple and mauve. Hanging on the walls were painted portraits and photographs of the dachshunds displayed in gilded frames. We picked our way between the beds and the toys and the dogs themselves, as she led us through her house to the backyard, where the in-law unit stood.

"Now, you have to come through the main house to access the unit," she said.

"There's no separate entrance?" Kyle said.

"That's correct," she continued, "and so you have to be careful not to let the dogs out when you open the front door."

Kyle pinched my arm above my elbow, but I refused to make eye contact; I didn't know whether I would laugh or cry.

"Here's the unit, then."

A structure that looked as though it had been built as a garden shed to house tools stood before us, one small window cut out of the wooden slats. Inside, a tiny kitchenette with a sink, hot plate, and fridge was shoved into the left-most corner, while a bed took up much of the rest of the space.

"I thought it was a one-bedroom?" I asked.

"It is," she said. "You see here that there's one bed here."

"But—" I began, before trailing off as Kyle pinched me yet again.

"Bathroom's there," she said, pointing to a door behind the mini-fridge, "and there's a closet for clothes and storage on the other side. Shall I let you take a minute to look around?"

* *

So, when we finally found the one-and-a-half bedroom on the bottom floor of a yellow corner house with three units—even though the bathroom was situated at the center of the apartment, with doors to both bedrooms and the kitchen coming off it, and even though the blinds were white and plastic and broken—we took out our checkbook and paid the deposit on sight.

We moved in at the end of the summer, just a week or two before school started up again. Between pooling together our hodgepodge collection of plates and bowls, pinning up the tapestries we had each gathered on our post-college travels—painted houseboats from Cambodia, embroidered hummingbirds from Costa Rica—the most exciting part of moving in together was combining our libraries. We exclaimed, laughed, and shared significant looks whenever two copies of the same book appeared—*Man's Search for Meaning, Silent Spring, East of Eden*—and rolled our eyes at the obsessions we each held, revealed by the large number of books on the art and form of poetry, on urban gardens and soil composition.

"How should we arrange them?" I asked.

"By author."

"By genre."

"By color and size."

"No way," I said, throwing a magnet I had just unpacked at Kyle.

"Just kidding."

We sat on the hardwood floor unpacking books from boxes. We made and remade piles, flipped through pages, got lost in chapters and the notes we had each left in the margins.

"You used a yellow highlighter in a novel?" Kyle said, flipping through my copy of *Sense and Sensibility.*

"Freshman year."

"Here's one in pencil," Kyle said, opening Chekhov's *Collected Stories*.

"Senior year," I said.

By the evening we had made little progress. The $99 mattress I'd bought with Monica when I first moved to the Bay lay on the floor in the bedroom, clothes and hangers piled on top; the little red couch we were borrowing long-term from my colleague Ted—"It's just sitting in our garage, Elena, you guys are welcome to it!"—was covered in books on permaculture and a waffle maker Kyle had gotten for his birthday the previous year.

"I'm hungry," I said.

"Pizza? We could order in."

"Or waffles?" I said, looking over at the couch.

While Kyle went off to plead an egg or two from our new neighbors, I rummaged through the kitchen boxes, pulling out a half-used waffle mix and an old, sticky jar of vanilla extract. I tacked up a picture of myself as a baby on the fridge—sitting in a high chair, naked except for a diaper, with half-eaten bits of beet plastered all over my face, and purple beet juice running like wine down my chest. My cheek-to-cheek smile showed off my two front teeth.

"Cute," Kyle said, when he came back.

We ate the waffles with our hands, sitting on the floor of the kitchen.

"It's so random," I said.

"What?"

"Where to put things. Which drawer the cutlery goes in, which shelf for the bowls, for the cereal."

"Totally."

"But it could be anywhere, anything. And then by next month it will feel inevitable, like the paper towels have to be under the sink, they couldn't be anywhere else."

"Don't be silly," Kyle said, "the paper towels go on the counter by the fruit basket."

Later, while Kyle placed pots of succulents and snake plants around the apartment, I pulled out my copies of *Zen Mind, Beginner's Mind* and *Dewdrops on a Lotus Leaf* from my class on Eastern philosophy and religion. I'd taken the class because my college boyfriend loved the professor, a kooky, white-haired, red-faced, older British man who started off each class with a five-minute meditation and talked about Pema Chödrön and Thích Nhất Hạnh as though they were his old friends (I suppose they very well might have been). Until that class, I had thought of meditation as something my mother had done with her gurus in the late sixties and early seventies; I pictured long-haired white people in crocheted crop tops sitting cross-legged on Mexican blankets in a field, eyes closed, while a man at the front of the crowd sitting next to a Ganesha statue hummed in a monotone.

When I told the professor I was moving to California after college to do TFA, he was thrilled.

"That's the stuff, Elena!" he said. "Get out of miserable old New England. Bloody cold here, anyway."

My college boyfriend was a self-proclaimed über-romantic. Grand gestures and little lies, anything was fair game. For our first date—the real date, not the chance meeting in a campus extracurricular, or the not-so-chance meeting in a dining hall a week later, but the real, let-me-take-you-to-a-movie date—he thought it would be romantic to bicycle our way to the movie theater with me sitting on the handlebars. Who knows why I agreed to this? I'm sure we both had some kind of *Daisy, Daisy, give me your answer do* picture in our minds, but the reality was that about two-thirds of the way to the theater I started to lose feeling in my dangling legs, and by the time we arrived I was making mental projections of my life as a double-amputee. I jumped—or rather, collapsed—down off the handlebars, blacked out, and came to a few seconds later slumped in my date's arms. But it did give him a pretty good reason to put his hand on my knee during the movie ("How's your leg?").

My college love flourished and ultimately disintegrated in dining halls and library stacks; three weeks into the relationship we were practically living together in his single (he was a junior when I was a freshman). I could still remember the feeling, though not the content, of our arguments at 2:00 a.m. outside my dorm room. We broke up over the phone because we were spending the summer apart—he doing research for his thesis, I serving coffee and trying to read as many of the classics in the Western canon as I could, weeping over *Madame Bovary* and *A Farewell to Arms*.

Lying on our mattress on the floor that night, Kyle told me how when he was little, he used to sit underneath the piano while his older sister practiced.

"I wanted to be inside the sound," he said, "so I would crawl underneath and sit beside the pedals."

"Didn't she get annoyed?" I asked. "Weren't you in her way?"

"I don't even think she noticed me," he said.

"What do the pedals on a piano do, anyway?"

"The only one I remember is the one that makes a note last longer; it sustains the sound."

"Did you ever want to live somewhere like this?" I asked, pulling out Kyle's *Sustainable Communities Around the World* reference book from underneath my pillow.

"I thought so," he said, "that's why I went to South America."

"You didn't want to stay?"

"I realized I didn't have to go abroad to do change work, that there are so many local communities in America that are food wastelands."

We turned off the lights and lay in the dark. The kitten we had spotted through our upstairs neighbor's window skittered cross the floor above our heads.

"School starts next week," I said.

"How are you feeling?"

"Nervous."

"You'll be fine," Kyle said, pulling me toward him. "Second year is always better than the first."

Chapter 15

I met Anna in homeroom on the first day of my second year of teaching. *Got a classroom!* I had texted my mom that morning, in response to her *Good luck today, sweetie.* On my desk was a stack of daily planners to hand out to the students, packets of pencils and erasers, gold star stickers. I had written "Ms. Berg" on the blackboard in multicolored chalk, the date in the top right corner. For my English classes I would arrange the chairs and desks into small pods of three or four students, but for homeroom on the first day of school, I set up a circle in the center of the classroom, just as we had been advised to do in our Restorative Justice training the previous year. "Circle time" would be a common occurrence in our classrooms—a time for processing, sharing, connecting. The point was to set the habit before a conflict made it necessary, so the kids would feel comfortable in a familiar process.

Anna was late that morning. She came flying into the classroom in the middle of our first circle, after planners had been distributed and permission slips for field trips and photographs tucked inside backpacks. We were sitting in our circle, the awkwardness of sixth grade showing in the dangling feet and the itchiness of new bras, introducing ourselves and sharing one thing from our summer vacation.

"I'm, um, Lily and um, I went to visit my grandparents in Honduras."

"Marco. I played a lot of soccer with my cousins."

"I dunno."

"That's okay, let's just start with your name."

"José."

"José, did you do anything fun this summer?"

José shrugged.

"Did you see any good movies? Or hang out with friends?"

"Nah."

"Miss, miss, José was in summer school."

"Yea, 'cause he failed last year."

"Shut up, Paul."

"Okay, okay," I said, holding up my hands. "Remember, in the circle only the person holding the buffalo speaks." I pointed to the Beanie Babies stuffed buffalo in José's lap. I had found it in Target the day before when I was stocking up on school supplies and remembering my own seventh-grade English teacher—Mrs. Pearlman—who used to start each day with a question, tossing us a stuffed animal when we wanted to answer. I had purchased the little brown creature in a rash moment of nostalgia.

Anna rushed in at this moment, long black hair pulled back into a messy ponytail, a blue-and-white headband perched precariously on top of her head. She wore large round glasses and carried a pink backpack that stood out against the school's maroon and khaki uniform colors.

"Sorry, miss," she said, out of breath. "Sorry I'm late, I'm new, I didn't know where to go and my mom had to take my little brother first and—"

"All right, that's all right," I said. "Come and sit down in the circle. Here, José, pass along the buffalo, please."

Anna plopped down into a chair. Shorter than most of the

students, she still had the baby face of a fifth grader. She turned the stuffed buffalo around in her hands and swung her feet.

"I'm Anna and I just moved here to Oakland. We were living in Arkansas before but we're actually from the Marshall Islands, but my mom brought us here to live with my uncle in the Fruitvale."

"Thank you, Anna," I said. "Welcome to Oakland."

"Oh, but can I say one more thing about my summer?"

"Sure."

"So, actually, one of the best things that happened this summer is I was in summer school, and they taught us about this poet, his name is Roger or Ralph Frost or something like that, and we read this poem about being in the woods and choosing which path to go down and have you heard of it, miss?"

I wanted to leap out of my chair and hug the big-cheeked, bespectacled, crooked-toothed girl sitting before me. I could hardly conceive of not knowing, of not having some familiarity with the poem she was referring to, "The Road Not Taken." The poem was part of my cultural consciousness, embedded in a backdrop of knowledge that included things like the phrase "One small step for man, one giant leap for mankind," and the fact that pine trees keep their leaves all year round, and that parts of Australia were once a British penal colony. Information I must have learned at some point in my life, but I couldn't remember when or how, couldn't remember a time of not knowing.

But here was Anna, discovering Robert Frost for the first time. I was almost jealous. I could only just retrieve a memory—more like an image, a feeling—of sitting on the floor of the public library while my mother roamed around searching for an obscure biography, flipping through the pages of an e. e. cummings collection, astounded at the restructuring of words, at letters and parentheses and commas rearranged, reorganized, remade into something new, unknown. The surprise of syntax shook me then, that which had been invisible in its predictability suddenly offering up surprise, mystery, magic. Just as this moment with Anna was offering now.

"Robert Frost, is that who you mean?" I prompted.

"Yeah, I think so. I think that's him!" Anna said.

"Yes, I've heard of him. I love that poem, too. It's a good one. Maybe we'll study it together in English class this year."

"Miss, Ms. Berg, I have to go to the bathroom," came a voice to my right.

"Me too," said another.

"I gotta sharpen my pencil, do you have a sharpener?"

Our circle paused, disbanded in the face of bathroom, pencil, and bell-ringing needs. Chair legs scraped across the floor—"Please put your chair next to a desk," I called out over the din. José slumped out of the classroom, trying to hide the height that betrayed his age by hunching his shoulders. Marco and Paul ran out behind him, shoelaces untied, pencils still unsharpened. The day had barely begun but already summertime seemed an age ago. Anna wandered out behind the rest of her class, a dreamer—unabashedly—and with a tendency toward tardiness, I predicted.

I took the ten minutes between homeroom and my first class of the day to rearrange the desks, rescue Roam the Buffalo Beanie Baby from the floor, rub the chalk from my hands, and take a sip of water from my silver steel bottle. As I heard my seventh graders line up outside the classroom and prepared to reintroduce myself to those I had taught last year, I found myself reciting the Frost poem Anna had discovered over the summer: "Two roads diverged in a wood, and I— / I took the one less traveled by." I smiled and walked outside to greet my students. It was going to be a good year—I was sure of it.

Chapter 16

I began the year with a memoir unit. Over drinks one evening in late July, Paula, a friend from TFA, and I had traded war stories, swapped strategies, learned mostly from the veteran teachers at our schools.

"How do you get them to be interested?" I said, scooping froth from my beer glass with my finger.

"Start with them; everyone likes to talk about themselves," Paula said, her lips stained red from wine. "Sneak in lessons about narrative arc and imagery and all that stuff in between getting them to talk about where they're from, about their families."

We started by reading excerpts from *The House on Mango Street* and made lists on butcher paper of descriptive words, sensory details, all the ways in which the author "shows" instead of "tells." I gave them prompts such as "What do you remember about your fifth birthday?" and "Who lives in your house with you?" and we threw Roam the Buffalo around the room as the students answered out loud, calling up images of pink icing and skinned knees and nanas and *tíos* and cousins who had recently crossed the border. I brought in garlic and cinnamon sticks and we brainstormed vocabulary to describe the way they smelled; we listened to recordings of crickets, of a baseball game, of rain over the ocean, of falling hard on slick pavements, of hail, of fallen leaves crunched underfoot, and made guesses about what each sound was, played a game of trying to describe each sound to an alien landing on Earth for the first time.

I created lesson plans out of memories. My favorite moments of English classes ranging from ninth grade through college; bits of that theater camp I went to in middle school; ideas that had shaped me, challenged me, obsessed me—all became fodder for my classroom, lovingly, albeit haphazardly.

My US history teacher in twelfth grade had handed out excerpts from *Let Us Now Praise Famous Men* and had us write response papers and journal entries answering questions such as "Who makes history?" and "What makes a narrative compelling?"

On the blackboard I wrote the words "Oral History" inside a bubble and drew lines coming off the circle.

"What do you think this means?" I asked my students.

"What's 'oral'?" Lucas said.

"Like your mouth," Antonia said. "You know, like when you go to the dentist."

"Yes," I said. "'Oral' here means 'spoken' instead of 'written.' So, what comes to mind when you see this phrase?"

"So, like not from a book?" Anna said, and I nodded. I wrote "Not from a book" next to one of the lines coming off the circle.

"Good," I said, "what else? If it's not from a book, where is it from?"

"History that someone says."

"Like stories your grandma tells you about when she was a kid."

"Things that maybe the people who write history textbooks don't know about."

"Things that aren't important enough to be written down," said José.

"Everything's important," Anna said.

"Yeah, right," José said.

"Okay, okay," I said. "It's an interesting question, though, right? How do we decide what's important? Who gets to decide? Is spoken history less important than written history?"

We didn't really answer the questions, but at night when I couldn't sleep, I told myself just asking them was worth something, that I was planting seeds that would sprout and grow years later.

I picked out my favorite StoryCorps episodes to listen to in class, searching for those long enough that they would take up an entire class period, and each student chose somebody in their own life to interview. We brainstormed interview questions—"Where are you from?" "What's your favorite food?" "What are you most proud of?" "What do you regret?"—and students translated them into Spanish, Marshallese, Quechua.

"A memoir can include not only your stories," I said, "but also the stories of people in your life, your family, your close friends."

"Because our story includes other stories?" Anna said, raising one hand while pushing her glasses higher up her nose with the other.

"Yes," I said, "exactly."

The memoirs took shape over the first months of the year. A chapter on "The Members of My Family," including an oral history of an "Important Person in My Life"; a chapter on "My Favorite Food." I taught a lesson on metaphor and simile, and we talked about our "first languages," our "mother tongues."

"What language do you speak at home?" I asked, and students raised their hands, calling out "Spanish," "Spanglish," "English."

"How would you describe your language?" I asked. "What if I said, 'My first language is picking blackberries with my mother'?"

In a creative writing seminar I had taken my senior year of college, the professor asked us this same question, had us do this same exercise. I wasn't yet prepared to teach poetry—though I wanted to— given how the previous year's attempts had gone. Still, I hoped to slip in a few of poetry's elements, prepare the scaffolding so that one day, perhaps in the next quarter, I could expound on about a line such as "Suddenly I realize / That if I stepped out of my body I would break / Into blossom," and the students would come along with me.

"That's not a language!"

"It's a metaphor, like she just told us."

"Who has an example?" I asked.

Anna raised her hand and said, "My first language is eating coconut and fish with my fingers instead of a fork."

Thank goodness for Anna, who felt almost like my teammate in the classroom; she was quick to understand my dreamy, disorganized lessons, somehow able to follow me through all my confusing tangents. She answered my convoluted questions, sentences that trailed off into ellipses. She seemed to bridge the gap between me and the rest of the class.

The students wrote twenty lines, all beginning with the words, "My first language is . . . ," although, likely because the examples I had offered all had something to do with food, most of their metaphors did as well.

Late into the memoir unit the first rain of the season fell. The halls were tracked with muddy footprints and bits of damp leaves dragged in on the heels of rain boots. I found Anna standing at the window in our classroom, staring out at the gray sky, the liquid drops. Although she was often late to school, she was usually early to class, her nose in a book she had borrowed from our classroom library.

"Everything okay, Anna?" I asked.

"Huh?" she replied, startled, blinking up at me. "Oh, yes, sorry."

"No need to apologize," I said, as I tidied up miscellaneous papers on my desk, trying to look the part of teacher, even though I still had trouble feeling it. "First rain in a while."

"It's strange," she said.

"What is?"

"That it can be raining but we can't hear it."

"Inside, you mean?"

"Yes," she said. "At home—in the Marshall Islands—you could hear the rain on the roof. So you knew it was raining before you saw it."

"That sounds like a good subject to include in your memoir project, Anna. For the 'Where Are You From' section."

"I should write about the rain?"

"Well, you can write about whatever you like. But sometimes it helps to start with a specific detail or memory. Hearing the rain rather than seeing the rain is an interesting difference between your home in the Marshall Islands and where you live now."

"Yeah," she said, "I guess."

At the end of the week, in a period that I had given my students as in-class work time to write and revise their final memoir projects, Anna handed me a sheet of paper.

"Here's what I wrote about home," she said, and skipped back to her desk.

Where I Am From
Namdrik—The Marshall Islands

Namdrik means "Little Mosquito" in Marshallese which is the language we speak there. There are lots of mosquitos on Namdrik. There are also lots of palm trees. My favorite time of year on Namdrik is Christmas because there are lots of dancing and everyone has been practicing for a long time. Then they do their dances inside the church but also outside and everyone watches. And also there is singing. Everyone in Namdrik is good at singing. I like to eat iuu which is coconut. My first language is eating coconut and fish with my fingers instead of a fork. We also eat a lot of rice. Namdrik is an island that is shaped like the moon, but actually it is also an atoll which means there is another island and it is called Madmad. Nobody lives there but sometimes we go for picnics and then we play races and explore and if it's a big celebration then they will cook a pig underground. On Namdrik when it rains you can hear it even if you are inside. Sometimes you can see the rain coming if you stand looking at the lagoon you can see sort of a column of gray and that's the rain. The rain makes big puddles on the sandy path through the island, and if it rains a lot then school will be canceled. Even though I was sad when me and my mom left Namdrik I am happy to live in Oakland because here you go to school even if it is raining and I like school because I like to read and learn.

Later that evening, over reheated leftovers, and in between our time spent grading and prepping for the following day of work, I told Kyle that I'd found my student.

"What do you mean?" he asked.

"Once I went to a book signing, and heard the author speak," I said. "She said she writes her books for one reader, as though she were whispering the story into that person's ear. So, I think I've found my student, the one student I'm really teaching to."

Chapter 17

On a weekend late in the fall—in New England it would have been considered winter already—Amelia, my roommate from college, came to visit on her way from London to LA, where she fully intended to become the next great indie flick's breakout female star.

"What do you mean, I'm sleeping on the couch?" she said as I stuffed a couch cushion into a pillowcase and piled several Mexican blankets on top of one another over the couch.

"Where did you think you were going to sleep?" I asked.

"In your bed with you, obviously."

"What about Kyle?"

"He can sleep on the couch."

"Don't be ridiculous, Ame."

"I'm not being ridiculous! I haven't seen you in a year and suddenly you're practically married. You can't go two nights without sleeping next to Kyle? What about me?"

The summer before our senior year of college, Amelia had gone to Buenos Aires to study Spanish and tango, while I went home to New England, picked fresh tomatoes off the vine, babysat the neighbor's kids, and dreamed up—ultimately unwritten—potential thesis topics on W. H. Auden and Robert Lowell. We would Skype at odd hours; Amelia would be lying on the top bunk of a hostel bed in a dorm room dimly lit by the Southern Hemisphere's winter sun, strewn with the drying socks of four strangers. A few weeks into her time she said to me, "Come! I'll pay for half your flight."

I flew to Buenos Aires two weeks later and got swindled at the airport, paying double what I should have for a taxi to Amelia's hostel. We walked through the cemetery in Recoleta at dusk, shadows falling over the marble and white stone tombs; we ate empanadas and spoonful after spoonful of dulce de leche; we wandered through El Ateneo, the bookstore housed inside a grand theater, and read aloud passages of Borges to each other while we sipped our *café con leche.* I went to the Jewish quarter alone, stood across the street from old synagogues cramped between neighboring buildings and brightly lit shops stuffed with rolls of colored fabric. At the Feria de San Telmo, the famous open-air market, we watched tango dancers perform in the streets, and I snapped pictures of baskets piled high with fruit, of red and green and purple scarves hanging beneath ornate window shutters. We agreed it was one of our most spontaneous and romantic adventures.

Although on one evening we did venture into a milonga—a tango dance club—and attempted to blend in with the locals, Amelia actually dancing, I standing on the side holding both our drinks, many of the nights found us snuggled two to a single hostel bed sharing a bottle of wine—not unlike how we spent many of our evenings in college.

"Can you believe this is our last year? What are we going to do after? What do you want to do?" I asked.

"I've got to travel. Maybe I'll go to Paris, or some tiny town on the Mediterranean coast and do nothing but eat olives and cheese."

"Me too," I said. "Travel first. Definitely."

"And then?"

"I'm going to California."

"You've been California dreamin' for ages."

"It's in my genes."

"Your mom?"

"All her stories are from California."

"All her stories are about tripping on acid."

I laughed. "She believed in something. She was trying to make changes, real, radical changes. That's the part I want to do. Forget the acid. Or . . . mostly."

"So, what are you going to do?"

"Teach. I'm going to teach."

"*Viva la revolución!*"

On the Saturday of Amelia's visit, Kyle went hiking in Marin and I took Amelia to Elmwood Café on College Avenue. She brought copies of Ibsen and Anna Deavere Smith's *Fires in the Mirror*, and I took out my students' response papers on Faulkner's short story "A Rose for Emily" and a red pen, circling comma-placement errors and tense-agreement issues.

"I'm trying to find a monologue I can memorize, you know, for auditions," Amelia said.

"Do you really think you'll land a movie gig?"

"Why not?"

"I mean, it seems like a total crapshoot out there. Do you have any connections?"

"Is that what you tell your students?"

"What?"

"That it's a crapshoot and if they want to pursue their dreams, they'd better have connections?"

"Come on, that's not what I—"

"Yeah, it is."

I sipped my chai latte, the foam clinging to the sides of the cup. Outside two young moms walked by holding coffee cups, hair tossed up in messy buns, their babies strapped to their chests in matching carriers.

"You know, you're different, Elena. You've changed."

"What do you mean? Different how?"

"I don't know . . . less something . . . more something else."

"That's descriptive."

"Your life. I mean, you go to sleep at 10:00 p.m. every night after watching a TV show in bed with Kyle and you spend Saturdays marking up student papers."

"So, you mean, I have a job? And a boyfriend? That's how I'm different? I'm an adult?"

"It's not just that. Look what you're doing right now. You're correcting your students' grammar in their essays but are you commenting on what they're actually saying? Or just pointing out incorrect subject–predicate agreement?"

"Grammar is important, Ame. If you want to have your voice count, to have it matter, you have to write well. You have to—"

"Follow the rules? Pass the test? That doesn't sound like you."

I believed what I was saying to Amelia—that it was important to understand, to fully grasp the structures of language. In order to feel ownership over our own stories, we need to be able to communicate effectively, articulately, beautifully. I was sure I was doing right by my students in focusing here.

"I'm growing up," I said. "I want my students to succeed in the real world."

"I thought you wanted to *change* the world through teaching, not just slot yourself into the system."

"It's not that simple. You sound so naive."

"I'm just reminding you what you used to say, of why you wanted to come out here. What about your mom?"

"I'm not my mother."

"No," Amelia said, "you're not."

There seemed to be a growing gap between story and reality, between the idea I had of myself, of what teaching could be, and the facts of it all. Days in the classroom spent struggling with fading whiteboard markers and missing bathroom passes, trying to counsel students who came to school hungry or angry, with third-grade reading levels in the sixth grade, seemed totally unconnected to my visions of teaching from a year earlier. When I walked with Monica by the marina or lay with Amelia in that hostel bunk bed in Buenos Aires or sat in the back of People's Café reading Paulo Freire, I dreamed up an image of the teacher I wanted to be. That teacher was a mixture of my grandfather (his spontaneity, his rambling stories that held his students captivated); my mother (her passion, her expectation that students could meet her unrelentingly high standards); and an amalgamation of my high school and college English and history teachers, those who asked questions I still turned over in my mind late at night, who gave me books and poems and essays to read that spun my brain into fire.

I looked down at Javier's response paper to "A Rose for Emily" lying on the table in front of me; I had written, "Use evidence to prove!" in red pen next to his opening line, "This lady was super weird and creepy." A paragraph later, next to the sentence that read, "After she died, the people found her boyfriend's body and a long strand of iron-gray hair next to it on the pillow," I had written, "Use proper citation when quoting from the text!"

Amelia's questions were forcing me to reckon with the fact that a year-plus into teaching, I didn't seem to be anywhere close to becoming the teacher I had hoped to be.

We invited Monica and Rae and my fellow TFAer Paula over for dinner so Amelia could meet my Bay Area friends. Paula brought the wine, Monica and Rae the kale, and Amelia, Kyle, and I simmered chickpeas and pine nuts into a spicy Moroccan stew. We piled the Mexican blankets and pillows from Amelia's couch bed in the corner, pulled the table into the middle of the living room, and combined our two chairs with the couch and a wooden bench borrowed from the upstairs neighbors.

"Have you been reading about Hurricane Sandy?" Kyle asked, after the wine had been poured and the salad tossed.

"There are blackouts all over New York City," said Paula.

"And fires. The subway's down; New Jersey is practically in ruins," said Kyle.

"Are your grandparents okay?" Rae asked me.

"Yeah, thank goodness," I said.

"I was supposed to be on the East Coast now," said Monica, "but my flight was cancelled."

"What for?" I asked.

"Well," she said, and looked over at Rae, "I'm applying to med school."

"You are?" I blurted.

"I thought you were more, I don't know, antiestablishment in your goals," Kyle said.

"I mean, I want to deliver babies," Monica said.

"Yeah," said Kyle, "but you could be a midwife or something."

"You're very opinionated about this," said Paula, "especially for someone who will never actually give birth."

"So, because I'm a man I can't have an opinion about the way the medical industry treats birth in this country?" said Kyle.

"Yes," said Rae, "that's exactly right."

Kyle laughed. "That's ridiculous."

"Whatever," said Monica, cutting in. "Isn't it important, though, to have ob-gyns who offer compassionate, holistic care?"

"Elena and I were just talking about this," said Amelia.

"We were?" I asked, confused.

"Sure," Amelia said. "Do you make change from inside the system or outside?"

"My mom definitely tried to go outside the system," I said. "Although it didn't really seem to work out."

"I think you have to focus on communities," said Paula. "Concentrate on empowering grassroots efforts on a local level—that's how you make long-lasting shifts."

"Are you from here?" Rae asked.

"Yeah," said Paula, "I grew up here."

"And you're also doing TFA, right?" said Amelia.

"Yep. I wanted to do something for my community before actually starting my career."

"Wait, so you don't want to be a teacher?" Kyle said.

"I mean, for now I do. It's a good way to give back," Paula said.

"And then what? What about long-term local change?" said Kyle.

"I also think we have to take advantage of new technologies. And this is the place to do that. Besides, not many TFAers actually keep teaching beyond their two years."

"Elena's going to," Kyle said.

"You're still planning on going the long haul?" Paula said to me.

"I—" I started to say, reaching for my glass of wine.

"Because if not," Paula said, "I might know of a cool opportunity."

"Come on," Amelia said, "this girl? She's a true believer. Right, Elena?"

I could feel my face start to flush, and I hoped that the others would attribute it to the wine and not the topic of conversation.

"Well," said Paula, "think about it."

Later, after everyone had left and the three of us were cleaning up, Amelia puckered her wine-stained lips and said, "Now, Kyle, don't be a home-wrecker. Be a good man and sleep on the couch tonight."

Kyle tossed a dish towel over his shoulder and bowed, laughing. "I thought you'd never ask," he said, kissing me on the side of my mouth.

Curled up on the mattress that had never made it off the floor of our bedroom, just as I was drifting off to sleep, Amelia said, "You could just believe in me, you know. The way I've always believed in you."

"I do believe in you," I said. "Invite me to your movie premiere; I'll be there."

She didn't respond, and before long I heard her breath change, slow, deepen. I turned over and stared at the light coming through the cracks in the white plastic blinds. It took me a long while to fall asleep.

Several weeks later, Amelia sent me an email:

To: Elena Berg
From: Amelia Carr
Subject: Theseus
Elena,

I have been thinking about that old story of the ship of Theseus, the Argonaut. Over the years, each part of the ship is rebuilt and replaced, until not one of the original elements remains. Is the ship, the story then asks, still the Argonaut? Or is it a completely new ship? What makes the thing itself, if it constantly changes and is recreated?

Isn't it the same with the self? Doesn't every part of the self change, renew, grow, decay? What is it, then, that keeps this present self somehow still identified with all the past selves?

Yours,
A.

Chapter 18

I had expected to have Sylvia as my coach again during my second year, but Jay found me in the first week to tell me that she had broken her hip over the summer and was home, "convalescing—or, in other words, she's actually retired now." Instead, my coach was Tori, a principal-in-training who had big plans for improving the school's overall performance on state tests at the end of the year.

"She started out in TFA, too," Jay said, "so she knows what it's like. You guys can bond."

Shorter than me by half a foot, Tori had a shock of dark curly hair cut just below her ears. Her wardrobe seemed to consist entirely of black slacks and white button-down shirts, and she wore large, rimless round glasses that magnified her brown eyes exponentially. We met in my classroom at the end of the school day, and there were no oatmeal raisin cookies or Vietnamese food—instead, Tori and I sat opposite each other, our legs squeezed under the student desks, with our laptops open, as though we were playing a high-tech game of Battleship. Tori sipped coffee from a flask and asked me questions that sounded open-ended but turned out to have correct and incorrect answers.

"Now, then," she said, toward the end of the calendar year, "what's your next unit of instruction?"

"I was thinking poetry," I said, chewing on a hangnail. "After the break, so we'd start in January."

"Poetry? Are you sure?"

"I think so?" I said, starting to ramble. "I mean, yeah, I've been kind of waiting to do it this year, you know—I made a few sort of unsuccessful attempts at teaching poetry last year but I think I'm much more prepared this year, and actually it's really the reason I wanted to teach in the first place, and—"

"Elena," Tori said, cutting me off, "do you really think that's what these students need? That a unit on poetry is what will best serve them?"

"Well," I said, "I think, I mean, yeah—"

"What state standards will you be meeting in your unit?"

"Oh, um, I haven't looked to see yet, but I can pull them up now on my computer, and—"

"Because the key here is to help these students get to high school and then into college. Do you agree? And in order to do that, they need to meet standards. These standards exist for a reason, and we can't just dally around in the classroom teaching to our whims—especially when we don't seem to understand the privilege that is poetry—and leave our students stranded. Do you see what I'm saying?"

"The privilege of poetry?"

"Yes. You do see how studying poetry is a privileged activity?"

"Not really—or. . . do you mean in a good way? What do you mean?"

"Think of it like Maslow's hierarchy. You need to get the fundamentals down first."

"You don't think poetry is fundamental—?"

"To what?"

"The soul?"

Tori raised her eyebrows up above the top edge of her glasses. My palms were sweating and I kept trying to wipe them dry on my pants. Tori took off her glasses and blew on the lenses. Without the protective shield of her glasses, I could see the deep purple half-moon shadows that sat under her eyes.

"I get it," she said, still rubbing her lenses clean.

"You do?"

"Sure, I remember when I was starting out. I had all kinds of notions. They bordered on a type of savior complex. Me and all my wisdom. Coming soon to a disadvantaged classroom near you. Sound familiar?"

She looked up at me and I shifted in the small plastic chair. My left butt cheek was growing numb. I thought about what Kyle would say in this moment, or what Amelia had said to me in the Elmwood Café. I tried to remind myself of my convictions, of why I was here in the first place. But Tori had hit a nerve, a silent doubt that had been festering all through the past year and a half in the classroom (and cafeteria). The truth was I didn't really know where I stood anymore.

Tori sighed. "Look, the point is this isn't a seminary and this isn't an Ivy League university. This is a middle school in Oakland. You need to teach to your students—you have to meet them where they are; otherwise, they won't get anywhere."

I nodded. "And the poetry?"

"Send me your lesson plans. Figure out how the unit is going to align with standards. I want to see graphic organizers and plenty of writing practice. How to build a logical argument. Don't just stand up there and recite your favorite lines and say, 'Isn't this beautiful?'"

Chapter 19

On the day of the shooting, I was late to work. I wouldn't have time to make photocopies of the poems I'd carefully chosen for the start of our poetry unit, nor of the graphic organizers I'd built into the lesson to appease Tori, and so I'd have to ask one of my kids to make the copies during homeroom. I hadn't eaten breakfast; Kyle had shoved a banana into my hands as I ran out of the apartment, and as I drove through the streets of Fruitvale, I felt the first stomach rumblings, the first signs of the hunger-induced bad mood and stomachache that would be sure to plague me for the rest of the day.

Usually, when I arrived at Bright Star, there were dozens of kids gathered on the sidewalks, on the corners, and in the parking lot behind the school. They'd be jumping rope, the younger ones, or giggling over texts and Facebook posts, groups of five or six gathered around the one with the phone to watch the latest music video or makeup tutorial on YouTube. We always had to corral them inside, and tell them to tuck in their shirts, take off their hats, put away the headphones before they were confiscated.

But on this day the streets were quiet, the parking lot and corners empty. I thought that it was because I was late, thought maybe I was later than I had originally guessed I'd be. The street vendors, usually selling the kids little plastic bags of spice-crusted nuts and popcorn, were nowhere to be seen, and the quiet sat heavily on the wooden gates leading to overgrown yards, on the bus stop advertising payday loans, on the streetlight that turned green and yellow and then red without a single car passing through. The quiet hung around the school building like a shroud, and I tried not to pierce it, not to set off alarms, as I eased my car around the back and into the spot marked RESERVED FOR TEACHERS AND STAFF.

It was Marta who opened the back door for me. Marta was one of the parent volunteers who staffed the front desk, signing in the late kids and sending the sick kids home. She wasn't supposed to open the door; protocol was to keep the school on lockdown for at least an hour after the threat. But she saw me through the window, locking Kyle's car with one hand, a pile of books and papers clenched in the other, and she hurried me inside, finger on her lips, and led me to the side of her desk, where several kids were crouching.

"What happened?" I stammered. "What's going on?"

"Shooting," Marta said, while a sixth-grade boy mimed firing a gun in multiple directions.

The papers slid from my hands; I felt the banana I had hastily eaten in the parking lot start to rise back up from my stomach to my throat.

"In the school?" I whispered. "There's a shooter in the school?"

Visions of Sandy Hook–like carnage played out in my mind's eye. I fought the urge to run back outside to the car and drive away.

"No, no," Marta said, grabbing my hand, "no shooter in the school. It was outside, on the street. A drive-by shooting. But it happened close enough to the school that we have to lock down for an hour."

I gripped Marta's hand and felt her rings start to cut into my skin. I looked back at the students crouching by her desk—they were finishing homework worksheets, eating by the handful the sweet, individually wrapped hard candies that sat in a dish on Marta's desk, braiding and re-braiding each other's hair. They were bored. Not afraid. I took my cue from them and slumped down on the floor, waiting for protocol to end.

While sitting there, my shoulder blades pressed uncomfortably against the side of the desk, I thought about the time, years ago, when my mother and I had found a baby mouse sitting in the shadows on the sidewalk. We had been walking home from a Saturday afternoon spent in the tiny downtown area of my hometown. We stopped at the public library to return a book, picked up half a dozen salt and sesame bagels at the local bagel shop, tried on and rejected about ten different new winter coats for me, and as we walked up the moderately steep hill that led back up to our house, we suddenly came across the tiny, perfectly still mouse.

We had been arguing about my plans after graduating from high school. I wanted to take a year or two off—to travel, to work, maybe I'd hitchhike across Europe, I had said the night before. I didn't want to take the SATs; I thought maybe I'd apply to college in a couple of years. My mother was adamant—I must apply my senior year of high school.

"But why?" I said, twisting the plastic handle of the bag of bagels around my wrist. "It's not like you did that. You went to California and had all these adventures after high school."

"Yes, and look how much time I wasted before actually getting started with my life," she said. "Besides, that was a different era."

"I'm sick of having the next step always planned out; I want to feel free."

I almost tripped over the mouse; I would have if my mom hadn't put out her hand to stop me.

"Look," she said, pointing to the sidewalk.

The mouse sat in the shadows on the edge of the sidewalk, its tail curled around its body. My mother leaned down toward it, swatting at the bees and summer mosquitos that were flitting around the grasses and tiny purple flowers growing up in the cracks of the sidewalk. The stillness of the mouse was startling, unsettling. We expected it to dart away, to twitch, to scamper into the safety of trees and brush. But it didn't move.

"Is it dead?" I asked.

"I don't know," said my mom. "It looks like it."

We stood and watched the mouse for some time. The smallness of it focused our attention, as though we were gazing through a one-inch picture frame. Inside was the perfectly unmoving mouse, the way the sidewalk was split in half between shadow and light, small curlicues of grass and leaves and flowers lining the edge of the frame. I drummed the bag of bagels lightly against my leg, and the plastic stuck ever so slightly to the sweat on my skin. It was only when we heard footsteps behind us that my mom and I looked up from the mouse and leaned our bodies out of the way of the runner coming up on our right—to give him space to pass, but also to shield the mouse and protect the quiet hum of the tiny sidewalk tableau.

We continued walking home, somehow agreeing to move on without speaking. The frenetic energy of our earlier argument was no longer in the air around us. Inside our neighbors' gardens, wild strawberries were opening up in hidden corners and between the wooden slats of picket fences and creaky gates. I could hear the stream that ran through the wooded area behind our neighborhood, could picture the green-blue ripples slicing over rocks, leaving them coated in a glossy sheen.

"Okay, Mom," I said, as we opened our front door, "I'll apply to college this year. It wasn't my plan, but . . ."

"Well," my mom said, "you know, 'the best-laid plans of mice and men' . . ."

"Yeah," I said.

"'Go oft awry.'"

The hour ended quietly, undramatically. Marta checked her watch; we started to hear footsteps and shuffling out in the hallways. I dusted off my pants, reminded the students to put away their headphones and take off their hats, and made my way toward my classroom. Jay was walking the halls, sticking his head into each classroom, checking in with the teachers.

"Ah, Elena—Ms. Berg," he said to me as we met in the sixth-grade wing, my stomach rumbling, my papers not yet photocopied. "Okay, there?"

"Yes, yes, all okay, thanks."

"No lessons today."

"Oh?"

"At least, not this morning. Circle up with your students and let them process what just happened."

Inside my classroom, desks were pushed aside, backpacks tossed in the corners and underneath chairs. We passed Roam the Buffalo around and around and talked about the way gunshots sound on an empty street at dawn, about how long it takes for ambulances to show up after calling 911 and how response times differed depending on which neighborhood the call came from, about the smell of hospitals, about the number of people each student knew who had died.

My poems and graphic organizers sat untouched on my desk for the remainder of the day, and when the final bell rang at three o'clock that afternoon, I tucked them into a drawer and rested my head in my hands.

Later that week my grandfather called me.

"Elenoosh," he yelled, having never quite accepted that he didn't need to shout through the telephone to be heard.

"Hi, Grandpa, how are you?"

"Your mother told us about the shooting, at the school. What a thing! With all the children. I don't know what the world is coming to."

"I'm all right, though, Grandpa. Everyone was all right."

"Yes, of course you are. Of course. And all the students, you know, they're lucky to have you."

"Thanks, Grandpa. I don't know sometimes. But thanks."

"What are you teaching them now?"

"Well, I was about to start with a poetry unit, but after the shooting, I don't know. It seems kind of silly."

"Silly? Poetry?"

Yes, Grandpa, *silly*, I wanted to yell into the phone. How could I justify standing in front of my students trying to teach iambic pentameter, or explain the structure of a villanelle, when there were drive-by shootings outside the school, outside the apartment complexes where my students lived, along the streets they walked each day? What had I been thinking? That I could recite some lines of Edna St. Vincent Millay or John Ashbery and valiantly defeat all manifestations of learned helplessness? A term—and a concept—I had only recently learned.

Shouldn't I be lobbying for gun legislation? For an expansion of food stamps and Medicare benefits? For free childcare? Shouldn't I be teaching my students how to do the same? Tori was right; they were all right. Students needed to learn to write thesis statements and conclusions, to write clear sentences and construct logical arguments. They needed to be equipped—armed—with good test scores and flawless records, so they could be accepted into universities and get well-paying jobs. With healthcare. And 401ks.

They did not need poetry. They did not need me.

This is what I wanted to say, to scream at my grandfather. But instead, I twisted a rubber band around and around my index finger until the tip of my finger turned red and purple and began to throb. Outside the front window of my apartment, I could see two squirrels chasing each other up and around the trunk of a tree that sprouted tiny pink-and-white flowers in February and sent showers of petals down onto the sidewalk like a spring snowstorm.

"It just doesn't seem very helpful," I said.

"Elena, don't forget what happened with Plato and the poets."

"Huh?"

"Plato! Oof, you know who he is, yes?"

"Yes, yes," I said, "but what do you mean what happened with the poets?"

"He kicked them out of the city, out of the Republic, that's what."

"Okay? So?"

"So! Don't you see? They were dangerous. Or so Plato thought."

"The poets were dangerous?"

"They incite chaos! Discontent! The first step in any totalitarian regime is to outlaw poetry, literature. Censor the imagination. Ban the visionaries. Burn the books."

"Grandpa—"

"You have a gift, Elenoosh, so you must share it. Not censor yourself."

"But, Grandpa—"

"A teacher's job is to disrupt the status quo, remember that."

"Grandpa!"

"What?"

"Here's the thing. I don't actually want my students to be kicked out of the Republic. I'm trying to help them get *in*."

Chapter 20

K yle and I spent the week of spring break that year holed up in a cabin near Montgomery Woods, a few hours north of the Bay. We booked the A-frame "Romantic Redwood Casita" on Airbnb for $500 for the week, packed up our car with lentil-and-bean soup mixes from Berkeley Bowl, and headed out of town, laptops left at home, cell phones switched onto airplane mode. We were going off-grid.

I could feel the breath I'd been holding since the beginning of the year start to exhale out of me as the six-lane highway turned to four, to two, as the billboards and bridges disappeared into fog, into ambling country roads, and finally into the dark green winding turns of the tree-covered paths that led into the California woods. The radio stopped working, the frequency turned into static ripples, and we turned off NPR, cracked the windows, and let the sweet spring air—the memory of rain held in the leaves, in the curled tendrils of bark—seep through the car.

The cabin was, as advertised, surrounded by redwood trees, tucked into a grove in what amounted to the backyard of a much larger property. In front of the little wooden house stood a white-haired, cardigan-wearing old woman, with a line of silver earrings going up each ear.

"Jane," she said, holding out her hand to us, as we parked on a mound of unused mulch and stepped out of the car, granola bar wrappers crinkling on the seats. "And Roy's just round the back."

We popped the trunk and pulled out our backpacks while Jane lifted up a heavy stone by the front door and retrieved the key.

"There's coffee and tea in the cupboards. If you need them, extra blankets are in the wooden chest by the couch. We like to make a fire in the firepit on Saturday nights; you're welcome to join. Some of the neighbors come over. Good people. Someone will have a guitar on hand. Anyway, if you need me—any questions about the house, or hikes to do, or anything—just come knock at the main house up there."

We murmured our thanks as Jane slipped out the front door, dropped our packs on the floor, and wandered through the tiny cabin. A hot plate, a mini fridge, and a kettle comprised the kitchen. A well-loved couch and armchair made up the living room. They were angled next to a large window through which we could see a jumble of thicket in between rows and rows of redwood trees. A narrow ladder led up to a loft, which housed a king-size mattress that took up most of the available space. The bed was piled high with an assortment of quilts and crocheted blankets, and the air in the loft was stuffy and close. A small window was cut out at the head of the bed, and while Kyle unloaded our soup mixes and granola bars and apples, I lay on my stomach on the mattress and looked out at the car, dusty and mud-splattered from the drive, the logs cut for firewood piled high next to the main house, and the needles of the redwood trees reaching up into the sky, combing out water droplets from the fog.

We changed into sweatpants, and I tossed my bra aside for the week, and we cozied up on the two-person couch with mugs of hot tea and thick slices of bread slathered with peanut butter. We read aloud passages from the books we were reading and sat in sweet silence, my feet tucked under Kyle's legs. One evening when it rained, we unearthed *The Matrix* trilogy from a bookshelf nailed into the wall and watched all three movies in one deliciously brain-numbing session. In the mornings, Kyle went running in the mist and I tried to piece together the yoga poses I could remember. I set a timer for twenty minutes and sat cross-legged in the armchair with my eyes closed, trying not to scratch every insatiable itch, counting my breaths and getting lost in thought after three, four, and then—minutes later—returning again to one.

For the first few days, we did not talk about school and instead listened to the birds calling to each other, wandered to a playground and swung on the creaking swings, and invented backstory after backstory about our hosts, Jane and Roy. We slept naked in the loft, with the window cracked, and had sex in the middle of the night when one of us would wake from the sounds of the forest. On one of those nights, the moon shone silver into the loft through the little window, and as we untangled ourselves from each other, we looked out to see a small herd of gray-white horses gathered below.

Toward the end of the week, we spent a morning hiking through Montgomery Woods, stopping to take photos of a French-speaking family of four in one of the groves, and then drove to Orr Hot Springs, which Jane had enthusiastically recommended. We paid at the entrance, grabbed towels, stripped off our clothes, and padded into the silent area, where three or four pools of different temperatures were housed within white stone walls, open to the sky. In contrast to the hippie wonderland of Sykes, there was something austere, almost monastic about Orr. Inside the pool I let my body sink down into the heat, tipped my head back, and rested my neck on the cool stone rim. I felt a type of unclenching, a tightness slipping out of my shoulders, and I realized that for many months now I had felt like a string on an instrument—a guitar, a cello, a violin—about to snap.

There is a story of Paganini, the great virtuoso violinist—so skilled he was said to be possessed by the devil—who was playing a concert when one of his strings broke. Undeterred, he played on, and kept playing as a second, and then a third string snapped midperformance. As the story goes, he finished the piece—and the concert—on just one string. *What of that last string?* I have often wondered. Did it hold on for the performance but break soon after the curtain fell? And what would it have meant to Paganini to watch his strings give up on him, one by one?

"Kyle," I said, when we emerged from the pool an hour later, hair dripping, nails blanched, "I don't think I'm going to keep teaching after the end of this year."

That evening, as promised, Jane and Roy lit a fire in the firepit and set up camping chairs in a circle surrounding the fire. They poured hot chocolate spiked with a little something extra into tin mugs, and a handful of gray-haired neighbors made their way along unmarked paths to join us. A guitar appeared, and a flannel-wearing man started strumming old Spanish love songs. I sat on a boulder, cupping the hot chocolate in my hands and holding the mug beneath my chin, so the steam would rise up and warm my face. I listened to Kyle's conversation with Jane about the drought in Northern California, how the reservoir by Yosemite was shrinking, about the increased danger of wildfire spreading with the earth so dry and cracked.

Roy pulled up a camping chair beside me and drummed his fingers on his knees in time with the guitar.

"We came out here about twenty years ago," he said. "We'd been

living in Oakland and then I read about this trail, this trek in Spain—
retracing a pilgrimage route. And I thought, we just have to do it.
Didn't know how we'd manage, how we'd pay; we had all four of our
kids with us at the time. But we managed to get over there, and we
started walking. You know, and then I got to thinking, and when
you walk everything kind of slows down, and I realized we were all
just living inside the Matrix, inside the corporate machine, and we
couldn't keep doing it. So that's when we came out here. To live with
our feet in the soil."

"And your kids grew up here?"

"Yeah. Well, they were all at different points of being grown by
the time we came out here, but the youngest, Noah, he knows the
land inside out. Still to this day he hates putting on shoes. Would
rather feel everything squish in between his toes, you know?"

Jane and Kyle came to sit next to us, and I lay my head on Kyle's
shoulder. I looked down at my feet, bundled up in socks and stuffed
into Birkenstocks. As the sky opened up in a whorl of stars, I slid one
of my feet out of my sandals, out of its sock, and buried it into the
dirt beneath me.

Chapter 21

We didn't talk about my decision to quit teaching until the next day, when the car was packed up and we were already off the one-lane road that wound out of the redwoods and back onto the highway. When we did finally start talking, all I could focus on were the full boxes of unsharpened, unused pencils I still had in my desk drawer at school.

"Is it because of the shooting?" Kyle asked. "I know it was a pretty jarring way to start off the year."

"No," I said, looking out the passenger window, "not really."

"Or because of Tori and her crusade against the soul?"

I laughed, shaking my head.

"Because you know you only have to deal with her for the rest of this year, while you're actually in TFA. You wouldn't have to go through her after this year."

"I know," I said, "but it's not that either. I don't think."

"Then, what?"

"It's just, I don't know. I have these pencils, boxes of them. I got them at the beginning of the year so I could hand them out—either if a kid needed one, you know, forgot a pencil for the day, or as a kind of reward system. You know, rack up this many gold stars or whatever and then you can go 'shopping'—I got pencils, erasers, stickers, all kinds of things."

"Okay, that sounds like a good idea—a little bribery never hurt, right?"

I laughed again, poking Kyle in the shoulder.

"So, what happened with these pencils?"

"Well, that's the thing. It's almost the end of the school year and I still have nearly all of them. I never actually handed any out. Kids would ask me for pencils and I just didn't give them."

"Why not?"

"I think I didn't believe they needed them. Remember last year how they nicked all the candy I brought for spelling tests?"

"Yeah."

"I was trying to make sure that didn't happen again."

"And the gold star shopping system?"

"Never got off the ground. We did it once or twice, maybe."

"Okay, I hear you. The pencil thing wasn't a success. But you're going to quit because of pencils?"

"It's more than that, Kyle, you know it is. It means I didn't—I don't—trust them. And if I don't trust them, how can I expect them to trust me?"

Kyle was quiet as we drove alongside the bay, boats bobbing in the marina.

"It's just becoming clear to me that I'm not actually doing what I set out to do; I'm not being the kind of teacher—or person—I want to be. And I'm afraid if I keep going, it'll just get worse—I'll go down the rabbit hole and never get back out."

"Yeah, I guess I see that."

I leaned my head back against the seat and rolled the window down so I could smell the slight saltiness of the air.

"How long have you been thinking about this?"

"I don't know exactly. A while, I guess, though not wholly consciously, if you know what I mean."

"Do you have ideas of what you want to do next?"

"I'm going to call up Paula. She said she might know of a good next step for me."

Kyle reached over and took my hand. I had always imagined that TFA would be the start of my teaching career—not its entirety. I remembered a conversation I'd had on that overnight trip to Ukiah, the summer before my first year of teaching. After our tattoo go-around, Ted, a math teacher who'd been teaching for close to thirty years, leaned over to me and said, "So, TFA, huh? What're you going to do afterward?"

"Afterward? You mean, like, after the two years?"

"Yep."

"Oh, well, I mean, I'm definitely going to keep teaching."

Ted raised an eyebrow and smiled. "Is that so?"

"Yeah. Yeah, of course. Why not?"

I closed my eyes in the car, still holding Kyle's hand. I didn't want to think about all the conversations ahead of me—with my students, with Jay, with my mom. I didn't want to think about the look Amelia would give me, or the way my grandfather would start yelling—probably quoting something from the *Tao Te Ching*. I felt tired suddenly, and all I wanted to do was sleep.

Chapter 22

Not long after Kyle and I had returned from our redwood getaway, I spent an evening walking around Lake Merritt with Paula. She told me about the new edtech startup she was going to work for in the fall, and how they were "actively hiring ex-TFAers," and how I "should definitely apply."

"Listen, it's right up your alley," she said, her hands stuffed into the pockets of her fleece Patagonia zip-up.

"Tell me about it; I'm interested," I said.

"It's a program to teach close-reading skills."

"For what ages?"

"I think it can be modified for any age, but probably middle school, so perfect for you."

"How does it work?"

"The idea is that kids can upload a picture of any text they're working on, and then the app will walk them through how to close-read the text."

"So, for example . . . ?"

"Right, so imagine you're supposed to close-read a poem or a short story. So you take a picture with your phone or the computer and it scans in the text. Then the program starts asking you questions, and you have different tools to underline and highlight and make notes in the margins. And it's all guided."

"I mean, it sounds awesome."

"Obviously it's still in the early stages, so I've seen a beta model, but it's not yet at full potential."

"What's it called?"

"CloseReader."

"To the point."

"But doesn't it sound perfect for us? That's why they want people who have classroom experience, to help write and design the actual guided reading process."

"How did you find out about it?"

"Jesse, one of my high school friends, is the lead engineer."

"And you're in?"

"Yes, I'm in. How much have you struggled to get your kids to read and analyze texts? I mean, in a single class I have students at a dozen different levels, and everyone works and learns at their own pace. It's impossible not to have some of them falling through the cracks. This can totally transform that issue."

"Yeah, that's been true for me, too."

"I want to be involved with bringing tech into the classroom—it's the future of learning. And there's already so much individualized, program-based learning for math. It's time the humanities got in the game too."

"You make a very compelling argument."

"So, will you apply? I can put in a good word for you. I mean, you'll definitely get hired if you want it. Plus, it would be so fun to work together."

I linked my arm through Paula's and watched the sun glint off the buildings of Oakland's financial district. We stopped to watch the ducks preen and dip in the lake while joggers, dog-walkers, power-walking women with gray hair and black sneakers, and stroller-pushing young dads carrying pouches of pureed fruit and vegetables and talking into their Bluetooths passed us. I remembered the San Francisco walking tour I had gone on soon after I moved to the Bay, and the idea of layers, of one generation making space for the next, one form of innovation encouraging another. Perhaps this was my next layer, I thought. Could I think of this as an opening that teaching had created for me, an opportunity, rather than an admission of failure in the classroom?

Listening to Paula, I could easily draw the lines between my two years in TFA and this new edtech company. If I wanted to, I could rewrite the narrative—leave out the story of the hoarded pencils and instead focus on how I'd seen the way humanities classrooms would benefit from more opportunities for individualized learning and self-pacing; how it was crucial to teach students today to be comfortable and adept with technology; how reading and analyzing texts was a particular passion of mine. I was excited, I could say, to work more on curricular development, on issues of scale, in a behind-the-scenes role, rather than front and center. Now that I'd spent time in the classroom, I could see that I would be better suited—more able to serve, to *help*—by working outside the classroom.

"It would be *so* fun to work together," I said, as we continued walking. "I'm in; send me the application."

Chapter 23

The school year ended without fanfare or fuss—most of my teacher colleagues smiled politely at me from across the hallways, shook my hand, and asked if I had any remaining school supplies that I could donate to the students for the following year. I followed Tori's directions and spent much of the final couple of months working through graphic organizers to create outlines for a five-paragraph essay. I signed out the laptop cart and my students practiced typing out their thrice-peer-edited essays. I brought in brownies for our final circle, and we talked about summer plans, but only Anna asked if I would be their teacher again next year. At the end of the last day, she handed me a drawing she had made of two paths going in different directions through a wooded grove of trees. On one path she had drawn a small stick figure with round glasses— "that's me," she said—and on the other, a larger stick figure—"and that's you." We never did get to Robert Frost, in the end.

Kyle and I sat outside at a bar by the MacArthur BART station on the afternoon after I left school for the last time, and I ate french fries with too much ketchup and drank two gingery cocktails, while Kyle sipped on craft beer. My backpack lay on the ground, and in between the gray clouds of a summer sky in the Bay, the sun glanced through, warming the back of my neck. I told Kyle I didn't want to talk about it and he nodded, squeezing my leg.

I had gone through CloseReader's application process, which included making a two-minute video of myself talking about a text I loved, as well as an interview over Google Hangouts with Close-Reader's founder, Andy, who asked me what I thought my greatest weakness was and how I felt about karaoke as a team bonding experience. He noted that I seemed nervous and asked if I wanted to comment on that observation. A few days after my interview, I was offered a job as a curriculum specialist. When I accepted, I received enthusiastically punctuated emails from the other five members of the team welcoming me on board.

I told Andy I could be ready to start two weeks after the end of the school year, but he cut me off, saying, "Nonsense," and that I should take at least four weeks to "decompress." We agreed that my first day would be in the beginning of August, which meant that after school ended, I spent several weeks lying on the couch in my pajamas, subsisting on apples and peanut butter and leftover pad thai, and watching every season of *Grey's Anatomy* on Netflix. I reasoned that this was my form of self-care.

At the beginning of July, my mother flew out to Berkeley to visit me. I offered for her to stay in our apartment, said that Kyle and I would sleep on an air mattress in the back room, but she declined and instead rented a room on Airbnb in a house about a half mile away from us. The room had a separate entrance, a private bathroom, a mini fridge, and a microwave. The owner of the house was an apparently prolific author that neither of us had ever heard of, who had left copies of her novels—romances set during World War II and mysteries taking place in the Arabian Desert—on every available surface of the rented room. On the night my mother arrived, I brought over a jar of olives, a loaf of cranberry walnut bread, and a packet of sliced provolone cheese, and she asked directions to the best place to get coffee in the morning.

It was my mother's first visit back to the Bay since she'd tripped out here in the late sixties, and we spent one whole morning wandering through Moe's Books on Telegraph while my mom marveled at all that had changed and all that was the same.

"You know, Mom," I said to her, as we walked along Telegraph toward Cal's campus, "sometimes, when I see older people wandering the streets here, yelling out crazy things, I wonder if they might be old friends of yours."

"Maybe," my mom said, pinching my arm. "Next time, you should introduce yourself. Tell them you're Sheila's daughter."

"Don't I look just like you did at my age? Maybe they'll recognize me and think I'm you."

"Well, send them my regards, in that case."

My mother wanted to visit her old haunts, so one morning she and I drove to Mount Tam, slipped cash through a slotted mailbox in a parking lot near the summit, and then hiked the four miles down to Stinson Beach. By the time we reached the beach town, our noses were freckled and red, and our breakfast of apple turnover and coffee was no longer sustaining us. We stumbled our way into town and found a beachfront restaurant where we ordered plates piled high with fried fish and salted chips. My mom scooped out the ice from her water glass and ran it over the back of her neck and the tops of her ears.

"So," I said.

"So?"

"So, what do you think of Kyle? You haven't said anything yet."

My mom nodded, as though she'd been waiting for me to ask, her mouth full of fish.

"Well?"

"Well, what, honey?"

"Well, what do you think?"

"He seems very dedicated to his work," she said.

"And . . . ?"

"And what?"

"That's it? He's dedicated to his work?"

"What do you want from me, Elena, I just met the guy."

"I've been dating him for almost two years, though! You must have some opinion."

"Of course I do, but it's your life, and—"

"Oh my god, Mom, just say it."

"Look, he seems like a good person."

"But?"

"But he also seems a little . . . I don't know, unemotional."

"Unemotional?"

"Yes. I just don't see a lot of passion in him. Not like you."

"He's Zen, Mom. He's not some firecracker about to go off at any moment."

My mom took a sip of water. A ring of condensation had formed on the plastic tabletop underneath the glass; every time the door to the restaurant opened, a rush of salty sea air came inside.

"I just want you to be happy," she said. "Don't lose sight of yourself. Never mind what you think I—or anyone else—might want for you."

With my index finger, I chipped away at a dried spot of ketchup or barbecue sauce or grease that was stuck to the table next to the salt and pepper packets. When I looked up, I found my mother looking out the window, toward the ocean.

"We can go to the beach," I said, "there's a shuttle that will take us back to the car."

"Yes," my mom said. "Let's go to the beach."

While my mom signed the bill, I chewed on the remaining ice chips in my glass.

"There's been a lot going on for me recently, you know," I said.

"I know."

"I mean, I just left teaching and I'm about to start a new job, so—"

"I know."

"I *am* happy with Kyle. He's great. I wouldn't have gotten through the last couple years without him."

"I'm glad for you," she said, reaching around to help lift my backpack up onto my shoulders. "Seriously."

"Okay."

We walked toward the beach, cutting through parking lots dusted with sand. At the edge of the beach, we stopped to take off our shoes, and I felt the hot sand rise up between my toes, get caught in the lines of my feet, slick with sweat from our hike down Mount Tam. Stinson Beach is a classic Northern California beach, so a breeze blew strongly out from over the ocean, and though there were many people in bikinis and shorts, lying facedown on blankets, corralling kids under umbrellas, or paddling a ball back and forth, there were just as many in jeans and leggings, wearing hoodies and zip-ups and big white scarves wrapped around their necks.

We wandered to the water's edge, where the sand starts to melt and squidge, and stared out at the gray-blue waves rustling like a thousand crabs running toward the shore. At the horizon there was the faint outline of a ship; I could feel the knots and tangles start to form in my hair. I thought about Amelia's email to me after her last visit, about the ship of Theseus, and the question posed by philosophers over the years—if each part of the ship is replaced by another, is it then still the same ship? It occurred to me that perhaps it was a form of this question that so terrified my grandmother's great-aunt Esty, the one who seemed to go mad looking at her reflection in the mirror. Perhaps it was not the *reflection* of herself that so upset her, that she refused to acknowledge as herself. Perhaps it was what the reflection told her about herself—that it was she, herself, who was the "other Esty," posing as the lost, almost forgotten, original.

On my mom's last night in Berkeley, she took us out to dinner at a restaurant downtown where the seats were made from recycled leather belts and they lauded themselves as a strictly "farm-to-table" establishment. We sat in a booth and ordered tiny plates of radishes soaked in marinade, a pizza on which lightly cooked quail eggs jiggled, and elaborate cocktails adorned with drenched cherries and lychees.

My mom asked Kyle about his hometown in Western Massachusetts, and he told her about the sledding races the kids in the neighborhood would have during the winter, everyone gathering at the top of the hill in the garden of a neighbor who had opened up his property for public sledding. We talked about movies and Kyle said he wanted to watch all of Ken Burns's Civil War documentary series this summer; he had watched his Dust Bowl documentary in high school and loved it. My mom asked if he was familiar with Dorothea Lange's photography. I told my mom I would need some more professional clothes for my new career in tech.

Toward the end of dinner, when the table had been cleared and we were drinking mint tea and sharing a plate of chewy, gluten-free cinnamon cookies, my mom asked Kyle about his future plans.

"What's next for you?" she asked.

"Actually," said Kyle, glancing at me, "I've been thinking I might like to teach. Maybe urban environmental development, or something like that. At a university."

"Really?" I exclaimed. "That's new. Since when?"

"I've been thinking it over for a while now," Kyle said, "but I wasn't sure what you'd think, you know, given all the recent shifts and things. I love the afternoons when the kids come to the garden. It's become my favorite part of the week."

I'd never felt jealous or competitive with Kyle before, but I wondered how I'd feel watching him become a teacher. What if he stuck it out, while I had cut and run?

"But what about all your advocacy work? I thought you wanted to go into public policy?"

"Yeah, hopefully I'll still do that work. I don't know, really; I've just been thinking about it as a possibility."

"Oh, don't teach," my mom said. "Don't go into academia, it's a bureaucratic nightmare. A real mess."

"Really?" I asked, surprised. "I thought you loved teaching."

"Besides, I'm sure there's more money elsewhere," my mom continued.

"Since when do you care about that?" I retorted.

"That's not really my focus," said Kyle. "Money isn't everything."

"It might be more than you think," my mom said. "Don't be lured into some romantic dream of the great professor. Most of the day-to-day is about grading hundreds of essays written the night before and appealing to the department for grants."

"Wow, Mom," I said.

So much of why I had applied for TFA in the first place was because my mom was a professor; I had often told Amelia that I wanted to feel as committed to the work I did in the world as my mom was to hers.

"Does that mean you're happy that Elena's leaving teaching?" Kyle asked.

"I'm excited for you," my mom said to me. "The startup sounds like it will be great."

"Thanks," I said. "Yeah, I think I'm excited too."

"Just don't forget about what really matters," Kyle said.

"What do you mean?"

"I know how important it is for you to be working to help others, and I don't want you to lose sight of that."

"No," I said, "of course not."

I looked toward my mom, who raised her eyebrows at me over her mug of tea. I tried not to catch her eye and instead reached for Kyle's hand underneath the table. When she finished her tea, my mom turned and signaled to the waiter to bring over the check.

Chapter 24

The evening before my first day of work at CloseReader, I opened my new work email account and found seventy-nine unread emails sitting in my inbox.

"Oh my god," I said, feeling a warm rush of panic, "was I supposed to be checking my email already?"

Kyle looked over my shoulder while eating peanut butter by the spoonful from the jar; I was having cereal for dinner.

"No clue," he said, "maybe?"

"Shit. But no one told me."

"Just go through them now, it looks like it's mostly calendar invites and things."

I had envisioned spending my evening in the bath with a homemade yogurt-and-honey face mask and then watching an episode of *Grey's Anatomy*. I needed to wash my hair; I intended to shave my legs. But there was no way I could go into work tomorrow with a full inbox; I poured a glass of wine and refilled my bowl of cereal.

Most of the emails were, as Kyle had pointed out, calendar invitations for repeating events. I understood what happy hour every Thursday at 5:00 p.m. meant, but what was "P2P" every other Wednesday at 2:00 p.m.?

"What's 'stand-up'?" I said to Kyle, as my weekdays were suddenly populated with a twenty minute block every morning at 10:00 a.m.

"Like, comedy?" Kyle said.

"Do you think I need to come up with some jokes?"

Later that evening I flipped through my old copy of *Dewdrops on a Lotus Leaf.* Underlined images and lines from my last semester at college jumped out at me, and I began to wonder: Who was that person who had circled that word in particular? Marked this line with a star? That there had been a version of me with pencil in hand, reading this little book of Japanese poems in the library, or in bed, or on a blanket on the lawn some spring afternoon, seemed now to be utterly strange and unreal. It was like visiting an old friend, flipping through that book of poems and seeing what had caught my eye years before.

With some lines, my current self agreed with my past self—yes, I would underline that now, too. So, yes, I am still the same person, the same reader, the same underliner. Yet others were less clear to me. What had so stood out to me then? What other thoughts or fears or loves were swirling in me, such that it was that line and not this, that was noted? Which self was going into San Francisco the next day to my new job? The same self who had just finished two years of teaching middle school? The same self who had traveled through Southeast Asia on overnight buses, eating plate after plate of bright green morning glory fried in garlic? Or someone new altogether?

The next morning, I began my new forty-minute commute into the city and discovered that, much to my surprise, I harbored germophobic tendencies. I was someone who would rarely pull out those paper toilet seat covers in airports and restaurants; I didn't carry around hand sanitizer when I traveled through Southeast Asia; I have some general opinion that kids should play in the dirt and eat things off the floor. But that morning, crossing the bay during the morning rush-hour commute, I watched as riders went through their daily makeup routine, applying foundation, blush, eyeliner, mascara, lipstick; I saw the particles of skin and powder flit into the air around them as they swirled their brush in the powder compact and then swished it over their cheekbones. My train car had no air flow, so I tried to wedge myself next to the door, afraid of growing woozy. I was terrified of passing out while we were under the tunnel, anticipating the announcement that would say, "Well, we're experiencing about a twenty-minute delay because of a medical emergency between Embarcadero and West Oakland. We'll be hanging out here for the moment, but we hope to be moving shortly." I couldn't bear the thought of being the medical emergency that caused a twenty-minute delay on BART.

CloseReader operated from the third floor of a coworking space in downtown San Francisco; Paula had texted me the code to the building the night before. I felt my new boots pinch as I walked the few blustery blocks from Montgomery BART to the office. Around me rushed the techie elite with Peet's coffees in hand, ordering their Sweetgreen salad lunches, setting up meetings in the public LinkedIn café. I passed by a bookstore featuring handmade greeting cards, beside which sprawled a man in an overcoat and little else, hair unkempt and dirty, mouth agape, eyes shut.

The elevator opened onto a large, open-plan office space; a fiddle-leaf fig tree perched in a woven basket leaned against a community bulletin board with flyers advertising the coworking space's weekly yoga and meditation offerings, the ten-minute neck-and-shoulder massages, and the various food trucks featuring the latest fusion food that would roll up in front of the building at lunchtime. Paula met me at the elevator—she had started working three weeks before me—and took me on a tour of the office, pointing out the small closed-door booths for private meetings and conversations; the array of red and blue couches and armchairs for working with your feet up; the kitchen, which offered complimentary tea and coffee and a hefty selection of snacks that were always on hand—peanut-butter-filled pretzels, yogurt-covered raisins, dried apple chips. The office had floor-to-ceiling windows lining one wall overlooking the street below, highlighting the silver-gray buildings around us, the silver-gray San Francisco sky above.

"But on a clear day," Paula said, "you can almost see the bay."

She led me to CloseReader's corner—four standing desks arranged in two pods, on which stood big desktop monitors, lined up against the window. There was a large whiteboard on wheels, which was covered in blue and red marker scrawl: "Primary Users = Students. Make design student-friendly (emojis??). Also: Teachers and Parents need to Buy In!!" On the corner of the whiteboard, held up with magnets, was a postcard of a black-and-white photograph: a man in a trench coat holds an umbrella above his cello case, which stands next to him. His gaze is away from the cello, toward the street. Perhaps he is waiting for a taxi or a bus. In the meantime, on the rainy Paris afternoon, the cello remains dry while the man gets wet. Amelia had once sent me that same postcard when she was living in London. On the back she had written: *How strange the things we claim as precious and must protect from the rain, while we get wet!*

"Here, this is your desk, this is our pod, the Curriculum team," Paula said. On my desk stood a water bottle with CloseReader's logo imprinted on the steel in white.

"A first-day gift," Paula said.

"Nice, thanks."

"We'll also go out to lunch all together today, to celebrate."

Nobody stood at the second pod of desks, but I could see notebooks open, half-eaten granola bars, a framed picture of a guy rock climbing, clad in red helmet, held up with straps. The chalk on his hands was visible, even in the photograph. A smile of brilliantly white teeth shone out of his sunburnt face.

"Who's that?" I asked.

"That's Jesse. So typical he'd have a picture of himself on his desk," Paula said, laughing. "He and Andy are in one of the conference rooms having a meeting with Julio."

"The other engineer?"

"Yeah. He's remote, lives in Brazil."

Paula rolled up a yoga ball and sat on it, bouncing up and down.

"So, how's it been going?" I said, slipping my jacket around a swivel chair hiked up to reach the height of the standing desk.

"So good," Paula said. "It's exciting. We're really here at the beginning of things. Most of Andy's time is taken up with investors right now, but he's also obviously involved in all the design and content stuff. Now that you're here, we can get going on developing some prototype lessons to try out in classrooms."

"Can you imagine being in school right now? All the teachers are back this week, I think."

"Honestly, I'm thrilled not to be prepping for fifty new students right now."

"Yeah," I said, sitting down, "me too."

I started thinking about my students, about those first-day jitters, about shiny new backpacks and empty notebooks. Over the summer I had cleaned out boxes of teaching supplies, random assortments of lesson plans, and essays and tests I had never handed back to my students. Looking through one exam from my first year, in which I had asked students to identify the different parts of a paragraph, I realized that what I had taught my students that year was to highlight in a certain order, use a particular color scheme, rather than to internalize what it meant to build an argument. They learned that evidence meant something in quotes and a topic sentence always came at the beginning of a paragraph. They did not—I was now sure of it—learn that their opinions about whatever we were reading mattered, were vital, nor how to unpack their opinions and figure out why they thought what they thought.

I looked up to see Andy and Jesse walking toward us, laptops tucked under their arms, still talking about the design specs Julio had laid out for them on their call.

"I still don't know about the sidebar option. Should it pop up? Or only if you click on it?" said Jesse.

"Hold that thought," said Andy. "Elena. Welcome. Great to have you here."

Andy was taller than I'd guessed from our Google Hangouts interview: pale, a little on the skinny side, with glasses that left deep red indentations in the sides of his nose and by his ears. Jesse, next to him, looked more like he was about to go rock climbing than sit at a desk writing code. We sat, the four of us, on yoga balls and desk chairs and a yellow polyester pouf that Andy pulled out from behind the whiteboard. While Jesse and Paula debated where we should go for lunch, Andy went over the calendar invites I had scrupulously accepted the night before ("P2P is a peer-to-peer coffee date or walk; No, you don't need jokes for stand-up") and let me know to expect an email invite to join the virtual HR network CloseReader used ("Just follow the instructions there to get set up with benefits").

My first day of work was a whirl of laptop shortcuts and

managing to eat a Mexican-Japanese fusion burrito while sitting on a bench outside without spilling any of the miso-mayo on my shirt; of cracking grammar jokes with Paula and getting used to the feel of noise-canceling headphones resting heavily on my ears ("Our norm is that if someone is wearing headphones, they want to do quiet, private work, so we leave them alone. If you want to ask them a question, send a message over GChat"); of watching a PowerPoint slideshow on the origins of CloseReader ("Ten years ago Andy was a teacher in a classroom in Detroit . . .") and selecting several middle-school-appropriate books, short stories, and poems to read over the coming days and weeks in order to start preparing sample guided close-reading lessons. I set up about fifty different passwords to various apps and programs and created my profile in Google, using, as my profile picture, a photograph Kyle had taken of me after a long evening hike in Tilden earlier in the summer, my hair in a braided tangle down my back, sunlight dipping behind me, my skin rosy and freckled.

When I left the office in the late afternoon, working my way through the throng of commuters, there was a man standing at the BART entrance playing the violin—I recognized the piece as the "Queen of the Night" aria from *The Magic Flute*, the opera I had heard years ago in Salzburg. I paused to listen and remembered a story my grandparents had told me about Joshua Bell, the famous violinist. A researcher placed him in the subway station, dressed in regular clothes, perhaps even slightly raggedy. I imagined him in a long black woolen coat, wearing gloves with the fingers cut off. He played in this subway station, his case open in front of him, and watched as people walked by without a second glance. Some tossed a few coins, a dollar bill or two into the case, but most took no notice. He was part of the scenery. A hard-on-his-luck guy who knew how to play a tune on the violin, asking for cash. I had some recollection that one person

did recognize him. That this person stopped and stared and marveled. How much, I wondered, had he made that day? Was it enough
for lunch, or liquor, or a place to sleep that night? My grandparents
always concluded the story by asking, "And what if every ragged
person on the street was, in fact, a Joshua Bell in disguise? Or what if
we looked at them that way?"

I dug into my pocket and pulled out a few coins, tossed them
into the violinist's open case, and continued down the stairs to the
platform, where the screech of the train's brakes drowned out the
music from above.

Chapter 25

About a month into my tenure at CloseReader—after I had adjusted to the midnight text notifications that would light up my phone on the bedside table, and after I had stopped going alone to the bookstore on my lunch break, instead heating up leftovers in the communal kitchen's microwave and squeezing onto a couch with Jesse and Paula to eat and chat—our team spent two days in the Marin Headlands on a "values retreat." Julio flew in from Brazil, and Andy—whom we saw infrequently in the office, as he was generally in meetings with advisors, investors, prospective investors—consulted with a few Silicon Valley gurus and planned out a two-day retreat filled with trust falls, a build-your-own-pizza dinner, and hundreds of sticky notes.

Paula and I, the East Bay residents of the team, drove up together. Paula picked me up in her dad's green Volvo, a string of beads hanging down from the rearview mirror and a tiny Buddha figurine wobbling on the dashboard. I had volunteered to bring snacks, and I piled the back seat of the car with goodies from Trader Joe's—salty popcorn and chocolate-covered pretzels and bags of trail mix. Kyle and I had fought the night before—about how I wasn't as interested in sex these days, and how he wanted me to initiate more—and I left while he was still in the shower.

"Which is the worse insult for a woman, do you think—to be labeled a slut or a prude?" Paula said, as we turned onto the highway. "I think for us, for millennials, it has to be the latter. I mean, think about it. We are post–sexual revolution. We've grown up in a world where there are condoms in campus bathrooms, where we've been on birth control since we were fourteen, where we could get the HPV vaccine for free as undergraduates. Our mothers fought for our rights to sleep around without consequences. The female orgasm is highly revered; there are seminars for both men and women to learn the intricate needs and infinite potential of the clitoris. 'Be free,' they all cry to us, 'you no longer have to restrain yourselves in the bedroom; you're free to be the porn stars we know you all are, deep inside.'"

"So, what does that mean for the restrained among us?" I pondered. "Liberated as we are, no longer bound into corsets or to making love behind a white sheet, or hidden away in a high-necked nightie, what are we supposed to do when we don't live up to the orgasmic promise that has been offered to us?"

"Have an affair," Paula said.

I laughed, and the Buddha figurine wobbled back at me, grinning from ear to ear.

We were staying in a rambling farmhouse-cum-retreat center that featured a long wooden table in the kitchen that looked as if it were cut straight from the tree and a garden with hemp-woven hammocks set up beneath overhanging wisteria, though the flowers had long since bloomed and died already that season. Paula and I shared a bedroom with a small sink and little glass mirror perched in the corner. In the living room, Andy had draped butcher paper up over the television and laid markers and notebooks on the marble coffee table in the center of the room.

We met Julio in the kitchen. He had an apple in his hand and a beard that suggested a guitar-playing, sandals-wearing kind of life-style. Together we put snacks into drawers and filled water bottles and talked about how his flight was, how he'd sat on the runway for over an hour before taking off and almost missed his connection. Jesse wandered in, a bunch of freshly picked chard in his hands, and Andy called us to come and sit down, get started, share a little gratitude. Again, I felt the relief of not being a teacher, standing alone in front of twenty students, wondering what on earth to do with them. I had spent the last month reading *Diary of a Wimpy Kid* and *Pride and Prejudice* and *The Hobbit* and *And Still I Rise* and excerpts of *Song of Myself*, taking notes for mock lesson plans, and now I was spending two days in a chard-and-hammock-filled garden, with these new colleague friends, all of whom were dedicated to teaching kids how to read and analyze literature, and making s'mores and drinking summer ale while they were at it.

"Okay, welcome," said Andy, as we arranged ourselves on couches and poufs and comfy chairs. "First, I just want to say that this is a safe space. It's important that we really hold the container, and even though we may challenge each other to push our boundaries over the next couple days, we also need to be able to sit with whatever comes up."

Julio nodded, sitting cross-legged on the floor with bare feet. My startup team retreat was starting off in the same way my mom described the Rainbow Gatherings she'd gone to when she was my age. I scooped a handful of raw Brazil nuts from a bowl on the coffee table and settled back into the couch.

"So, let's start off with a gratitude circle. Anyone want to begin?"

"I can start," said Jesse. "I'm feeling grateful to have some women on our team, finally!"

We laughed and Paula rolled her eyes.

"No, but seriously," said Jesse, "I've been with Andy since the beginning and it's nice to be growing, have new people joining the movement."

"Well," said Paula, "I am feeling so grateful not to be in a class-room right now. I mean, don't get me wrong, I'm into curriculum development and everything and getting tech into schools, but, wow, teaching can be a real bitch."

"I'll go," said Julio. "I'm grateful to be here with you all, and not stuck sleeping in an airport in Houston."

We all nodded our heads.

"Oh, and apples. I'm grateful for apples."

Andy and I made eye contact, and he raised his eyebrows at me. *Sure*, I nodded, *I can go.*

"Yeah," I said. "So, I think I'm feeling grateful to have found a way to still be doing something I believe in, even though it's different from what I imagined a few years ago. Does that make sense?"

Again, everyone nodded.

"Thanks, you guys. I resonate with everything you all shared," said Andy, "and I'll just add that I am grateful for all of you being open and willing to work hard to make this product and this com-pany the best it can possibly be."

Julio led us in a collective breath and our retreat officially kicked off.

That evening, an early-season rain started to fall. The mist had been collecting all afternoon, and by the time we had finished with the first round of sessions on "What is a value?" and "How values create culture," and eaten our make-your-own pizzas—mine included rips of mozzarella cheese, pine nuts, and butternut squash—our retreat house was surrounded by clouds and the rain could be heard drizzling out of a drainpipe. I slipped away to shower. I hadn't checked my phone all afternoon, and as I toweled off my hair, I saw several missed calls and texts from Kyle.

Kyle: *hey*

Kyle: *chat later?*

Me: *hey, not gr8 service here so cant talk but retreat going well and c u tomorrow xox*

I plugged the phone in and changed into my elephant hippie pants—the ones I'd purchased outside of a pagoda in Siem Reap—and went back downstairs to the living room. Julio was sitting cross-legged in front of the electric fireplace, strumming on a guitar and singing a medley of Simon and Garfunkel songs. Paula and Andy had dug out a deck of cards and were deep into their third or fourth round of gin rummy. I went into the kitchen to boil water for tea and found Jesse sitting on a barstool by the counter, reading a well-worn copy of the first book in the Lord of the Rings trilogy. I turned on the kettle, pulled out a mug and a nettle-and-hibiscus tea bag I found in one of the drawers, and sat down next to him.

"I've never read it," I said, pointing to the book in his hands.

"You haven't? It's a classic; my absolute favorite," he said, laying the book facedown on the counter.

I shrugged. "I've seen the movies."

"Oh, come on," Jesse said, "Miss Literary Genius over here, you know better than that."

"I've never gotten into fantasy or sci-fi or anything like that."

"Fantasy's the only fiction I like to read. Who wants to read realistic fiction? I'll just read nonfiction to find out what's going on in the world. But fantasy makes you think; it makes you dream."

"So, you dream about hobbits?"

Jesse laughed. "Sometimes."

"I don't know," I said, pouring my tea, "it seems kind of escapist. I read because I want to understand human experience more, you know? Not aliens or robots or whatever."

"You know what you suffer from?" Jesse said. "A lack of imagination."

"I don't think I've ever been accused of that before."

"First time for everything. Seriously. Sci-fi and fantasy go deep into what it is to be human, to be alive. You should read some before you knock it."

"Okay, okay, I surrender."

We sat quietly for a few minutes while I sipped my tea. We could hear Julio singing the same verse of "The Sound of Silence" over and over again while Paula and Andy switched to playing Bullshit.

"So, did you get those pants in Vietnam or Cambodia?" Jesse asked.

I laughed. "How could you tell?"

"I spent six months in Southeast Asia a few years ago," Jesse said.

"Oh, no way, I was there after college. Where did you go?"

"Yeah, I did it all. I did Vietnam, did the motorbike tour. And I did Thailand; I did Myanmar too. Amazing country. I went in the off season and there were basically no tourists."

"Nice, wow. How long were you there?"

"In Myanmar? Two weeks, or something like that. Love the Burmese people—they are so nice! But I spent most of my time island-hopping in Thailand."

"Cool, yeah, I only spent a few months traveling, but I was in Thailand and Vietnam, too. And Cambodia."

"With your boyfriend?"

"Kyle? Oh, no," I said, "we only met after I moved to the Bay."

"Ah, I see," said Jesse.

"Did you go to the Full Moon Party?" I asked.

"On Koh Phangan? Definitely."

"You jumped the fire rope, didn't you?"

Jesse laughed. "Of course I did. After way too much to drink."

"Insane."

"Yeah, but you have to do it, right? That's what traveling's for. Come on, what crazy things did you do?"

"True, yeah, I love that about traveling. I met this German girl in my hostel in Phnom Penh and totally changed my plans to go with her on this multi-day Ayurvedic cleanse in the middle of the rainforest."

"How was it?"

"Awful. I spent the entire time either on the toilet or lying on the bathroom floor next to the toilet."

"Ouch!"

"Yeah, I still don't think my microbiome has recovered."

"At least you had a toilet. I once had to take a shit on the side of the road because I wasn't going to make it back to my hostel in time."

I snorted tea out of my nose. "Oh no!"

"Yes. I was literally pissing out of my ass on someone's geraniums. Or, you know, coconut tree or something."

"Gross, gross," I said, laughing. "Okay, do you have any good bug stories?"

"Duh—my best one is about a spider the size of Godzilla. I had just finished a several-day trek and hadn't showered or slept in a real bed in days. So I decide to splurge on the 'fancy' hostel option and get myself a private room, and there I am lying in bed airing out my feet when I see these legs—these huge, hairy legs—start to crawl up the wall, and—"

"Stop!" I said, grabbing Jesse's arm. "Oh my god, don't. I'll have nightmares."

"Okay, well, suffice it to say that in the battle between me and the spider, the spider won."

"What happened?"

"At first, I thought maybe I could flush it out, kind of shove it out the door. So I got my water bottle and I started pouring water down the wall into the corner where the spider was, hoping it would scurry out and I could sweep it out of my room. But instead, it ran the opposite way. Toward my bed."

"Oh no, oh no."

"Yeah, anyway, then it was all over. There was no way I could sleep in that room. I checked and there was an empty room across the hall from me. I grabbed all my stuff and literally ran into the other room. I stuffed my sweatshirt in the crack under the door and didn't come out again all night."

"Did you sleep at all?"

"Yeah, barely."

"My bug story is not nearly that bad."

"Tell me."

"I was staying in this little cabin room–type thing in Thailand. You know, on a cliff overlooking the beach."

"Heaven."

"Yeah. Sort of. Except this cabin had all these cracks open to the outside, so every time I went into the bathroom, I had to face down half a dozen flying cockroaches."

Jesse shuddered. "No."

"Just zipping around the sink and the shower and the—"

"I can't. What did you do? Did they ever land on you?"

"Yeah, they did once or twice. Until I figured out that that thing, you know, the hose or whatever next to the toilet? I figured out that I could grab that as soon as I walked into the bathroom and then spray at those bastards till they ran back outside."

We were both laughing now as I mimed firing at my cockroach foes; we laughed until tears started streaming down my face and Paula, Andy, and Julio wandered into the kitchen to find out what was so funny.

"Bugs," Jesse said.

"You had to be there," I said.

The rain was falling steadily outside, and it was coming on midnight. We said good night; I put my mug in the sink and headed to bed. On the way up the stairs, Jesse put his arm around me and gave my shoulders a squeeze.

"Good times," he said. "Night."

"Good night," I said.

In the morning, the rain had stopped and the sky had cleared. Paula woke me by throwing a pillow at me when I didn't turn off my alarm, and we pulled our hair back into messy buns, exchanged our glasses for contact lenses, and made it downstairs in time to see Julio getting up from sitting in lotus position on a cushion on the back porch. Breakfast was a do-it yourself affair, and we brought our bowls of yogurt and chia and coconut flakes and crunchy peanut butter into the living room, where Andy stood, hair still wet from the shower, marker in hand. I settled myself on the floor, pulled out my notebook, and was ready for "Day 2: Creating Our Values."

We had been tasked with bringing our favorite stories of our team and how we worked together, and from these stories we would identify the values that guided our organization. Andy asked us to write our stories down on Post-it notes, and we would then arrange them into categories. I took a stack of blue Post-it notes and jotted out bullet points—of how when I had joined CloseReader everyone on the team had sent me a welcome email; of how Paula and I spent a significant amount of time each day making jokes about the books we were reading; of how often Jesse or Julio asked for my opinion about a design spec they were working on; of the fact of this retreat itself.

We cleared space on the floor in front of us, moved aside the coffee table with the discarded card games and empty cereal bowls, and started laying our notes on the ground, organizing and arranging them into similar categories. Alongside my story of the welcome emails, Paula placed a note about how she had gone to coffee with both Jesse and Andy in her first week working and had a get-to-know-you Zoom call with Julio. Next to a story that Jesse wrote about working late, Julio put his note about Andy following up extensively with him on questions he hadn't known the answers to. Almost all of us had stories about laughing together and sharing ideas across teams and disciplines.

"Clearly, one of our values has to be about humor and fun," Jesse said, grouping together a handful of Post-it notes recording inside jokes and happy hours.

"Great," said Andy, turning to the butcher paper hanging over the television, "let's write that down. One: we will laugh often."

"And something about dedication," Paula said, gathering up the stories of late nights spent refining programs.

"Yes," said Andy. "How about this. Two: we will strive for excellence."

"We should have something about our mission," I said, "about how we're trying to serve students."

"Great," said Andy, "I love it. Let's say, three: we put students first. Or maybe this is better: our goal is to serve."

"I like the one about students," I said. "It's more specific."

"True," said Julio, "but I think the service one might be better because it's about a quality we're trying to cultivate, you know? Rather than just identifying who we're serving."

"That makes sense to me, too," said Jesse.

We sorted through Post-it notes and wrote and rewrote our values all through the morning and into the early afternoon. We paused briefly for lunch, and I walked outside and checked my phone again to find another missed message.

Kyle: *want to go out to dinner tonight when ur back? Love u*

I texted *yes!* and went back in for our closing. In alternating brown and blue marker, Andy had rewritten our cleaned-up, final list of values on a fresh sheet of butcher paper that hung over the television:

> *We laugh often*
> *We strive for excellence*
> *We are here to serve*
> *We challenge each other*
> *We ask for help*
> *We adapt and evolve*
> *We think BIG*

I took a photo on my phone, and then the five of us squeezed in front of the list and took selfie after selfie.

"I feel like we just got initiated," Julio said.

"Do we need a handshake?" asked Paula.

"Or should we all run around the garden naked?" Jesse joked.

Andy laughed and handed us each a glass. "Let's just raise a toast," he said, pouring whiskey into each of our glasses. "This is good stuff. Straight from Scotland."

"To CloseReader!" we all said, and clinked our glasses together. As I tipped the whiskey down into my throat, I felt it slowly start to burn and tears popped into my eyes. I looked around at the others; Jesse and Paula were in mock agony at the alcohol's taste, while Julio was calmly onto his second drink. I remembered the feeling I had at Orr Hot Springs earlier that year with Kyle, when I realized that I was like a string on an instrument about to snap, and that story my grandmother loved to tell of Paganini, whose strings snapped one by one throughout a concert. I started to think about what happened after the concert was over, when he had to replace each string. Later, perhaps the soundboard and the bridge—and eventually the pegs, which would have grown rough and sticky over the years—would also have needed some upkeep. After each different part of his violin had been replaced and repaired, I wondered, would it have still been the same violin? Would it even matter?

Suddenly, Paula poked me in the ribs, and I coughed, laughed, and held out my glass for another shot.

Chapter 26

I started to ease into the culture of a tech startup. Although technically Andy was my "boss," he reiterated again and again how he wasn't in favor of top-down management and how he wanted us to feel that we were all responsible to each other. He was rarely in the office, often checking in with us by phone as he drove to the South Bay for meetings, and so it was really just me, Paula, and Jesse in the office on a day-to-day basis. Julio worked his own odd hours, showing up on Zoom calls eating breakfast or dinner, or on his porch with a beer in hand. Although Paula was an early riser, neither Jesse nor I were morning people, and so, over the course of a few months, we settled into a rhythm of showing up at the office closer to ten or ten thirty, and leaving after the evening rush, around six thirty. By the time I'd arrive home, it would be after seven or sometimes eight, if I worked late, and I'd find Kyle reading on the couch, having already eaten dinner.

In the first few months of our new routine, Kyle would make a plate for me and leave it in the fridge, ready to be heated up when I came home. He'd sit with me at the table while I ate, and we'd catch up on our days. I told him about researching state standards to show how CloseReader's offerings aligned, about creating draft after draft of guided text analyses, how we had to come up with questions that could be applied to any text, but not be so generic as to be rote or uninteresting. I told him he should come join us at a happy hour one week, and that Paula and Jesse and I wanted to go hiking together on the weekends, that we should all go together. Kyle told me about the politics of the nonprofit that ran the urban farm, and I nodded along, trying to think of the right questions to ask.

On the weekends, I got together with Jesse and Paula and went hiking in the Oakland redwoods, or walked around Lake Merritt, and then had brunch, sipping on orange juice and champagne and eating omelets stuffed with sun-dried tomatoes and caramelized onions, and I felt as if my life had suddenly turned into an episode of a nineties television show, set against the backdrop of Silicon Valley. Kyle didn't join us, saying he had to do inventory for the farm instead. We would snuggle in bed on Saturday nights and watch movies, the way we'd done when we first started dating—although now, Kyle would often fall asleep before the movie had finished, and I'd check my phone, scrolling through the pictures Amelia sent me of her bike rides along the beach in LA and the elaborately stylized lattes she seemed to drink every day. I stopped feeling the Sunday evening blues that were a feature of my TFA years, when I'd dread going back to the classroom on Monday morning after a weekend of trying to forget my ineffective lesson plans and not-yet-graded quizzes. Instead, I looked forward to the start of the week.

At the end of the year, I finally convinced Kyle to trek into the city one Thursday afternoon and join us at our regular 5:00 p.m. happy hour.

Me: *come, itll be fun*

Kyle: *ok* ☺

Me: *great! and u can finally meet jesse, don't think andy will be here*

Kyle: *cool*

We had already ordered our drinks by the time Kyle arrived, and he found us standing around a table, looking at the local artwork and photography posted on the walls of our neighborhood bar.

"Is that a banana?" I said, pointing to a blurry black-and-white photograph.

"I think so," Paula said, "and a wine bottle, maybe?"

"But more importantly," Jesse said, "what do you think the banana is feeling in this moment?"

"That it needs a drink," said Paula.

"Cheers to that," I said.

"Hey," said Kyle, and I felt his hand on my back as he edged his way through the happy hour crowd.

"Hey," I said, leaning in to kiss him, his unshaven beard scratching my lips. "You're here!"

"I'm here."

He turned to hug Paula, who kissed him on the cheek and said, "Long time no see!" and then held his hand out to Jesse, as the two of them exchanged rounds of, "Hey, man, good to finally meet you."

For a while we chatted awkwardly, in little spurts, about the photographs on the walls and the winter projects on Kyle's urban farm and the big push we were making to have a CloseReader prototype ready for classroom demos in the spring. I saw Kyle fiddle with his hair, pulling at the curls sitting on the back of his neck, which I knew he did when he felt uncomfortable or distracted. I felt the strangeness of bringing two distinct parts of my life together, and the way I was suddenly out of sync both with Kyle and with Jesse and Paula. The intimacy I had with each sputtered when they were brought together, and I felt nostalgic for the evenings of my first year in Berkeley, when Kyle, Monica, Rae, and I would eat plates piled high with pasta and drink glass after glass of cheap Trader Joe's wine in the living room of our South Berkeley apartment. I was only sporadically in touch with Monica since she'd moved back East to start med school; she and Rae had broken up and gotten back together several times and I could never remember their current status.

"So I read this article last week about Bitcoin," I said, "and honestly I'm not sure I understood half of it."

"I'm so into Bitcoin," Jesse said, "I think it's going to be huge. Take over everything. A bunch of my friends have invested."

"Really?" Kyle asked. "Why do you think so?"

"It's the future," said Jesse. "Decentralized money, independent of government backing or regulation."

"Okay," said Paula, "but isn't it just numbers on a screen? It seems made-up."

"Well, what do you think cash is? Or your credit card?" said Jesse. "Just symbols that we've all decided to interpret in the same way. It's just one big fictional agreement."

"So, what if we opted out of the agreement?" I mused.

"Exactly," Jesse replied. "That's what Bitcoin's offering."

"Isn't it just a new agreement, though?" Kyle said. "Just another exchange of trust? I mean, it seems like it's just moving the power from the old guard of Wall Street to the new guard of Silicon Valley and tech."

"No way, man, you've got it all wrong," said Jesse. "It's radical. A new form of exchange, a new type of market."

"Wouldn't radical be getting rid of the market altogether, though? Finding an entirely new way to cooperate and exchange goods?" Kyle asked skeptically.

I remembered Kyle on the day we had met, marching together in the blazing September sun at an Occupy rally. I knew he had been disappointed when the movement faltered, when the slogans were spent, the windows smashed, the community microphones hoarse and gone quiet. He had hoped—we had all hoped—that things were going to change. I wondered what Jesse had been doing while Kyle and I were holding up hand-drawn signs and chanting "We are the 99%" over and over again. Traveling maybe, or attending a coding boot camp.

Paula indulged him, "Like what?"

"What about a gift economy—" said Kyle.

"Like at Burning Man?" Jesse interjected.

"I've never been," said Kyle, "but yeah."

"Oh, you have to go," said Jesse.

"Have you been?" I asked.

"Yeah, a couple times."

"I'm so curious about it," I said.

"You are?" Kyle asked.

"I would definitely go again," said Jesse.

"Yeah," I said, "I mean, we see all the Burners getting ready in August, with their sparkly bikes and gallons of water and leopard-print bikinis, and—"

"And it's interesting," said Paula.

"It's a whole different world out there," said Jesse.

"I didn't know you were into that kind of thing," said Kyle.

"Well, I couldn't even consider going before," I said, "because of school."

"But now?" Kyle replied.

"I don't know," I said, "maybe."

"Amazing," said Jesse, "let's all go! We can have a CloseReader camp."

"What would be our offering?" said Paula. "Free text analysis?"

"Maybe we could pass out poems," I said.

"You'll fit right in," said Jesse.

I looked at Kyle, who was looking at his phone. Our drinks were mostly finished; the ice was melting in the glasses, diluting the last golden dregs. Jesse and Paula took out their wallets and laid cash on the table, tucked it underneath the coasters.

"Back to the grind," said Jesse.

"Yeah," said Paula, "let's go."

"Oh," said Kyle, "you're going back to work?"

"Yeah," I said. "Sorry, we still have some things to finish up, and—"

Jesse and Paula looked at each other. "We'll meet you at the office," Paula said, squeezing my arm as they walked out.

"You've been working late so much," said Kyle. "Can't you call it for today and come back with me? We can go out to dinner or something."

"No, I can't. I mean, that sounds nice, but I really do have a lot to do."

"I wish you'd told me beforehand," said Kyle. "I wouldn't have come all the way out here for a forty-five-minute drink."

"I wanted you to see Paula, though, and meet Jesse. You know, these are the people who I spend my days with, and it's important to me that you all know each other."

Kyle was quiet. He ran his hand over his stubble. Outside the light was fading and the techies on Market Street were zipping up their fleeces, warming themselves with glasses of whiskey and Styrofoam cups of coffee, gearing up for the evening stretch. We stood in the street just outside the bar, still and unmoving in the cold air, as around us parents rushed to get home for bedtime, taking an hour-long break from answering email to wash spaghetti sauce out of their kids' hair and read *Goodnight Moon*.

"Kyle," I said, "I'm sorry. I have to go, though."

"Yeah," he said, "okay. I guess I'll see you later, at home."

I walked back toward CloseReader's office building, my hands in my pockets to ward off the cold. As I turned around, I saw Kyle unlocking his bike and heading to BART. For a moment, I considered running after him and blowing off the last few tasks on my to-do list. I waited to see if he would turn around, but he kept his face turned down, collar up, threading his bike quickly through the crowd. I punched in the code to the office building and went inside.

Chapter 27

In the spring of my first year at CloseReader, we set up demonstration days at various schools around the Bay. I called up Jay at Bright Star Academy and arranged for us to spend an afternoon in several different English classes, trying out our guided close-reading programs on my former students. In the weeks leading up to our demonstration, I worked late into the evening most days. I would slide into bed after Kyle had gone to sleep and we would lean into one other, finding each other in dreams if not in daylight. He left for the farm early, and we wandered in and out of our yellow-painted apartment on opposite schedules, passing each other in the doorways, kisses pecked on cheeks, hands squeezed under the blankets.

Kyle wanted us to go back to Roy and Jane's cabin in the redwoods in the spring, but I couldn't take the time off, I said, not so close to the first demos. So, Kyle drove to Yosemite with three friends and spent a week camping and hiking through the meadows, up the sheer cliffs. He didn't have reception in the park, so we didn't call or text. During the week that he was gone I luxuriated in our empty apartment, sometimes staying up until 2:00 a.m. watching Netflix, leaving the dishes piled high in the sink and the bed unmade; when I came home from work in the evenings, everything was exactly as I'd left it that morning.

Amelia and I sent a flurry of emails to each other during that week. I would wake to find new emails delivered in the middle of the night, some just of poems with no subject or commentary, others filled with descriptions of her recent adventures.

To: Elena Berg
From: Amelia Carr
Subject: Zen
Elena,

I spent a day at the Zen center here. It was mostly unre-markable. I tried to sit in full lotus throughout each for-ty-minute meditation session. I have always wondered if other people are somehow built in such a way that their legs do not fall asleep in this position, or if they are simply not as bothered by it as I am, but throughout most of the day, the main thing I was focused on was my feet starting to twang with the pain of pins and needles, and then the experience of them falling fully asleep in my lap. I had vision after vision of my legs and feet falling off, or being stuck in lotus position permanently, and so eventually I succumbed to my body's resistance to discomfort, and pain, and its intense need to run away. To change position.

My biggest insight/takeaway from the day: If I just stretch out my leg, everything will be okay.

Love always,
A.

I read her emails on my phone on the way to work, cramped in the train car, and I knew exactly what she meant. If I could only stretch my legs out, everything would be okay.

* *

I hadn't felt nervous about returning to BSA until the day of the demonstration itself. Paula and I met on the corner outside the school, which was now both familiar and unfamiliar. We arrived after classes had already started, so we missed wading through the throngs of kids gathered in groups outside the school, splitting a breakfast roll or sharing headphones while listening to music. I was grateful not to bump into any of my old students just yet. It had been less than a year since I'd walked in and out of the single-storied, red-and-beige building every day, and yet I was surprised at the sight of the newly planted tree saplings around the perimeter of the parking lot. They had not been there last year. I tried to imagine the story behind the saplings—were they the efforts of one of the science classes? Or a parent-teacher initiative to beautify the school grounds? Had they been planted by landscapers on the weekends, or during spring break? For a moment I wondered if they were a community project by a new TFA teacher at the school and I felt a rush of guilt and jealousy, and wondered why I'd never followed through on my own plans to introduce an after-school reading program, or a dance class for the mothers of my students.

"You okay?" said Paula, wiping the fog off her glasses.

"Fine," I said. "Yeah, fine."

"Weird to come back here, right?"

"So weird."

We checked in at the front desk, still set up in the catchall cafeteria, and hung lanyards around our necks with the word "visitor" scrawled in dark letters. I didn't recognize the parent volunteer at the reception desk this morning and checked myself from blurting out, "I used to teach here," over and over again.

"This was where I taught my first year," I said to Paula.

"What, here? In the cafeteria?"

"Right over there, by the photocopier."

"You're kidding."

"They didn't have a classroom for me."

"You should have complained to TFA right away."

I had had that same thought multiple times, but what should I have said? How could I have known then that having class in the same room as the photocopier would mean that roughly every hour some teacher or student would wander in and stand at the copier for twenty minutes, and that each time that happened my own class rhythm would be lost to the noisy light show that was that ridiculous machine? Could I have predicted the disastrous effect of trying to teach—worse still, trying to give a quiz or a test—in the same room where other kids were eating lunch, listening to the music outlawed in their own classrooms, and making weekend plans with their friends? And even if I had known all this, what could I have said? How could I have protested? What was I—or Jay—to do in the face of too few classrooms and too many students to properly attend to?

We walked through the hallways to our first classroom, and I was reminded of my first day at BSA, when I was so moved by the book reports on biographies of Rosa Parks and Cesar Chavez plastered to the walls. I pointed them out to Paula; she shrugged.

"It's the same at every school around here. It's not that impressive."

"You grew up here, so you're used to it. I think it's amazing that students are reading books about people who look like them."

"True, but there's more to change education than the books you read."

"Like what?"

"Think about it. You say it's helpful for kids of color to read books that feature people of color. But what about the teachers standing in front of them? What percentage of teachers here are white?"

"I don't know. Yeah, most of them, I think."

"Right. How do you think that impacts students? When the authority figures, the people with knowledge, are all white?"

"Do you think white people shouldn't become teachers? Do you think I shouldn't have done TFA?"

Paula shifted her bag from one shoulder to the other. "No, it's not that simple. But you have to be aware of yourself in relation to those you're trying to teach. When I was a kid, I don't think I had a single teacher who looked like me. Come to think of it, a lot of the other students didn't look like me either. I went to a fancy prep school in Oakland, and there weren't a whole lot of other biracial kids there."

"That must have been strange."

Paula laughed. "Yeah. That's one way of putting it."

"Is that why you did TFA?"

"It's a big part of it."

We knocked on the door of our first classroom, and a young teacher sporting a tie, an oversized mustache, and sneakers opened the door for us; I didn't recognize him. He shook our hands and introduced himself as Mr. C., a first-year TFA teacher.

"Good to have you here," he said. "Remind me what you're testing out?"

"It's a program to help kids close-read a text; it walks them through the process."

"Well," he said, "we sure could use that around here."

I remembered the moment in my first year of teaching when I realized that my kids would probably not have read the poem or story or passage I had assigned for homework; that they did not know how or why to mark up a text; that they wouldn't place questions or underlines and exclamation marks beside remarkable or surprising or interesting points. What I didn't know then was how to actually teach my kids to close-read—I didn't understand how to make it explicit. I thought that it was impossible to teach interest, to teach being curious about the words, to teach attentiveness to the lyricism of a passage—I figured it was all innate, that it was there or it wasn't, that my job was to ask the questions, not provide instruction and scaffolding for how to give the answers. I didn't know that beneath my curiosity and my instincts were layers upon layers of specific—and wholly teachable—comprehension of the way language worked, of its varied structure and meaning, of the nuances and shades of connotation that were attached to each word. It was from working with CloseReader that I'd finally broken apart the process, learned the steps, and thought about how to guide students through them.

I wanted to say all this to Mr. C., but instead we walked into the classroom and stood on the side as Mr. C. clapped his hands together, gathering up the attention of his students. I had turned to ask him whether he'd remembered to check out the laptop cart when I saw Anna sitting at a desk at the front of the room.

"Anna!" I said, leaving Paula to figure out the laptop situation.

"Hi," she said, looking from her desk to me to her desk again.

"Do you remember me?" I asked. "It's Ms. Berg. I was your ELA teacher last year."

"I remember," she said.

"How are you?" I asked warmly. "Have you discovered any new poets since last year?"

"Oh," she said, "no, not really."

The change from sixth grade to seventh grade is profound. Whereas the year before, Anna had still been closer to a child than a teenager, peering out from her oversized round glasses, her feet dangling off her chair, just one year later, she was touched with a newfound self-consciousness, her hair in a low ponytail instead of two braids, a few scattered pimples across her forehead.

"How's school going? Do you like the seventh grade?"

"It's okay," she said, shrugging.

"How's your mom?"

Anna bit her lip and looked down at her desk. "Okay," she said, barely audible.

"Elena!" Paula hissed at me. "Let's go, we have to get started."

"I'm happy to see you," I said to Anna. "My friend and I are going to show you guys something fun, and I'm counting on you to let us know how it could be better. Okay?"

Anna nodded, and I turned back toward Paula. We passed out laptops to each of the students, and then Paula stood at the front of the classroom and told the students that we needed their help.

"You are the very first students to see what we're about to show you," Paula said dramatically, and I could see how captivating she must have been as a teacher in her own classroom.

"Really?" the students murmured from different corners of the room. "We're the first?"

"Yes," said Paula, "and it's really important that you tell us exactly what you think about it. We want to know if it's boring, if it's silly, if it's helpful, if it's fun, if you think you'd use it to do your English homework . . ."

"But don't worry about that just yet," I said. "After you go through the exercise, you'll see a form with a few questions, and you can tell us what you think about it then."

"Right," said Paula. "Now, do you all have a short story or a poem that you've been reading with Mr. C. in class together? The first step is to open up the program and take a picture of your text—"

"We can take pictures with our laptops?" said a boy in the back. "Awesome!"

Several students turned their attention to the computers in front of them and began making silly faces and obscene gestures into the built-in cameras. We heard the click and swish as photographs were captured one after the other.

"My laptop camera isn't working!"

"Neither is mine!"

"Maybe you can use your phone?" Paula said. "I can show you how to download the app and then you can just transfer the picture to the computer."

"Woah, wait a minute," said Mr. C. "No phones allowed in the classroom."

"Oh, right," said Paula. "No phones in class?"

"Mr. C.," I said, "any chance we can make an exception today?"

"Yes!" said several students, rummaging through their backpacks.

"How did we not think about the no-phones-in-class thing?" I whispered to Paula.

"Well, but who knew the laptops wouldn't work?" she said. "They seem ancient."

"Okay, okay," I said, waving my hands to quiet the room down. "Here's what we'll do. If you're having trouble with your laptop, Paula and I will come around and take pictures with our phones and then we can upload the pictures to your computers. Raise your hand if your computer's camera isn't working."

Paula and I scrambled to the four or five students whose hands were raised, snapping photographs with our phones and trying to upload them to the computers. In the meantime, I watched as many of the students began taking photographs of each other, of pages from their math textbooks, of their hands spelling out gang symbols, of Mr. C. looking much older than his twenty-some-odd years in the back of the room.

"These are awesome pictures," one student called out.

"Yeah, can we keep them?"

"They're better than my iPhone camera."

By the time everyone had a text photographed and uploaded, the class time was halfway over.

"So, just follow the prompts on the screen," Paula said. "It's going to lead you through an analysis of the story or poem you uploaded."

"There's a dashboard on the side," I said, "where you can take notes, or underline, or highlight passages you want to remember."

"Check it out," a voice behind me said, poking her neighbor in the ribs, "you can use the little pen thing to draw on top of the picture."

"No, wait," I said, turning around, but it was too late. I heard giggles from all corners of the classroom, as students began doodling, scrawling, and graffitiing on top of the text they had uploaded. On top of a Langston Hughes poem, a student had drawn a cartoon image of a bomb exploding; on top of a page from the Maupassant story "The Necklace," another had written "FAKE" over and over again in the various different highlighter colors CloseReader had provided. I watched as Paula tried to steer a couple of students through the set of guided questions we had spent months working on, and even Mr. C. got into the fray, with ten minutes of class left to spare.

"See here," Mr. C. said, "it's asking you to highlight the images in the poem; what images are here?"

"But that's what I did," said a student, "I drew out the pictures of the poem, see? What explodes? A bomb."

"Okay," said Paula, "this is asking you to underline any passages that are important to the plot."

"I don't know."

"Well, what happens in the story?"

"She borrows a necklace and then she loses it."

"And what sentences here help you understand that?"

"This is dumb."

The bell rang and there was a flurry of scraping chairs, computers shutting, and backpacks hastily grabbed. Mr. C. looked relieved as his students left, and I remembered that same feeling, as though I had been holding my breath for the fifty-minute class period, or the entire school day, and how when the bell rang it would release slowly, noisily, without me having been aware that I had been holding it in the first place.

"Wait, so can we keep the pictures? Can we print them?" a chorus of voices called out.

Paula and I looked at each other from across the classroom, shaking our heads at each other. Then, as the classroom emptied, I saw Anna standing in the doorway, waiting for me.

"Anna," I said, walking toward her.

"I liked it, Ms. Berg," she said.

"You did?"

"Yeah, I thought it was fun. I finished it."

"Oh, thank you, Anna; I knew I could count on you."

"Okay," she said, shifting her backpack from one shoulder to the other.

"You're all right?"

"Yeah, fine. Okay, bye," she said, and wandered out into the hallway.

"That was a disaster," Paula said, collecting the laptops and placing them back on the cart.

"How is Anna doing?" I said to Mr. C., who was shuffling papers on his desk in a way that reminded me of my own attempts to seem busy and purposeful in moments when I felt completely out of my depth.

"I mean," said Paula, "they didn't even go through the questions."

"She seems kind of quiet," I said, "and I remember her as so bubbly and exuberant."

"It seems like she's having a hard time at home," said Mr. C. "That's what Jay told me."

"Oh no, what's going on?"

"Her mom is out of work. They're probably going to go back to the Marshall Islands at the end of this year."

"Are you listening to me, Elena?" said Paula.

"What?"

"We have to go; we need to process."

"Yeah, hold on." I turned back to Mr. C. "She's a great kid, really special. I think if you—"

"Seriously, Elena. Let's go," Paula said, heading for the door.

"Okay, I'm coming."

As we left Mr. C. to his desktop shuffle, Paula whipped out her phone and began texting the team to tell them what a total failure our first demonstration had been. She wanted my input, kept asking me for my notes on the experience, but I was distracted by Anna. I had told Kyle that she was "my student," the student I was teaching to, and yet I had left—left teaching, left her—and here she was in someone else's classroom, so unlike the girl I remembered. I recalled all the times I had felt as though she had rescued me last year, somehow piecing together something meaningful from my inexperienced lesson planning. Now, it seemed to me that she was the one who needed rescuing. For a moment I considered telling Paula to go back to CloseReader without me, that I wanted to stay—to rush back into the classroom, back to teaching, to return to BSA. Jay's office was down the hall; surely, all I'd have to do would be to knock on the door and tell him I wanted to come back.

"I feel so guilty," I said.

"What? Why?" said Paula.

"For leaving. That student, Anna? She was really important to me. And it seems like she's struggling."

"And you think it's because of you? Because you left?"

"We had a connection. And there's so much inconstancy in these kids' lives. Maybe if I had stayed, I would have been an anchoring force in her life."

"Elena, we have a real problem here. Did you see what happened in there? Those kids tore us apart. We've been working on this together almost a year and in one afternoon it totally fell apart. We need to get back to the office and figure it out. You made your choice about teaching last year. We both did."

"Is it really that simple?"

"No, of course not, but it's also not as simple as saying if you had stayed in the school, then everything would be great for her. Would you staying have helped her mom get a job? No. You're not her guardian angel."

"But what is my responsibility toward her?"

"Right now, your responsibility is to get CloseReader up and running so she can have access to great learning tools from anywhere in the world. Okay? Now, let's go. Andy's going to be pissed."

Chapter 28

O ver the next month, Paula and I dragged ourselves from one middle school classroom to the next around the East Bay and San Francisco. We had written off the failed demo at BSA as a fluke; there had been tech issues, nostalgia issues. "Besides," I had told her, "that's how the kids were with me as a teacher, too." Jesse and Julio fixed some of the design bugs, now asking students to choose whether they'd be working on a poem or a short story excerpt; Paula and I called ahead to the next schools to make sure the laptops had functioning cameras. We figured we were covering all of our bases; Andy wasn't so concerned.

It soon became clear, though, that BSA hadn't been a one-off disaster. In classroom after classroom, we discovered flaws in the design of CloseReader. In one private school in San Francisco, the kids whipped through the questions in ten minutes, bored at the level of instruction, and their teacher questioned the value added; in another, although the teachers liked the click-on definitions of terms such as "imagery" and "rhyme scheme," the students didn't bother to read them, and hands shot up around the room in a flurry of exclamations of "I don't understand" and "I don't get this." Even as we hustled to address each issue as it came up, there were others that arose. We were trying to create a generic close-reading model, which meant the prompts were not text specific; "This doesn't fit my story!" students called out constantly during our demonstrations. By the beginning of the summer, and the end of the school year, we were exhausted.

I told Kyle about my encounter with Anna at BSA, and the guilt I felt at leaving my teaching job for CloseReader. I had some wild idea that he and I should bring her to live with us, sort of sponsor-foster-adopt her through her high school years, so she could stay in the United States and take advantage of the education system here.

"She's such a special kid," I told him. "We have to do something."

I expected Kyle to jump at the idea. It was just radical enough, I thought, to appeal to his romantic sense of duty and idealism.

"Are you crazy?" he asked me, which was not the response I had anticipated. "You want Anna to come live with us?"

"Well, yeah, I know it can be done. And, I mean, you know how I felt about her. She could thrive here, I know it."

"Where is this coming from? This is your attempt to feel less bad about quitting teaching?"

"No, I don't know, I mean, I'm trying to make things right here."

"But there are so many things wrong with this idea!"

"Like what? What on earth could be wrong about wanting to give a kid a shot at a great education?"

"For one thing, do you know how to raise a preteen and teenager? And are we going to skip like a hundred steps in our relationship to suddenly become parents together? And what about her actual mother?"

"Obviously there are things to figure out, but isn't it worth it?"

"You're so caught up in your own guilty savior cycle you can't see that you're not actually trying to help Anna; you're trying to help yourself. She's just a pawn in your story."

We didn't talk for several days after this fight, and I spent long days at the office, making up things to do into the evenings to avoid hours of silence at home.

At CloseReader, our summer was spent in reckoning. Paula and I spent days poring over our guided reading lesson plans, refining the prompts, speaking with old teacher colleagues about best practices. Jesse and Julio rewrote code, tweaked and redesigned the layouts, updated the colors and the fonts and the entire user interface. Andy, however, went radio silent. There were weeks on end when we didn't hear from him, and I felt our operation coming slightly untethered, a ship without its captain, the rest of us steering blindly into the wind.

Toward the end of the summer, near my one-year anniversary working at CloseReader, Andy called an all-hands meeting. We reserved one of the conference rooms in the coworking space and set up Julio on Google Hangouts on a large monitor. He was growing his hair out, and before Andy arrived, we spent several minutes admiring the shaggy curls tumbling over his forehead. Jesse brought in a bowl of yogurt-covered raisins, which I promptly devoured, while Paula sat with her head in her hands, reading *Times* article after article about the Ferguson unrest and the shooting of Michael Brown.

"Are you following this?" she said, looking up from her computer. "The city's on fire. The police are shooting rubber bullets at the crowds."

"Jesus," I said.

"They're shooting at the protesters?" Julio asked.

"It's a post–9/11 thing," said Jesse.

"What is?" I replied.

"The militarization of the police. It's to combat terrorism."

"And I suppose Black people protesting count as 'terrorists'?" retorted Paula.

Jesse shrugged. "I don't know."

"Don't you have a right to protest in America?" interjected Julio. "Isn't that the whole point?"

"Different rules for different races," said Paula.

"Hey everyone, how's it going?" Andy greeted us, walking into the conference room.

"The country is going to shit," said Jesse, "and how are you?"

"Yeah," said Andy, "and Ebola is spreading across Africa."

"Jesus," I sighed. Paula closed her laptop.

"Well," said Andy, "I'm not sure this will be a real pick-me-up."

"Great," said Paula, letting her head fall back into her hands, "that's great. I knew it."

The air had grown thick and stale inside the conference room and I had started to develop a yogurt-covered-raisins-induced stomachache. Andy didn't sit down. Instead, he stood in front of the door, twisting the cap on and off a pen.

"Guys, first of all I want to thank you for the tremendous work you've done over the last year."

"Oh boy," Jesse said.

"And especially in the last few months, I know you've been working like crazy to respond to all the feedback we've gotten from students and teachers."

Paula reached out under the table and grabbed my hand. I squeezed.

"But here's the thing. It's become apparent to the board—and to the investors—that CloseReader as we originally conceived of it is not actually meeting a clear need."

"What—" said Julio, but Andy held up his hand.

"We've been doing a lot of listening over the last few months," said Andy, "and this just doesn't look like it's on its way to real success."

"So—what? We give up? The people with the money get to decide this for us?" said Paula.

"We're not giving up."

"It sure sounds like it."

Jesse elbowed Paula.

"Listen," Andy said, "we're not giving up, but we are learning about what our customers want. The one thing that we've gotten consistently positive feedback on is the actual technology of CloseReader, the high quality of the document scanner. Right?"

Paula and I looked at each other and nodded. In every classroom we'd visited, students and teachers had commented on the quality of the photography.

"And we've been seeing some amazing innovations in the way students and teachers are using the technology. We're hearing that kids are scanning all the handouts they get in class and keeping them in one digital folder, which is making it easier for them to stay on track and study for quizzes and tests. We're seeing that teachers are using it to scan student work and keep portfolios for each student without the hassle of physical papers that can get lost or destroyed."

"That's true," I said, "I did hear from some of the teachers at BSA that it's been great for both students and teachers to organize their work."

"Exactly," said Andy, "and we started thinking, what else could this technology do that we haven't predicted? How could it help people outside the classroom?"

"We could offer add-ons, too," said Jesse, "like organization systems or something, tabs maybe, so people can create filing systems."

"Exactly," said Andy. "It opens up a lot of possibilities. So, this is what we're going to do. We're going to step back from the lesson planning and the guided reading, and instead we're going to refine our technology platform. Rather than predetermine what our technology should be used for, we're going to let others decide how they might use it. If that means students and teachers want to practice close-reading on a text, then that's great, but we won't dictate their user experience."

"So, essentially," said Julio, "we're becoming a scanner app?"

"We'll be providing high-resolution photography capabilities," said Andy, "with a focus on document preservation."

"Sorry," I said, "but what?"

"Like I said," said Julio, "a scanner app."

"How exactly is this not giving up on our mission?" said Paula.

"Remember our values," said Jesse. "Didn't we say that we are 'here to serve' and that we will 'adapt and evolve'?"

"You're on board with this?" said Paula.

"We're not giving up," said Andy, "we're pivoting."

"Pivoting," said Julio.

"Yes," said Andy. "Pivoting."

"And where does that leave us?" said Paula, gesturing to me. "We're the curriculum team. Are we out of jobs?"

"No, no," said Andy, "all of you will have jobs here—if you want them. I know this is a big shift, and not what you originally signed up for. So, I want you all to take Friday and Monday off. We're going to close the office and I want all of you to do some thinking and processing and figure out if you still want to be a part of this team. If you don't, no hard feelings. I'll give you great references. But if you do, this is a hugely exciting moment for us, and you'll get to be a part of transforming this organization."

"But seriously," said Paula, "what would we do?"

"We'll figure all that out," said Andy, "but trust me. You've got a place here. You guys are smart and creative and reliable, and that's exactly what we need."

"I'm in," said Jesse. "You know that, man. We've been together since the beginning. I'm not bailing now."

"Thanks, Jesse," said Andy, "awesome. That's awesome. But still, I want you to take the long weekend. Do what you need to do to make an informed decision about this. Talk to your people. Go to the beach. Think on it. Because if you're in, you're in."

"What are we—what's our new name?" said Julio. "I assume we're not CloseReader anymore."

"Right," said Andy, "great call. No, we're no longer CloseReader. Now, we're CloseR."

Chapter 29

Paula, Jesse, and I left the office at the end of our meeting; we switched Julio off, grabbed our bags, and left Andy to a few days of solo work.

"Let's eat something," Jesse said. "All this talk of pivoting has made me hungry."

We sat down at a small metal table that tipped back and forth over the uneven concrete of the sidewalk, our elbows bumping up against each other, and ordered too-large salads that we wouldn't finish and a plate of fries to share.

"So," Jesse said, "thoughts?"

"I want to know what Elena thinks," said Paula.

"Me?" I said. "What about you?"

"You barely said anything up there," Paula said.

"You said plenty for all of us, though," Jesse replied.

"And you're definitely in?" I asked Jesse.

"Yeah," he said. "Yes. I mean, I love Andy. He's the real deal; whatever he does will ultimately work out. I'm sticking with him."

"And you don't care about the scanner thing instead of an ed program?"

"I mean, does it sound better to be working on curriculum than a photo app? Yeah, definitely. But I'm not trying to prove anything to anyone. I still get to work with code, still get to be a part of a developing startup. Still part of the tech scene. That's really what I want."

"Plus, still have a job," Paula added.

"Wait, you're in, too?" I asked.

"I don't know," said Paula, "I have to think about it. I'm not that excited about the scanner app. But, then again, maybe my new role would be cool; I was kind of tired of lesson planning, anyway. And am I excited about being jobless and having to go into that mode again? No, definitely not."

"And you?" Jesse prompted. "Our silent holdout?"

"Yeah," I said, "I have some thinking to do."

"Come on," Paula pleaded, scooting her chair close to me, "you can't leave us!"

I laughed as Jesse scooted in, too, and they both put their arms around me.

"I love you guys, you know that," I said.

"So, you'll stay," said Jesse.

"We'll see," I replied, drowning a french fry in ketchup.

"Anyway," said Paula, "now we have four days off. What are we going to do?"

I bowed out of the afternoon excursion to Golden Gate Park and crossed the Bay in an empty BART car. Back in Berkeley I wandered along the side streets, pausing to take in the purple-and-white checkered flowers, the vine-covered gates, the overhanging fuzzy red flowers that dropped little crimson spines all along the pavement. The houses in Berkeley don't seem to follow much of a pattern. Two or three in a row will be small bungalows made of earth-colored and white stucco with cauliflower-shaped succulents poking out of a mulch-covered yard. Then, across the street, there are suddenly houses that remind me of New England—tall, made of wooden slats, with porches snaking around the sides. A redwood tree in one garden; a palm tree next door.

The Berkeley summer had been overwhelmed with plums. Trees were bowed under the weight of the little red jewels; neighbors were leaving bowls full of plums on each other's doorsteps. All through June and July we had eaten plum jam, plum and apricot crumble, plum cake, and plum scones. Earlier in the summer, while walking through the wide, tree-lined streets, on the border of Berkeley and Oakland, Kyle and I had heard a voice say, "Do you want any plums?" We looked up and saw a woman collecting plums from a tree into her T-shirt. She piled them into a plastic bag and handed them to us. When we thanked her, she said, "Oh, this isn't my tree. I've knocked on the door of this house a few times and nobody's answered. And the fruit is just rotting to the ground, so I figured . . ." We all nodded.

I walked into a secondhand bookstore and headed toward the back, where the poetry anthologies were collected on a narrow shelf, next to cookbooks and Moleskine journals. I ran my hands over the slightly tattered spines and remembered how, when I was in high school, I would stay awake through the night writing essays and memorizing equations, and in between I would read poem after poem after poem. Sometimes I'd spend an entire night on a single poet, reading sonnet after sonnet or ballad upon ballad. One spring in college, two friends and I stayed awake for three days and two nights reciting poetry, studying for a final. I don't remember what grade I got on the test, but I do remember those nights, and the sense that together we were falling, unveiling, drinking, reveling, revealing.

I found a copy of Milan Kundera's *The Unbearable Lightness of*

Being tucked away in the poetry section. I had read the book twice, once the summer after my senior year of high school, when I went through my mom's bookshelves, and I had reveled in the romance between Tomas and Sabina. The second time was in a class in college on "The Politics of Literature," and it was only then that I realized just how little I had paid attention to the ways in which their love story was tangled up in the Soviet Union's invasion of Czechoslovakia. "Context!" my professor used to cry out, banging his hand on a desk; "We exist in context!"

At home later that evening, Kyle found me in the kitchen chopping tomatoes and ripping up strips of basil leaves.

"Listen to this," I said, holding up a book of Wendell Berry poems I had purchased at the bookstore that afternoon, "'Found your hope, then, on the ground under your feet. / Your hope of Heaven, let it rest on the ground underfoot.' Also, 'Be still and listen to the voices that belong / to the stream banks and the trees and the open fields.' Isn't that amazing?"

Kyle threw his backpack in a corner and sat down on the kitchen floor, resting his back against the fridge.

"You're home early," he said.

"Yeah," I said. "Actually, I have some news."

I turned and saw Kyle rubbing his eyes, the dirt that was perpetually in the creases of his hands making shadows on his face.

"What's wrong?" I asked.

"Minor disaster at the farm today," he said.

"Uh-oh. What happened?"

"One of the kids ate some pokeberries."

"Some what?"

"Pokeberries. They look like blueberries or grapes. But they're poisonous."

"Oh, shit," I said, and sat down next to him. "Is the kid okay? What happened?"

"It was my fault," Kyle mumbled. "I was with the little kids this afternoon, you know, the preschool group. I don't know why that pokeberry bush was even there in the first place; someone should have caught that. But anyway. One of the kids had tripped and I was helping her, wiping her knee and getting a Band-Aid on, and so I took my eyes off the others for literally one minute. But when I turned around there was this little boy with purple juice running down his chin and all over his hands."

"Oh god."

"I knew exactly what it was. It's the telltale sign, that purple juice."

"So what did you do?"

"It was a whole mess. The kid started puking. We had to call poison control."

"Oh, Kyle."

"Then we had to get the parents to come, obviously. They took him to the hospital."

"And do you know how he's doing now?"

"Yeah, I waited around to hear. It seems like he'll be okay, just needs to get it all out of his system. But I feel awful, you know?"

"Of course you do."

"I just sat in the office literally rocking back and forth on my chair. So anxious."

"I'm so sorry. Why didn't you call me?"

"I mean, you were at work."

"Right. Well, weirdly, today I actually wasn't. There's been a whole thing."

"What happened? Did you quit?"

"Quit? No, why would I do that?"

 Kyle didn't say anything.

"No, but Andy's given us a long weekend."

"Why?"

"It turns out the company is going to pivot."

"What do you mean?"

"Like, it's not going to be a curriculum-design company anymore."

"What's it going to be?"

"It's going to focus on the technology we've developed, the scanning and photography functions."

"It's going to be a photo app? Aren't there a million of those already?"

"Well, no, it's more than that. We have this awesome scanning capability that we developed for kids to upload the texts they were working on, and we have all these ways of marking up the texts. So now we can offer that to everyone, not just students."

"Sounds dumb."

"It's not dumb."

"You're going from having a mission to help students to not having a mission at all. I knew Andy was just in it for the profit."

"That's not true, Kyle."

"You said Andy gave you some days off? Why?"

"Yeah. To decide if we're in, if we want to stay on."

"Is there even anything to think about? Are you really going to stay on with a company that isn't doing anything worthwhile in the world?"

"It's not *not* worthwhile."

"Oh, come on, Elena, you can't be serious."

"Think about it. Everything's moving online, to the cloud, right?

The world is moving away from paper. We're going to help facilitate that."

"I can't believe you."

"What?"

"The world is literally falling apart and you're going to devote yourself to better scanning opportunities?"

"Don't be so dramatic."

"Have you been reading the news? Are you seeing what's happening in Ferguson?"

"Yes, I know, it's crazy. Paula was reading about it today. They're shooting rubber bullets into the crowds."

"And tear gas," said Kyle. "They're tear-gassing the protesters. What kind of country sends police in to attack citizens?"

"It's not like it hasn't happened before," I said. "My mom was tear-gassed in the sixties."

"Things are completely fucked up," said Kyle, "and it's not the same thing, Elena."

"I know it's not; I'm just saying that—"

"Your mom is white and educated and rich, and she did just fine after her little stint as an antiwar hippie."

"What? Kyle, I know, I'm just trying to point out that—"

"Stop romanticizing. This is a different reality."

"You're accusing me of romanticizing? While you criticize my job for not being radical enough?"

"Is working in some random tech company really what you came out to California to do? What's happened to you? Where's the Elena I met at the Occupy march? The one who wanted to change the world with poetry, one kid at a time?"

"Oh, just like you're doing? One pokeberry at a time?"

"That's low, Elena."

I went back to the counter, where the basil leaves had started to wilt and the tomatoes were oozing juice and pips all over the cutting board. My hands were shaking.

"Why can't you just be happy for me?" I snapped. "I finally like what I'm doing. I have friends at work. My team loves me. My boss values me."

"Because it's not you. It's not the you I fell in love with."

"Maybe I've changed."

"Maybe you have."

"And if I have? Can you accept that?"

Kyle got up from the kitchen floor and dusted off his work pants. He looked at me, dirt under his fingernails, curly red hair matted and unkempt.

"I guess that's the question," he said.

Chapter 30

Kyle and I barely spoke to each other over the weekend, and on Tuesday morning, when I woke up at my regular time, showered, got dressed, and headed out to the office, Kyle lay on his side of the bed with his back toward me, an arm flung over his face. At the office, Paula, Jesse, and Andy greeted me with cheers and hugs. Julio had emailed us all over the weekend letting us know he would be moving on, and I already missed his slow gentleness, his unintentional humor, and his long, curly locks.

"Game on," Andy said, and we all agreed.

Our first week at CloseR involved a major design sprint, turning our cubicles into something resembling an art studio, with construction paper and markers and scissors strewn all around. Paula and I still didn't fully know what our roles would be, but it didn't seem to matter.

I had planned a visit to Amelia in LA during the last weekend of August, and I took a Friday off to make the trek down south by bus. As I stood at the bus terminal, I watched a homeless man crossing the street combing his hair. He had a beanie tucked into his pocket, and as he trundled his belongings over the crosswalk, comb in hand, the hat fell out. I felt myself flinch, as if to get up and call to him, run after him, pick up the hat and hand it to him; but instead I stayed where

I was, feet still and unmoving on the ground, iPhone in hand. Once on the bus, I settled into the polyester seats, stuffed my headphones in my ears, and tried not to think about the stilted unease that had settled over us since I told Kyle I was planning to stay on at CloseR.

Amelia met me at the bus terminal. She had cut her hair short, with asymmetrical bangs, and her feather earrings brushed the tops of her shoulders when she moved her head.

"You look skinny," I said, tossing my backpack in the back of her car.

"I do yoga every day," she said.

"And then do you eat anything?"

"Does coffee count?"

We drove to her apartment, a small white box with a little balcony from which you could just make out the ocean. Palm trees swayed on every corner. I kicked off my shoes and collapsed on Amelia's couch, while she opened a bottle of wine and handed me my first glass of the evening.

"Okay," she said, "talk."

"Kyle," I groaned.

"I figured."

"I just feel . . ."

"Suffocated."

"Yeah, I guess."

"What's he done now?"

"It's my new job."

Amelia laughed. "Right, I bet he hates it."

"It doesn't align with his values."

"Or his idea of you."

"That's just it. He's got this image of me. And I seem to keep disappointing him."

"Well, of course you do."

"What?"

"Meaning, he's not actually in love with *you*. With the real—imperfect—you. He wants you to fit the ideal. Or his version of the ideal."

"Maybe he's right, though. Maybe I've totally lost my way."

"Oh, come off it, Elena."

"Isn't that what you thought too, though? Last time you visited."

"I don't love you because you're some vegetarian peacenik selling Greenpeace donation subscriptions on the corner. I'd love you if you were a meat-eating sloth who sold vacuum cleaners."

"Thank you."

"I mean it. If that's what you wanted, then that would be fine with me."

"Yeah. I know."

"But not with Kyle."

"No," I said, "I don't think it is."

"So," she said, "what are you going to do?"

"Right now," I said, "I'm going to drink more wine. Top me up."

The next day we rented bikes and cycled along the boardwalk by the beach. We stopped to drink multiple cups of coffee to soothe the wine-induced headaches we'd woken up with, and wandered in and out of bookstores while the wind blew salt crystals in from the sea. Amelia told me about her recent love affairs, and the older man she'd started seeing at the beginning of the summer who wore a leather jacket and played blues guitar on Thursday nights at a local bar.

"I really, really fell for him," she said.

"So, what's the problem?"

"Two things. One: he's old."

"How old?"

"Old, Elena. Like, maybe could date my mom old."

"Aha. And the second thing?"

"He's married."

"He's married?"

"Yes."

"So, he's cheating on his wife with you?"

"No, they have an open relationship."

"A what?"

"Ethical non-monogamy. They're married, but they also date other people."

"Have you met her?"

"We had dinner one night. With her boyfriend, too."

"My head is starting to spin."

"From the wine or my amorous adventures?"

"Unclear."

We bought a hodgepodge of foodstuffs—cheese and freshly baked rolls, nectarines and the bougiest stuffed olives we could find—then parked our bikes and sat on a blanket on the beach. I took off my shoes and slid my feet into the warm sand. Amelia whipped out leopard-print sunglasses so large they covered the top half of her face. For a while, we read and ate in quiet. We took pictures of the waves rolling onto the beach, of our picnic spread, of Amelia's perfectly manicured, red-painted toes, and of my prominent Teva sandals tan.

"I could get used to this," I said.

"Maybe you should just stay," said Amelia.

"Dreamy," I said.

"Seriously," she said. "Ditch Kyle; work remotely."

"Kyle," I repeated.

"Yeah."

"I'd almost managed to forget."

"I think you should call him."

"And say what?"

"You'll figure it out."

"Now?"

"Yeah. I think you should call him now. Go for a walk. I'll be here."

I got up from the blanket, grabbed my shoes in one hand and my phone in the other, and walked toward the ocean. I paused at the place where the sand meets the water, feeling the sun on my neck, tasting the salt on my tongue. I had the feeling that I was both forgetting and remembering something, and I started thinking of my grandparents. Between my grandfather's stories and my grandmother's songs, they had fallen in love with opera. Instead of going to synagogue, they used to take my mother and stand in the lines outside the Met on Saturday mornings to buy the last-minute, discounted tickets and then stand in the back of the concert hall, peering through the spaces between the audience members' heads. They became expert at seeking out a straight line of sight to the stage, avoiding getting caught behind the tall men with broad shoulders and the women who wore their hair high and wide.

"Music takes off where language fails," my grandparents always said. "Listening to the greats," they said, "can make you feel as though you are remembering something you had once known intimately but forgotten. This type of music pulls away the veil, seems to wipe away the mirages of this world, of this thin slice of reality we walk through day by day."

When I finally called Kyle, my feet had sunk into the marshy patch of sand at the water's edge, held in place by tide and shoreline, by cowrie shells and sand dollars and bits of broken glass rubbed smooth. I started to cry almost as soon as he picked up, salt mixed with salt, streaks of crystals tracing lines down my face like the silver shimmers left behind by snails on a garden path. Our conversation didn't last long; we had already rehearsed our fights. I looked out at the white-capped sea, and though I had imagined yelling, had imagined needing to battle our way out, in the end it was quiet, gentle. Not with a bang, but a whimper.

I told him I would stay a few extra days in LA, and he said he'd be packed up and gone by the time I was back. The wind picked up as I turned to look back at Amelia, who was clearing up the picnic and rolling away the blanket, leading us toward a night of bingeing *Sex and the City*, and I heard squeals as sandcastles crumbled and messages written with sticks were blown away and washed over. My feet released themselves from the wet sand with a pop, a squelch, and I remembered our time in Jane and Roy's cabin, when I had dug my toes into the mulchy earth of the redwood grove by the campfire and later announced to Kyle that I was going to stop teaching. Feet in the dirt, in the water, in the sand. We had been holding each other still, stuck in place, and now it was time to move.

Chapter 31

I moved into a small basement studio underneath a ramshackle Berkeley craftsman home. It opened onto a garden that reflected the eccentricities of my landlords, an older couple in their sixties who lived above me. The garden's main exhibit was a battery-operated fountain featuring stone sculptures of hummingbirds in midflight. Around the fountain grew a mess of wild irises and African lilies. Lemon and apple trees hung heavy with their loads, and the uneven brick patio was often covered in rotting scraps. A large vegetable plot took up most of the rest of the garden, and the tomato and chard plants grew tall and thick throughout the summer months. Sandy, who suffered from a chronic cough, would stand on the balcony above me and call down instructions to her husband, John, on how and where to hack at the weeds that were starving the vegetables' roots.

My studio was sparse and slightly lopsided, but clean, with a toilet that didn't run after it was flushed and a new refrigerator. It came partially furnished, which suited me, and while it was nearly impossible to come in or out of the studio without running into Sandy and entering into some all-too-personal conversation, she would regularly leave baskets of zucchini or a selection of documentaries on DVD on my doorstep.

"You just moved to Berkeley?" she asked the day I moved in.

"No, I've lived here for a few years," I said.

"Why are you moving then? And why are you living alone?"

"I just broke up with my boyfriend."

"Ah," she said, "jumped in a little too quick."

"No, I—"

"Help yourself to apples!"

Sandy and John were well-established hippies and had been living in their house for the last thirty years. They regularly threw "revolutionary evenings," during which speakers came to lament the state of healthcare or gun control or higher education in the United States. Sandy whipped up platters of deviled eggs and potato salad and handed out glasses of white wine, and at the end of the night everyone who was still there had been cajoled into participating in the next phone bank Sandy and John were organizing for one cause or the other. On Saturday afternoons, neighbors would pop over and sit in the garden with their guitars, and Bobby from around the corner would bring his accordion, and they'd croon old peace songs and Simon and Garfunkel, and I'd wonder where they had been and what they had been doing when my mom was fumbling around with wires and bomb parts and stealing packets of ramen from the grocery store.

The studio was just around the corner from a hole-in-the wall café that served vegan donuts and hot milk flavored with saffron and rose. I started going in the mornings on my way to the city, squeezing into the tiny rectangular space decorated with framed LP record covers and a mirror on the back wall to make the room seem larger than it was. I could never have justified spending $4.50 on a cup of steamed milk to Kyle, but in my nascent singlehood, it felt like a necessary comfort. The vegan donuts tasted like sugary cardboard, as most were also gluten-free, but the handsome, bespectacled barista always asked if I wanted one, and I couldn't bring myself to say no.

I felt Kyle's absence in all my new indulgences. The steamed milk; the late-night Netflix binge sessions; the way I stopped reading the news and instead started reading Facebook updates. He had been my conscience, my moral compass, my Zen meditation teacher walking through silent rows of seated practitioners, using a stick to slap those whose spines curved, whose heads hung low, who moved to scratch the itch on their shoulder. Without him, I ate spaghetti every night for a week, stayed in bed until noon on the weekends, stopped going to yoga classes and hiking in the hills. I felt my freedom in the way I did not have to explain myself, defend myself, in the way I did not have to live up to any semblance of "goodness."

I heard he moved in with friends in Oakland, close to the urban garden where he worked, and for a while I was sure we would accidentally bump into each other, steeling myself every time I left my studio for a possible chance encounter. After a while, though, I stopped expecting to see him, no longer looking for him at the BART station or Lake Merritt. We texted each other briefly on our birthdays and New Year's, but otherwise I didn't hear from him.

Soon after pivoting, CloseR moved out of the coworking space into our own office. We hired an office manager and several sales reps, and Paula headed up the new marketing efforts. I became a project manager, which appealed to my love of organization and spreadsheets, but it was difficult to explain to my grandparents exactly what my job entailed. We tightened up our systems, moving from Excel and GChat to Slack, Asana, Dropbox, Dropbox Paper, 1Password, and TextExpander. I got a salary bump at the beginning of my second year with the team and selected a 401k with a matching program. Paula, Jesse, and I, by virtue of being on board since the beginning, were all promoted to the leadership team, and every three weeks or so we'd meet early in the office to go over the numbers and the long-term vision. Happy hours continued weekly, and we also added a monthly karaoke night to the mix as the team grew.

Chapter 32

In late summer 2015, Monica and Rae got married at an old summer camp in upstate New York. They planned a whole wedding weekend, replete with dodgeball and ropes course options and a Friday night bonfire by the lake. I tacked up the invitation on my fridge, which featured a picture of them eating a Nutella-filled crepe in Paris, and I took a week off from work to head to the East Coast. In one late-night moment of panic, I texted Monica to see whether Kyle had been invited and felt embarrassingly relieved when she said that he had, but he couldn't make it.

I had forgotten the sticky heat of New York summers, accustomed as I had become to the cool summer mornings and evenings of the Bay, and when I stepped off the plane, I was hit by a wall of blazing-hot air pulsing against my skin. I took a train up to the camp, leaving behind the sweating bricks and concrete of the city and winding out into green, open spaces alongside water that glistened beneath the white afternoon sun. It was my first wedding of a friend. "Welcome to this phase," Jesse had said before I left. "You're going to need a whole separate bank account just to fund all the weddings you're about to be hit with." It had occurred to me late in the process of packing that I hadn't purchased them a gift. But, I reasoned, I was flying across the country. And paying for my lodging at the camp. Surely that was enough.

On the way up to camp, I thought about the year I had lived with Monica, about our sunlit apartment with its seventies floral curtains and orange walls. I remembered the time I'd complained that our toilet wasn't working, that we needed to call the landlord, and how she had laughed and laughed and said she wasn't flushing it intentionally. "We're in a drought, girl! No need to overuse the flusher. It's a whole thing here. Everyone does it."

I would never hear Monica and Rae having sex at night or in the evening—they were exclusively morning and afternoon lovers, it seemed. I had overheard plenty of my roommates having sex in college, all heterosexual couples, all characterized by a few gracious moans on the part of the women and then the inevitable heaving grunts of the men. But Monica and Rae lingered in their lovemaking. Their panting exploration of each other's bodies would reverberate around the apartment and at times, I admit, I crept closer to their closed door, stood outside, and felt myself grow warm as they, unhurried, unchecked, and clearly unashamed, teased and tantalized each other for (what seemed like) hours on end.

I don't know that I was ashamed of sex or my body. But I had to admit, on those lazy, sensual weekend afternoons, that all the sex I'd ever had—with Kyle or otherwise—while often sweet and loving, and at the beginning even quite passionate, was, on the whole, fairly tame. And fairly quiet. I have wondered whether I was, in some way, rebelling against my mother's promiscuity, the stories of her teens and twenties that she told to me, uncensored, from the time I was in my early teens. I myself was a product of said promiscuity. But— unlike my mother—I had always been tentative around sex, around my body and my partner's body.

At the camp, I checked in and received a name tag, a bunk assignment, and a welcome bag filled with a mini sunscreen and bug spray and neon-colored sunglasses. I was directed to a sheet of stickers that clarified our preferred pronouns. I pulled off a pink "she/her" and stuck it onto my name tag. It was disconcerting and strangely nostalgic to find myself at a wedding—this monumental ritual of adulthood—inside a camp, inside the secret world of childhood and adolescence. I had flashbacks to the few summers my mom shipped me off to the Jewish summer camp in the Berkshires, to color wars and soggy quiche and shaving my legs for the first time next to six other girls. I remembered nights when a girl would sneak back in after dark, giggling as she washed her hands and gargled with mouthwash, and the notes we wrote to each other at the end of the summer, filled with rapturous expressions of everlasting friendship.

I found my way to my room and claimed a bottom bunk by the window. On the top bunk sat a woman wearing headphones and scrawling a note on a card.

"Hey," I said, as I unzipped my bag and looked over the weekend's schedule of events.

The woman waved and took out her headphones.

"Hey," she said, "I'm Jackie."

"Elena," I said.

"Just have to finish writing this card to Monica and Rae."

I pulled out my dress for the wedding and hung it on the edge of my bed, willing gravity to smooth out the creases.

"Okay," said Jackie, "done. Sorry. Nice to meet you!"

"You too. How do you know Monica and Rae?"

"I'm part of Monica's med school crew. There's a bunch of us here. A few of us in the singles bunk and some on the couples' row."

"Is that how we got our room assignments?"

"How do you know them?"

"From the Bay. Monica and I were roommates for a year when we first moved out there."

"Oh yeah! She's told us so many great stories from her time in Cali. You guys lived together?"

"Yeah."

"So, you're the teacher, right?"

"I was," I said, my mouth going slightly dry.

"Not anymore? What do you do now?"

"I work at a tech company."

"What does it do?"

"Essentially, it's an app that lets you scan documents and save them directly in the cloud."

"Huh," she said, "interesting."

"Yeah. You're a doctor?"

"On the way, anyway."

"What kind of medicine do you practice?"

"I'm a pediatrician. I really love kids."

"That's great."

Over the course of the weekend, I ate tiny mushrooms stuffed with cheese and got bitten by a thousand mosquitos and jumped into the cool lake to escape the afternoon heat. I had conversation after conversation that mirrored the one I'd had with Jackie: How do you know the couple? Where are you from? What do you do? Amid a crowd of medical professionals and Burning Man devotees, I was the "techie." I figured out quickly that although Monica and Rae were the reason I was there, I wasn't actually going to spend much—or any—time with them over the course of the weekend. We hugged quickly the first time we bumped into each other, and I brought Monica a plate of bagels and lox at the breakfast buffet the morning of the ceremony, but that was basically it.

The ceremony itself took place at the edge of the lake, amid a grove of sugar maple trees that, in just a few months, would turn brilliant red and orange and gold. We sat on blankets laid out in a semicircle, fanning ourselves from the heat and the mosquitos and squinting into the sunlight. Rae wore a long, white, sleeveless dress, with gold bangles circling up her arms and matching gold earrings. Monica wore a white jumpsuit and an old-fashioned hat veil, and they both looked stunning and untouchable and like they hadn't slept or eaten in several days. I felt a deep sadness while looking at them holding hands among the trees, for it seemed to me that while they had stepped out of our dreamy, pasta-eating, joint-smoking early twenties into solidity, into commitment, into love, I had tumbled out of that era alone and unanchored.

They had written their own vows, and they read them into a microphone punctuated by gusts of wind that sent ripples through their hair and the pages in their hands. They quoted Rilke, claiming their relationship was one that protected each other's solitude, and I cried when Rae said she was committing to bearing witness to Monica's life. Someone scooted around the rows of blankets handing out little hemp bags filled with rice, and when they kissed and the band lit up, we all stood and showered them with the white grains. I overheard a little girl behind me whisper, "There are going to be so many rice trees here!"

At the reception we danced to the best of the nineties and ate chocolate truffles and skewers of salmon drenched in butter. There were toasts I did not pay attention to, but I drank the champagne quickly and felt my lingering sadness from the ceremony lighten and shift to the background. On the dance floor I found myself in between the crowds, the various circles, and for a moment I just twirled alone, my hair falling out of its bun, sweat dripping, shoes off. The photographer snapped a photo of me, which, many months later, Monica sent to me in the mail along with a roughly scrawled, "Thanks so much for coming and celebrating with us!"

Chapter 33

Sandy and John's radical gatherings started taking on a more urgent tone about a year before the election. They plastered their windows with signs calling for Bernie for President 2016 and Cooperation Not Corporation and Black Lives Matter. Every weekend I heard the parties start up. The aging hippies of North Berkeley would drive over to the flats in their Priuses and Teslas and gather upstairs in Sandy and John's living room—the same living room, Sandy often reminded me, where she had birthed each of her three children, right there on the rug, yes, this same rug, there was even a bloodstain that she'd never been able to get out—to fret about Hillary and Jeb and shake their heads in exaggerated despair at Trump's latest gaffe.

"Thank goodness for Trump's absurdity. The Republicans are going to run themselves out of the race with this large a lineup," they'd say with satisfaction. "It's Hillary and the establishment we need to worry about."

Sandy would knock on my door in the evenings and tell me to "come on up." I'd be just home from work, shoes kicked off in the corner, deliberating between Mexican and Thai takeout and there she'd be, calling out "Elena! Elena!" before she was halfway down the stairs from her balcony.

"I brought you a bowl of fresh tomatoes," she'd say, "and what are you doing just sitting around here in the evenings? What do you do all day?"

"I work, Sandy," I'd say.

"You work?"

"Yes. I work."

"Oh. Well, listen, come on upstairs, we're having an evening, and Bernie is going to call in from the campaign! You can hear what's going on straight from the horse's mouth, so to speak."

I followed the initial stages of the primary loosely, with vague terror at the prospect of a Ted Cruz ticket. I had some general sense that it was "Hillary's turn" after the Obama upset in 2008, and didn't think much about it until Berkeley's gardens and cars started exploding with Bernie signs and bumper stickers. I watched the debates on my laptop at home, sitting on the couch eating popcorn and texting Amelia or Jesse at the same time. When I talked to my family, my grandparents said they'd vote for whoever was "best for Israel," and my mom pointed out every time Hillary was called "cold" or "unapproachable" by the media, complaining that all America seemed to want was a president you could have a beer with.

Over New Year's, a bunch of us from CloseR went up to Tahoe. I didn't ski, although I had grown up in New England, but most of my new colleagues did. We rented a house near a ski resort on the north part of the lake, and I brought books and slippers and a swimsuit for the hot tub and a large tin of cocoa powder. I drove up with Paula, Jesse, and Kat, our new head of design; a few of the sales team drove up a day earlier. We wound our way slowly through the snowstorm that hit an hour or so outside of Sacramento, watching as the snow started to pile up on the hood of the car and in the edges of the windows.

"Snow!" Kat said, pressing her nose to the passenger window.

"Do we have chains on our tires?" I asked.

"You're such a New Englander," Jesse said.

"Yeah," said Paula from the driver seat, "way to take the romance out of snow."

"You guys can thank me later," I said.

We pulled into a gas station thirty minutes from the rental house and Jesse, Kat, and I wandered through the tiny convenience store while Paula stood at the pump. There was a young couple in the store with a basket full of canned chicken soup and Gatorade. Jesse and I stood in front of a turntable rotating pizza slices while Kat strongly considered a blue slushy. From where we stood, we could hear the couple approach the checkout counter and begin to chat with the cashier.

"I'm telling you," the man's voice said, "Trump is exactly what this country needs."

"Oh, I know," said the cashier.

"He's the only one of the lot I'd actually vote for," said the woman.

"Things need to change," said the man.

"Trump's a businessman," said the cashier. "He knows how to make a deal, how to get things done."

"And he tells it like is," said the woman. "He doesn't mess around with political correctness. He's real."

Jesse eyed me and we slunk behind a shelf of toothpaste and bottles of aspirin. I pinched his arm again and again and he peeked around the shelves to get a better look.

"Don't," I said. "Don't do it."

"Toto," Jesse said, "we are not in Kansas anymore."

"We found the outer limits of the bubble," I said.

"What should we do?"

"Run."

Jesse snickered and grabbed my hand, and we ran out of the gas station laughing, into the icy chill of the snowstorm. Kat followed a few minutes later, slushy in hand.

"Guys," she said, "this tastes like childhood."

"Let's go," Paula called, honking the car's horn. "I'm freezing; come on."

The door to the house opened up into a mudroom, where snow boots and thick socks and the various layers of scarves and hats and fleeces and winter coats were stored, and then continued into one large open-concept room, with couches lining the walls, a kitchen with a six-burner stove and a fridge that beeped if you left the door ajar, and a circular dining room table and chairs. The bedrooms were all downstairs, and Paula and I threw our bags into one of the unclaimed rooms with a queen-size bed covered in a paisley duvet.

It was dark by the time we arrived, and the sales crew—Neal, Claire, and T.—had already claimed their spots in the outdoor hot tub for the evening, so our car picked at the large pot of pasta left for us on the stove and stretched out on the couches in the living room. Kat flipped through the channels on the TV and Jesse rested his head in my lap while I slurped spaghetti from a bowl hovered above his face. In the morning, everyone would head to the slopes to rent equipment and purchase tickets while I would make a haphazard attempt at doing an online yoga class before giving in and watching a rom-com at 10:00 a.m., hot chocolate in hand.

"Can you believe that couple?" Jesse asked, after Kat had given up on the television.

"Which couple?" Paula replied.

"We overheard them in the gas station," I said.

"Overheard who?" Neal chirped, as he, Claire, and T. walked in from the hot tub, wrapped in towels, the tips of their hair wet and dripping.

"Trump lovers!" Jesse exclaimed.

"I didn't know they actually existed," said Claire.

"And in California," said Kat.

"I felt kind of scared," I admitted.

"Yeah," said Jesse, "like maybe they'd pull out their guns and start comparing."

Paula snorted.

"But seriously," T. said, "how many people on your Facebook feed are Trump supporters?"

"Um," I stammered.

"Entirely zero," said Neal.

"That kid from my freshman-year dorm . . ." said Claire.

"And yours?" I returned.

"Yeah, tons," said T. "I grew up in gold rush country. Small town. Real, real small town."

"So, you understand them," said Paula.

"Sure," said T., "although they definitely don't understand *me*."

We laughed and nodded.

"The Trumpers are crazy," Neal declared, "but kind of irrelevant, right? I mean, the real question is Hillary or Bernie."

"Hillary," Claire said definitively. "It's about time a woman became president."

"Glass ceiling and all," said Kat.

"Exactly," said Claire.

"I don't know," said Paula. "It feels like you have to choose between being a feminist or being a progressive. Like, do I want a woman to be president? Yes. But do I want Hillary to be president? Not really."

"You're for Bernie?" I asked, surprised.

"I am definitely for Bernie," said Paula.

"Huh," I replied.

"You're not?"

"No," I said. "Well, I don't know. To be honest, I'm not sure I'm entirely comfortable with having a Jewish president."

"What!" Kat exclaimed.

"Woah, woah, woah," Jesse said, sitting up.

"Are you allowed to say that kind of thing?" Claire asked.

"I'm Jewish," I said plainly.

"Can you also make Holocaust jokes?" Neal said.

"Yes," I shrugged.

"But hold on," said T., "why would you say that?"

"I don't totally know," I said, "I don't have a whole manifesto on it. It's just, I feel uncomfortable. The spotlight would be on Jews in such a big way. There'd be a whole thing about Israel. I just . . . I'm not sure I want to deal with it. Like, it doesn't feel totally safe."

"Elena," Jesse declared, "that is some major internalized antisemitism there."

"What?" I said.

"Seriously," said Paula, "that's like if I said I didn't want Obama to be president because he's Black. That I didn't want someone who looks like me in the White House."

I thought of my grandparents' dining room table. Half of it was always littered with *New Yorker* magazines and unopened solicitations for airline miles, credit cards, requests for donations to AIPAC and Hebrew Free Loan. At the other end, where we'd sit and eat, the wood was rubbed smooth and there were wine stains and unidentified splotches from years and years of Friday night dinners and Passover seders. "Be exemplary," they always told me, "so that nobody can find fault with the Jewish people through you." But also, "Don't be too exemplary," they cautioned, "so that the goyim won't notice us. Make no mistakes; keep your head down."

When I was a freshman in college, the Hillel hosted an event that caused my grandfather and my mother to stop speaking to each other for several months. Although I almost never set foot inside the Hillel, eschewing student-led Friday night services for dorm room socials and later, when I turned twenty-one, the local bars, I was intrigued by the event description, and I went. Displayed around the Hillel dining room were large photographs and testimonials from current and former soldiers in the Israeli army. The diary entries talked of atrocities committed by the Israeli army on Palestinians, detailing each soldier's personal shame in stark language. When I told my grandfather about the exhibit, he threatened to stop contributing to my college tuition. The exhibit was titled "Breaking the Silence," but my grandfather was clear: the silence must remain unbroken.

"How can a country—a people—change without discourse?" my mother argued at the time. "We're just trying to survive," my grandfather responded. "Why does this discourse of yours need to happen in the public square? Who needs to see all our dirty laundry? What good can that possibly do?"

"I don't know, guys," I said again.

"You're afraid," said Jesse.

"Yeah," I replied, "maybe."

"Inherited trauma," Paula said solemnly, "that's what you're suffering from."

"I blame the Holocaust," I said.

"Definitely," said T. "This is definitely the fault of the Nazis."

"Reincarnated as Trump?" Neal smirked.

"Too real," Claire said with a shiver.

"Seriously," said Kat.

"Now that we've reached this part of the night . . ." said Jesse.

"Which part? The Nazi part?" I asked, reaching out to poke his arm.

"Yup," said Jesse, intercepting my hand and holding it in his. "Now that we've reached this part of the night, I'm pretty sure it's time for a drink."

Later, I lay in bed with Paula, my head woozy, cheeks flushed from one too many drinks.

"So," she said, just as I was drifting off to sleep.

"What?"

"When are you and Jesse going to hook up?"

"What are you talking about?"

"Come on, Elena, the tension is *thick* between you two."

"Stop it, we're just friends."

"He wants to, you know."

"He told you so?"

"Not in so many words. But I've known Jesse a long time."

"Kyle and I just broke up."

"Ages ago!"

"We were together a long time."

"Have you been with anyone since him?"

"No."

"Well, maybe it's time."

"Yeah, maybe. But with Jesse?"

"I'm telling you; it's going to happen."

"And I'm telling you . . . I'm going to sleep. Good night."

Chapter 34

The first time I slept with Jesse was on the night of the election. We were watching the results in my little studio, Jesse, Paula, and I, because I wanted to be close to Sandy and John when Hillary won. Their house was one of Berkeley's gray-haired hippie central meeting points, and I could only imagine the unique combination of joy and sorrow that would mark a Hillary victory in their community. They'd raise a glass to say *thank god* it wasn't Trump, and then immediately get on the phones to batter Hillary's moderate platform with progressive demands. They had spent the summer mourning Bernie's presumptive loss in the primaries, and I couldn't imagine a better place to be to watch the election results roll in.

Paula left as soon as they called it, before all the votes were tallied. She couldn't bear it, she said, needed to go for a walk, to make sure her passport was in order, to make an appointment at Planned Parenthood to get an IUD inserted. I could almost hear the wails coming from upstairs as Sandy and John and the neighborhood took stock. Jesse and I stayed curled in our corners on the couch, the laptop between us, the remnants of dinner distributed in bowls and takeout boxes sitting on the windowsills. Even my succulent seemed to droop. We stayed awake watching the interactive map of the United States turn red, even when it was clear there was no mistake and that there would not be a recall or a recount or a revote.

In the days and weeks to come I would read and reread Michael Moore's essay from the beginning of the summer predicting Trump's victory; I would fill my Kindle with the *New York Times*' suggested reading list, books to explain "how we got here"; I would attend Sandy and John's weekly vigils upstairs, drinking and eating with the over-sixties crowd, desperate for some wisdom or perspective or any hint of grace. But in the moment itself, at two or three in the morning, whenever they called it, whenever Jesse and I shut the computer and blinked into the new darkness, all I could do was reach out across the space between us and place my hand on Jesse's face.

He turned to me quickly, like Trump's victory was some terrible pickup line, some cue for switching from the drinks-and-flirting part of the evening to the making-out part of the evening. We fell into each other, frantic, fumbling. It was awkward; our teeth mashed together, my leg was stuck under me, and Jesse's fingers got caught in my unkempt, unwashed hair. There was a moment when we paused and I felt Jesse hesitate, his chest sweaty and heavy on top of mine, my tongue on his collarbone.

"What are we . . ." he started to say.

"Shh," I said, pulling him closer to me, embarrassed by the cliché of it.

I could have told him that it was okay, that yes, it was desperate and comforting and reckless and inevitable, but I didn't want to speak. I just wanted his hands, his face, just wanted to relieve some of the tension, some of the build-up, just wanted, honestly, to be fucked without having to think about it or anything else, before facing the undercurrent of shock and sorrow and Trump-induced anxiety and sleeplessness that lay ahead.

It was quick, the way the first time often is; we had been waiting for each other and it was over almost before it began. We lay on the couch together afterward, slowly disentangling, breath heavy.

"Well," I said.

"It's a new world," said Jesse.

"In more ways than one."

"I've been wanting to do that since you told me about the flying cockroaches you battled in Thailand."

"I know."

Jesse left soon after. He offered to stay but I wanted to shower, to lie naked on my bed with the windows cracked, to try to separate out the different churning sensations in my stomach: Trump's victory; my first time having sex since Kyle and I broke up; Jesse, Jesse, Jesse. To my surprise I slept deeply and woke up late the next morning, having already decided to "work from home." I scrolled through Slack in bed, tried to catch up with emails; all anyone could talk about was the election. Andy wrote to the team and told us to "take the time we need to process and then get back to work."

Jesse texted me in the early afternoon. We wrote *hey how r u* back and forth until one of us said, *it's okay*, and the other, *you're one of my best friends*, and then, *I love you*, and finally, *I'm not looking for anything serious*. It was sex born of disaster, the body still attempting to live, to hope, even though the brain was in a state of despair. What was the current thinking on the relationship between the body and the mind? Were they separate entities? Or was there unity between them? I thought about people falling in love in North Korea, or the Warsaw ghetto; of having sex in hiding, in the dark, under siege. Maybe we had been trying to orgasm our way out of reality, out of annihilation, into some chance of survival, and into the next day.

* *

Not long after the election, Amelia announced that she was moving to Europe.

"I'm going," she said, "to Barcelona. To walk along Las Ramblas and stand inside La Sagrada Familia and see the light come in through the stained-glass windows. To see Gaudí's higgledy-piggledy, Alice-in-Wonderland buildings and remember that the truth is sometimes slant."

"When are you going? Why?" I asked.

"I'm getting out of the Matrix," she said. "As far away from this crazy, unhinged, gun-toting, racist country as I can get. As soon as I can."

"Come on, Amelia, you can't just cut and run."

"I can. Yes, I can. And you could, too. There's a sickness at the heart of America. You know that, you saw it when you were teaching. Where else do little boys go to schools with AK-47s and shoot their classmates and their teachers? It's all a myth, America. I want to live somewhere where being responsible for one another, taking care of one another, is part of the national narrative, the consciousness of the place, the policy of the place. I don't want it to be a radical notion that everyone should be able to go to a doctor or get their prescription medicine without going bankrupt. I'm so sick of this individualistic, capitalistic bullshit that says we're all just in it for ourselves and nobody else. I'm done. I'm done."

"But by leaving, isn't that exactly what you're saying? That you're only in it for yourself? That you're saving yourself while the rest of us are here trying to make some kind of a difference?"

"What difference are you making, Elena? No, honestly. Did you do any phone banking for the election? Did you get anyone else to vote for Hillary who wasn't already going to?"

"No, probably not, but . . ."

"You're too plugged in to see. You're in the belly of the beast."

"It's a privilege to leave."

"Yeah, that's true. But it's also a privilege to stay and live the way you're living. As though everything that's rotten about America won't really touch you. As though you're immune."

Later, after she had already gone, she sent me a postcard from the Picasso Museum gift shop. On the back she had written:

Darling,

I am in a whirlwind of chocolate and churros, sangria and tapas, tango and art. It's everything we dreamed about when writing those awful art history papers in college. The evenings start at 10pm and go all night. Siesta is part of the flow of the day. I met a group of Chileans and Argentinians last night who laughed when I said I was a Trump refugee. "Now the US is just like everywhere else," they said. "You're not so special—not even in your grief." This was strangely comforting.

This afternoon I went to the Picasso Museum and was transfixed. There was a special exhibit, Cubism and War. I am thinking about how artists begin deconstructing their subjects, their places of perspective to show different viewpoints; same time as Einstein, same time as Joyce, Woolf, cummings, deconstructing language and form. The discovery of perspective—the rejection of traditional perspective. This is the key. Wondering how I might write a Cubist play? Short scenes— flashes—that create a whole world. The main character would be a construction worker who has worked on a single cathedral his whole life—hundreds of years, then finishes it. What does he do when it is over?

Barcelona—home of the tiny shower.

Besos,

Amelia

Chapter 35

We started to notice some changes in Andy, and, by extension, CloseR. By the summer of 2017, the company had grown to almost fifty people. We had weekly all-hands lunches, catered by local restaurants and usually featuring a presentation from someone. One week, the head of sales walked us through a slideshow that showed how a conversation between two people at a college alumni networking event the previous month had led to a massive contract with a company based out of Sacramento that none of us had ever heard of.

"All it takes is a conversation," he said, "from any one of us. We all need to be out there talking to our network."

Another week, Paula talked about the power of "likes" and "retweets," and how our personal social media accounts also reflected on CloseR's brand. Every quarter, Andy would give an overview of the financials.

"We value transparency," he said, "and so I want you all to know where we stand."

Details about salaries were never included in these presentations, but graphs denoting our increasing credit line over the years stood out prominently.

Over time, though, the presentations started to shift in content. While we filled our paper plates with *dosas* and curried chickpeas or kale salad doused in cranberry vinaigrette, balancing them precariously on our knees in the common area, the presentations went from the generic "Nuts and Bolts of the Organization" to a form of "Self-Help 101." We did breathing exercises, closing one nostril and breathing through the other, and Andy walked us through a twenty-minute PowerPoint on "How to Have Difficult Conversations with Colleagues." Louise, our office manager, printed out affirmations in large, bold lettering and stuck them on the walls around the office. Posters calling out "I AM BOLD," "I AM PRODUCTIVE," and "I AM VALUED" accosted us from every angle.

"Why do I feel like I work in a yoga studio?" Paula said to me in the mornings.

"Pour me some green juice and let's get on with it," I replied.

In the late summer—a time I still associated with back-to-school, even though it had been years since I'd structured my life around a school schedule—Andy organized a company off-site focused on the Enneagram, a system of nine personality types and their supposed psychological motivations. In the weeks leading up to the retreat, we were all emailed a long, multiple-choice test, which asked us questions about how we'd respond to specific conflicts, whether we preferred to be alone or with others, and a whole slew of other seemingly unrelated scenarios with what-ifs attached. Jesse stood behind my chair as I filled mine out, peering over my shoulder and breathing into my hair.

"Stop cheating," I said.

"I didn't study," he said.

We had been sleeping together since the election—our "Trump affair," we called it. We had sex in response to anything related to Trump—the inauguration, the Women's March, when he hired Steve Bannon, when Mueller's Russia investigation started. "Therapy," we said, "an act of resistance." We got off on the malaise, the despair that hung over the Bay like a thick fog that wasn't going to break at noon. It had gotten less awkward since that first time, more languorous and playful. Because we weren't actually in a relationship, sex wasn't an afterthought, done hastily and tiredly after dinner once or twice a week. We maintained some of the boundaries of friendship—I didn't brush my teeth while he took a shit; he didn't clip his toenails on my kitchen floor. Keeping those boundaries helped dissolve others.

We received the results of our Enneagram questionnaires several days before the retreat. A long pdf packet filled with information about my "type" showed up in my inbox. I was a Four, otherwise known as "The Individualist," and I spent a whole morning avoiding work and reading through my analysis. "Fours want to distinguish themselves from others," I read. "They want to feel that their taste, their self-expression, and their emotional depth are *unique*." Later, when Jesse and I compared our results, I pointed out the line that read, "Sexual Fours go through tremendous shifts of feeling about their loved ones—everything from idolization to unbridled hatred."

"This is ridiculous," I said. "Why are we being personality typed at work? I don't even believe in this kind of thing. How can you put a box around a person and say, 'this is you'?"

"That's because you're a Four," Jesse said.

"What are you talking about?"

"It says so right here in your analysis—you think you're special."

"What's going to happen next? Are we all going to have to wear our types as badges on our shirts or colored armbands, and then only get to talk to other people who are the same type? I feel like I'm suddenly living in *Brave New World*."

"Does it also say your type is dramatic?"

Louise had rented out a conference center on Treasure Island—
between the city and the East Bay, she said, to appease us all—and
we drove over the bridge and the bay to arrive at the nondescript,
gray concrete building, a mirror of the steely gray September sky. The
room had been set up with a semicircle of chairs facing a lectern.
On each chair was a number between one and nine, and we realized
quickly that we were expected to sit according to our Enneagram
type. We started arranging ourselves, the numerous Twos taking up
half the circle. Paula was a Three and we looked for the break between
the Threes and Fours so we could sit together. Jesse was a Seven and
waved to us from across the room. It was only once everyone had
arrived that I realized I was the only Four. I was both mortified and
gratified.

Our facilitator was a silver-haired woman named Deborah who
had flown in that morning from Denver. She walked slowly around
the circle, making eye contact with each person and giving a slight
smile, a nod of the head. When she returned to the lectern, she turned
on the projector behind her, revealing a bold-printed quote by Don
Richard Riso, which she read aloud:

"The Enneagram is, at its most abstract, a universal mandala of
the self—a symbol of each of us."

"Oh boy," I said, sitting back in my chair.

Paula elbowed me in the ribs, and I hid my face behind my
notebook.

We spent the day as students in a lecture hall, while Deborah
read aloud from her slide deck. There were elaborate charts, circles
intersected with triangles, and lists upon lists of famous people organized by their "type."

"How can they possible know what type Abraham Lincoln was?"
I said to Paula during the morning break.

Around the snack table, one of the Twos asked Andy, "Should we use this as part of our hiring procedures?"

I felt for the first time that we had gone too far in our crunchy-granola, green-juice-drinking, Tevas-wearing, om-chanting approach to the workplace. That we were spending all this time on the appearance of self-improvement and fulfillment and enlightenment, not realizing the alt-scene was becoming the establishment. All this collective soul searching had started when CloseReader became CloseR, when the mission got hazy, when the substance started to fade out. We had wanted to help kids become better readers, but instead we were helping people upload files to the cloud. Not to worry, though; we were simultaneously cleansing our chakras. And now here we were, personality typed and sorted, everyone handed a card detailing their personal journey to nirvana; just follow these steps. All thanks to the privilege of getting to work in the Bay Area tech scene.

"The Enneagram doesn't put you in a box. It shows you the box you're already in and how to get out of it," Deborah quoted after lunch, and I felt her gaze rest on me.

The problem was not the Enneagram itself, although I was convinced that it was pseudoscience at best and a woo-woo cult at worst. The problem was that my workplace had taken on the aura of a New Age religious center. The boundaries between work and life had become fluid, without my full awareness or consent. In the hierarchy of our organization, I was being pulled along a trajectory set for me by others. The Bay: where CEOs flirt with being self-actualization gurus. What would have happened had I refused to take the Enneagram test that arrived in my inbox? Or if I had bowed out of the retreat? Would I have been demoted, fined, or fired as a result? Would I have lost the trust of my teammates, my direct reports, my supervisor? The fact was, it hadn't even occurred to me to refuse, to protest, to challenge.

The Kool-Aid was being administered, sip by poisonous sip, all in the name of "workplace culture." At the Enneagram retreat, I looked up and realized everyone was drunk on it.

Chapter 36

That fall, fires raged in Napa and Sonoma, and the smoke filtered through the skies and hung over the Bay, thick and gritty. The first couple of days I mistook it for the usual fog that sat on the Berkeley Hills most mornings when I woke, but that fog was gentle, light, and gray. It trailed off in cloudy wisps along the tree lines, over the bridges, until, by late morning, it had floated clear away and revealed blue skies. But the smoke in September never left the air; it sat, an ashy weight, stinging my eyes and making my nose itch and skin crawl. By the time I figured out that it wasn't just tourists or hypochondriacs around the city who were wearing masks, all of the FDA-approved face masks—the ones that would really keep the ash out of your lungs—were sold out in my local CVS stores and Targets and Walgreens. So I bought a pack of cheap knock-off masks, ones that slipped over your ears and smelled like cotton and antiseptic, and only had the appearance of protection.

The sunsets during those days of fire were among the most striking I have seen. I could see the red, shimmering blaze of a ball through the window of the BART train as we came up at West Oakland, and when I got off at Ashby, I'd run up the steps to the street and stand alongside the other weary workers, watching the sun slice through the ash and the smoke, sending off reams of pinks and reds and yellows over the horizon, over the Bay. I took pictures on my phone that didn't come out well and sent them to my mom at home, who wrote back things like, *wow! stunning!* and then five minutes later: *are you safe?*

Sometimes, we'd wake up to an orange, ashy sky. The streets were quiet, everyone hushed inside their homes, staring out the windows. The trees were silhouetted dark against the orange glow. On weekends, I found myself lying on Jesse's mattress on the floor beneath the window, staring out at the apocalyptic sky. The orange tint coated San Francisco in sepia tones, as though we were living inside an Instagram filter trying to make the world seem like a vintage postcard or an old silent film.

The fires seemed to shake some things loose, the way the wind picked up the ash from Wine Country and dusted it down over the city and the East Bay. They were one more stone thrown, one more crack in the veneer of California. They sat atop an earthquake that woke me in the night and sent my books tumbling off the shelves; atop shootings in Oakland; stabbings at a BART station; rising rent prices; mudslides in SoCal; the fact that the opioid crisis had reached California. People made rash decisions during the days of smoke that played out later. I got a text from Kyle saying he was headed back East, back home to Western Mass where he had an opportunity to be the manager of a community farm. And Paula decided to leave CloseR, quitting just as the smoke began to clear.

I hung on, clinging to my routine, head down, mask on. Sandy and John yelled down to check on me and I gave them a thumbs-up through the bamboo curtains hanging over their deck. I went to work. I got my sweet, frothy milk from the café around the corner. Jesse and I plugged our noses and held our breath as we kissed in the gritty air, our Trump affair now extending to include local disasters, every burned grape another reason to press against each other. I woke in the mornings feeling nauseous, seasick; I ate saltines for breakfast and blamed it on the smoke curling its way into my lungs.

I talked to my grandparents on the phone; they had seen photographs and videos of the orange skies, the rising plumes of smoke, the scrambled evacuations.

"Elena," my grandmother said, "this is madness. What are you doing there?"

"Write everything down," my grandfather said. "Take pictures! You're living through history."

"I'm fine," I said. "Thank you for the apple cake; it was delicious."

When the first rains came during the night midwinter, I stood outside in Sandy and John's garden in the morning, tasting that sweet, thick after-rain smell in the air. Sandy pulled aside a curtain; she came out onto the deck in a flannel dressing gown, coffee mug in hand.

"Elena," she said, "how old are you, anyway?"

"Twenty-nine."

"When are you going to get yourself a boyfriend?"

On the counter in my bathroom, two pink lines blazed into being.

PART 2

Chapter 37

Here they are, those skies above West Oakland, orange clouds settling over shipping crates and wrapping around the gangly, white industrial cranes, the ones they say inspired characters in *Star Wars*. Here's how I know spring is on its way—we have come out of the tunnel, out from under the bay, and light still hangs on the day. The sky over West Oakland BART tells me that the earth is spinning, that time has continued on, that winter is ending. More than the rolled jean cuffs of the skinny white techies and the sudden proliferation of Allbirds woolen shoes, the fact that the skies still hold the sun after those long minutes between San Francisco and the East Bay tells me that the seasons are changing.

They didn't want to let me go alone, the nurses; they wanted me to call someone, to have someone pick me up. But who could I call? Who would be willing to drive back from the city at 5:00 p.m.? "I'm fine," I told them. *Fine, fine, fine.* They didn't look at me during the procedure. I lay there, legs spread, my cervix being dilated one millimeter at a time, while they bustled around, checked the screen, hovered in the background. So why should they care how I leave? How I get home? I didn't take the Valium or Vicodin; I'm not jacked up on opiates; I'm in my right mind, so I can take myself and my empty uterus and get on BART. That's what I told them.

On the way to work I usually listen to *The Daily*, a podcast from the *New York Times*, which gets me only halfway there, and I'll be squeezed between a hundred different armpits, silently fuming against those who keep their backpacks on instead of putting them on the floor between their feet, while I hear about Parkland, and Harvey Weinstein, and simultaneously scroll through my Instagram feed. I usually fill the rest of the commute with podcasts from *The Moth* or *This American Life*, but today I don't need stories; I need poetry. So, I'm listening to *On Being*, which I usually avoid because by living in Berkeley I'm inundated with so much pseudo-spirituality that I no longer seek out the real thing. But today, today I think I could use some Krista Tippett.

It's been a long time since I sat with a poem, since I unraveled a stanza line by line, word by word, letter by letter. Reading a poem, really reading it, feels like getting high. It's like what happens on shrooms. Colors become more vibrant; the hillside breathes.

Now I'm with Krista Tippett as she interviews Naomi Shihab Nye, and it feels like an act of rebellion for me, granddaughter of Holocaust survivors, just to be listening to a Palestinian American poet. Nye says, "You are living in a poem," and I want to believe her, but I'm distracted. I'm distracted by the older Black man stumbling toward me outside West Oakland BART in an oversized red zip-up, beard scraggly, jeans ragged, nails chipped and dirty. My Lyft app is spinning into gear and the thing is, I am still bleeding. I can feel it dripping out of me, onto the hefty pad they gave me to stick onto my underwear, and here's Nye whispering in my ear about kindness, and I just start shaking my head at him.

There's a paramedic's van parked in front of BART, and even though it's spring, the sky has started to darken, and, because it's the Bay, the temperature is about to drop ten degrees. I've got my fleece zipped up to my chin, underneath the blue puffy vest Andy handed out at the Enneagram retreat. As the Lyft app pings to tell me my driver is just three minutes away and I should be on the lookout for a silver Toyota, I see that the man hasn't gone on to one of the dozen or so other weary twentysomethings waiting for their rides, as I expected him to, but is still talking to me. Except now he has started gesticulating with his hands, his bushy eyebrows have furrowed, and lines are deepening in his forehead. His eyes have narrowed, and I can see he's upset. *Me too.* But I take out an earphone (just one) and start to say:

"Oh, I'm sorry, I didn't hear—"

"Why you gotta shake your head at me? You didn't even know what I said—"

"Sorry, no, I just had my headphones in, and—"

"You think just 'cause I'm a Black man I'm gonna ask you for money? Why'd you shake your head at me? I didn't even ask nothing. What'd you do that for?"

"You're right," I say, "I'm sorry."

"Hey, that's all right, that's okay. Let's start over, why don't we?"

The little black dot on the Lyft app inches closer and closer; the man puts out his fist and we pound.

"Do you know where Fruitvale is?"

"Oh, yes, it's in Oakland," I say, I point, my hand waving in the general direction.

"Yeah, so I gotta get to Fruitvale now. I'm trying to get home, you know, and I only got ten cents on me. I only got ten cents, so, can you help me out?"

This is when the cramping starts up again, just at this moment. They said there'd be some cramping in the next forty-eight hours, "as the uterus contracts," so I've been expecting it, but suddenly I can't breathe out here in the blustery evening winds of West Oakland. The Lyft app pings: my driver is here; I've got fifty-nine seconds before he leaves and Krista Tippett is asking Naomi Shihab Nye about what it was like growing up partly in Ferguson, Missouri, and partly on the road between Ramallah and Jerusalem. But what I want to know, what I want her to tell me, is what I should do in this moment, this bleeding, privileged, infuriating moment right now, with this man standing here, hand out, indignant and begging, and me, fleece zipped up, blood oozing out, my uterus clamping down against the flow, the feeling of the suction tube still reverberating inside me. Forty seconds, thirty seconds, my driver is about to leave, and I have to go, and how could he, but also how could I, and maybe it's not his fault or my fault but here we are at fault, and no.

I shake my head again, stuff my earphone back into my ear, and get into the back seat, my cheeks burning. The seats in this silver Toyota are leather-smooth and sleek; water bottles are perched in their little round holders on the middle seat, and there are Altoid mints at the ready. The music is low, radio tuned to the jazz station, something melodic with no words. We're waiting for another passenger to join but then we're off. I can see that the old man has already moved on to the next waiting woman, wireless earbuds jutting out of her ears, her light spring jacket that was warm enough this morning no longer sufficient to ward off the cold.

It is warm in the car and Nye is finishing up her last poem, and I pull out the picture in my pocket. It's a little black-and-white printed photo with my name on it and the date stamped at the top. Here it is—proof that there is nothing left inside me. It's only tissue, they said, not even the size of a plum. Yes, and it's only a dollar or two I could have fished out from my wallet; it's only a few weeks away from my thirtieth birthday; it's only so many things. And now, even as I try to shake off the last minutes, the last hours, as I settle back into these leather seats, dreaming about the unopened bottle of Trader Joe's wine in my kitchen, and the episodes of *Portlandia* I still have left to watch, still, I can't shake the question that has started to rage inside me: *how the hell did I get here?*

Chapter 38

This is how they emptied me: millimeter by millimeter I was opened, legs spread, dangling over black stirrups. It was a male doctor who did it, the "D&C"—the abortion. An older man, with silver hair and an awkward bedside manner, sticking me with pins, as though I were at the tailor's having a dress taken in. I didn't take the drugs because I was more afraid of not feeling than feeling pain. The local anesthesia numbed some of the pain but not the pressure. Pressure like deep aches shooting up into my uterus. As I lay there, I imagined my cervix was a sea anemone that had closed up tight and was now being coaxed open. I imagined it unfurling, tentacle by tentacle, defenseless. When the doctor placed the suction tube in me, my uterus felt like a dirty carpet being vacuumed. I felt the waves pulse inside me, and I cried while the nurses looked away, checking my vitals on the screen. The doctor said, "Yes, yes, you are likely to feel sadness," and I wondered at what point in his career he had read this line in a textbook and memorized it.

I didn't tell Jesse—haven't told him. Things have been winding down anyway, with us, in an unspoken, mutually agreed upon way. Our foray into a sexual relationship has felt the way it did to travel at twenty-two—we explored the main attractions, stayed close to the tourist route, and then declared that we had "done it." The pregnancy was collateral damage, like picking up a parasite or getting diarrhea on a train after eating the unadvised street food.

I found the clinic location online—in the seven years I've lived in the Bay, I've never really gone to see a doctor. My mom deposits me at her nurse practitioner's office every other year or so when I'm home in the summer, and I get the requisite Pap, slip my arm through the blood pressure cuff, and lift my shirt so she can press around the contour of my breasts, looking for lumps. When we first moved in together, Monica gave an impassioned monologue about the benefits of the IUD, so I went to the Berkeley Women's Clinic and lay on the hospital bed, shivering with cramps. I almost passed out the first two times I tried to get up. The gray-haired old woman who inserted it told me not to worry, that it wasn't an indication of how I'd respond to childbirth. I thought it was an ironic comment, given the reason I was there. The same IUD that failed me now. Outside of that one time, though, I've never had a reason to go. So when I saw the two pink lines appear in my bathroom on the night of the first rains, the first person I thought to call was not Jesse, but Monica, even though she was three thousand miles away.

At home, finally, I lie on the couch with a cool towel over my eyes for a while, trying to breathe my way through each cramp, through the absurdity. I hear the "yoga voice" that so many teachers put on, reminding me to stay in the discomfort, to just stay for one more breath, and then another. I practice half sun salutations in my mind. Repeat over and over again to myself: *Inhale, arms up. Exhale, fold forward and touch the earth. Inhale, halfway lift. Exhale, fold. Inhale, raise the arms overhead toward the sky. Exhale, hands to the heart.*

Earth. Sky. Heart.

Breathe.

Chapter 39

I never knew my father—my "progenitor," as my mother likes to say. My mom told me it was a short-lived romance, a fling on the other side of her hippie years, when she was back in school, studying the concept of revolution in historical narratives and navigating her way through sexism and antisemitism and ageism to get herself on a tenure track. So it had always just been my mom and me—and my grandparents on holidays and summer trips into the sticky heat of New York, when we'd go to baseball games and eat knishes hot off the street and go to little hole-in-the-wall Italian restaurants where I'd order plates of spaghetti piled high with Parmesan cheese and we'd split slices of cheesecake, pushing aside the syrupy strawberries. Mostly, though, it was just my mother and me.

Whenever we'd fight, after I'd sequestered myself in my bedroom with my books, my mom would come in and sit on the bed, some kind of offering in hand—tomatoes fresh off the vine that she'd picked from the garden, the last square of the chocolate bar we'd been eating that week. It was always after our fights that she'd tell me stories about when I was a baby. I think fighting with me made her nostalgic, sentimental in a way she normally wasn't.

While I pretended not to listen, my mom would start talking about how I was a terrible sleeper as a baby. She used to celebrate on the nights that I'd sleep two or three hours in a row. A colleague had handed her an article that lauded the necessity of sleep-training infants, and she'd tried it one night, when I was six or seven months old, placing me in my crib and walking out the door, coming back after five-, ten-, fifteen-minute increments. Others who had used the technique said to expect thirty, maybe forty minutes of crying. But not me, my mom said. I wailed and cried all night long.

She gave up trying to change my sleep habits and instead brought me into bed with her, snuggling us up together so that I would sleep tucked into her armpit, my body curled around hers. She would wake in the mornings with a stiff neck, aching shoulders, arms that had no feeling left in them. Sometimes in the night I would sleep talk, using baby babble. Other times I would roll and twitch and fling my arms and legs until they came to settle, usually half on top of my mother's body. She would be desperate to pee, but waking me was the worse outcome, so she'd lie still, stomach aching, slipping in and out of dreams. When I would stir and wake during the nights, she would put her hand on my back, or hold both my hands together in hers, and try to breathe me back into slumber.

All through my childhood I would regularly crawl into bed with my mom, after bad dreams or nights when I just couldn't sleep, when I couldn't get comfortable, when it was too cold or too hot, wandering, half-asleep, from my bedroom into my mother's. She was so used to me being next to her that she wouldn't wake up at these midnight visits, but just as when I was a baby, she'd put her hand on my back or hold my hands in hers, and within minutes I would be in a deep sleep.

I haven't been sleeping well since the abortion. Night after night I lie in bed, trying to count backward from one thousand, diffusing lavender essential oil and listening to recordings of waves. In the night, I think about summers as a kid, when tomatoes would grow heavy and ripe, the vines taking over every yard in the neighborhood. My friends and I would be sent into the gardens with bags to collect those that had fallen, overripe, to the ground. We'd empty sacks of them onto the kitchen tables, try to keep them from rolling off the edge and onto the floor, and laugh as they tumbled around like billiard balls.

Recently, my mom called to tell me that she had given up planting tomatoes the last couple of summers and had let the vegetable boxes in our garden grow over with grass. It was less the work of growing them that became too much, and more the work of eating them. So many, and so constantly, it was hard to keep up. They were growing rotten, tumbling off the vine of their own accord, and mulching into the earth. She had thought about turning them into sauce or stewing and canning them and lining the jars up along the pantry, the way my grandmother would have done, letting nothing go to waste. She said she had thought about collecting them in little baskets, tying a string around them, and passing them out to neighbors and students and old high school friends of mine. But day after day they fell to the ground, sweet and stinking. She had one of the neighbor boys come to even out the land where the planter boxes had been, remove the wooden barriers, and patch up the grass so you couldn't tell that there had ever been anything but lawn.

Chapter 40

I stopped bleeding just a few days before my thirtieth birthday. It went on for weeks, starting out as a thick gush, gradually tapering off into a trickle, a few spots, and then, one day, it stopped. I threw away the pads, those monstrosities with wings that thirteen-year-olds use when they first get their period, walking through middle school hallways bowlegged, trying to get comfortable on metal desk chairs. I've been taking advantage of CloseR's work-from-home policy these last few weeks, eschewing my trek across the bay for answering emails in my pajamas, taking Zoom calls on the couch. I ordered mac 'n' cheese takeout, and my apartment has smelled like melted cheese and garlic for days. Monica texted to see how I'm doing; I am ignoring Jesse's infrequent check-ins.

I've taken up drinking whiskey in the evenings, right at five o'clock, when I sign out of Slack. I mix it with ice, pull out old, esoteric books I bought in college but never read, and sit sipping the amber-colored liquid until I can no longer feel it burn. Amelia and I used to talk about that moment when traveling—like when you're on top of the mountain or your hands are in the dirt or you're finally drinking the latte in the café tucked in the cobblestone alleyway—when you look up and find yourself in the place you dreamed about being in. The dreaming self meets the dream. It can be terrifying, dizzying, euphoric, anticlimactic. The selves reach across time, the dreamer and the dreamed. There must be a Borges story that describes this.

My transition into thirty is not feeling graceful. I have been thinking of the ways in which those dreams fulfilled can make way for new dreams to emerge, but then, too, the opposite—the way an unfulfilled dream nags and tugs, gets in the way of moving forward. How all the myriad disappointments, all the small missteps add up, clog the system, like hair stuck in the shower drain. I remember how, in my freshman-year college dorm, the shower in our bathroom got so clogged with hair that one day, at the beginning of the spring semester, the drain essentially threw up. Black muck oozed and spluttered out of the drain in protest, coating the walls and floor of the shower. We couldn't use it for days and days, and after it was fixed, someone on the hall wrote a friendly reminder in permanent marker on the shower wall: "Good morning! Please clean out your hair!"

It feels like I haven't been cleaning out my hair. It keeps shedding; I keep shedding certain choices, certain hopes, certain intentions, and just stuffing them down the drain, out of view. But it's starting to feel clogged. I think I might throw up.

When my mother calls this evening, I almost don't pick up. I'm on the last season of *The Great British Baking Show* and considering starting over at the beginning; it feels like Xanax in a television show; it helps me fall asleep. I haven't yet told my mother about the abortion, though I'm not sure why—she'd probably be thrilled. But I don't want to deal with avoiding her questions, with coming up with half-truths to describe what I've been up to recently, to talk about my upcoming birthday.

She calls twice, one after the other, without leaving a message.

And late—it is after midnight her time. So, on the second call, I answer.

"Mom, you're calling so late."

"Elena, what are you doing?"

"I'm watching my baking show."

"That British thing?"

"Yeah."

"Listen, turn it off a minute, will you?"

"What's wrong?"

"It's Grandpa."

"What happened?"

"He's had a heart attack."

"A heart attack?"

"He's in the hospital."

"What? Mom, is he—"

"No. But you should call him. I'm going to drive down next week when the semester ends, spend some time there, help Grandma out."

"Should I come home? Mom, what—"

"Just call him, Elena. Talk to him."

"I will, okay, I'll call him tomorrow."

On my computer screen, Paul Hollywood cuts into a gingerbread cake sculpture in the form of the Colosseum—bits of gingerbread cookie crumble and fall as the spun sugar that holds it all together grows hot and melted. I've been wearing the same pajama pants for three days; Sandy finally comments this evening when I go outside to catch my breath after my phone call with my mom. *Things are unraveling*, I want to tell her. There was a baby and now there isn't; there was Jesse and now there isn't; there was Kyle and now there isn't. Monica and Paula have gone on to the next things; Amelia is in Spain. I was going to be a teacher, but now I'm not. And my grandpa—my yarn-spinning, opera-loving, won't-stop-talking, Israel-defending, slightly sexist grandpa—is in the hospital. There is a heart that beats—and one day it will stop.

My grandmother has a new smartphone and with it comes FaceTime. When I call them, I am still wearing my glasses and my hair is wet from the shower. She puts her face up close to the phone and starts yelling; I can see the deep creases around her eyes, the wrinkles chiseled into her skin along her cheeks, her forehead, the ridges of her nose. She asks me about my glasses, are they new? I tell her she can stop yelling, I can hear her just fine. Her breath fogs up the phone and the little jade beads in her necklace bang against the screen, making a *clack-clack-clack* sound.

"Put Grandpa on," I say. "Let me talk to him."

She holds the phone up in front of my grandfather. His face is wan and slack, and his head is resting against the white pillow on the hospital bed. He has a blanket tucked around him and his long, knobby fingers are resting on the blue wool. His eyes are open, his eyelids heavy. He looks sedated.

"He's full of drugs," my grandmother hisses to me over the phone.

"Can he hear me?"

"Yes, yes, you just talk to him like you would normally."

I can't conceive of it. Our normal was my grandfather talking and me listening, snickering, asking questions, taking mental notes. Our normal was him asking me one question and then before I could properly answer, going off on tangent after tangent, reciting old nursery rhymes in Yiddish he'd learned as a boy, noting the weather patterns over the Andes, reflecting on the latest theories on pedagogy. In the image of my grandfather that I held in my mind, he wore a blue beret with the words "Philosophy Rules" embossed on the bill, a glass of red wine on the table, butter in the white ceramic butter dish, a book or three or five laid out before him. The radio was always on, and he went through his days listening to the news or classical music or a BBC program about bird-watching, somehow internalizing all the new information as he sipped his wine and buttered his bread and underlined his students' essays. There is nothing normal about the image of him on the screen in front of me, mouth open on the hospital bed, eyes glazed and gazing off somewhere just to the left of the phone. I can't think of anything to say.

I call him back this morning, determined to ramble.

"Grandpa," I say, and he blinks his eyes at me.

"He can hear you," my grandmother shouts from his bedside.

"Grandpa," I say, "everything's okay here. I'm still working at the tech company, you remember? It's not the most fulfilling thing I've ever done but I don't mind the work and I like the people. I'm still in the little studio apartment underneath Sandy and John; I think you'd like them. You'd have a lot to talk about, anyway. The weather here is pretty warm; we're having a spring heat wave, you know, and everyone's talking about how again we had very little rain and what fire season will look like this year. Um, and I'm reading some old college books that I never finished. I'm finding notes in the margins that I don't remember writing and bookmarks two-thirds of the way through the book . . ."

I go on like this for five, ten minutes, telling him about the mugs of tea Sandy has started leaving for me outside my door in the mornings, about the hummingbirds I can see outside my kitchen window in the afternoons. I tell him about my commute, about the fog on the hills, about Amelia's latest letter from Spain. I do not tell him about the abortion, about my newfound whiskey habit, about how it is getting harder and harder to get up and dressed and out the door in the mornings. Over and over again I say I am well, and happy, and healthy, and okay.

Eventually, when I pause to take a breath, my grandmother brings the phone back to her face.

"He's tired now, *bubbeleh*, he needs to rest."

"Okay, Grandma, I'll call again soon."

"You do that. Oh, and Elenoosh—"

"Yeah?"

"Happy thirtieth birthday!"

Chapter 41

I start taking long walks on the weekends, often ending up at one of my old spots in the East Bay. The first time I set out is the day after my birthday, after the rambling call with my grandfather. I find my way to People's Café in downtown Berkeley, where, when I first moved here, I used to sit and read poetry in the back, sipping on Mexican hot chocolate and watching the Occupy movement start on the sidewalk just out front, next to the Bank of America building. I almost can't find the café at first—it's moved across the street and has swanked up. It's no longer made up of scratched and slightly battered wooden chairs and tables, held in place by scraps of cardboard stuck under the base to keep the wobbles out. It's classier, cleaner, and altogether less appealing.

I wander in and sit down, but the view is all wrong; I am facing the wrong direction. Or, rather, People's is, now that it has moved locations. I can still remember the baskets of individually wrapped vegan baked goods sitting at the counter, next to the over-the-top lefty bumper stickers, and how, when I'd order my drink, I'd end up slipping a slice of banana bread or pumpkin bread onto the counter as well. Those were the days when I still underlined the books I was reading, collected lines of poetry, dreamed up lesson plans, and gradually built out a mental web of connections between Adrienne

Rich and the psalmists of the Hebrew Bible and John Milton; when I was sure that the sonnet form held the key to understanding human potential, and that all I had to do was recite beautiful lines of poetry over and over again to a group of twelve- and thirteen-year-olds, and their lives would be transformed in a single, supernova instant.

People's had been my landing pad in Berkeley, my cozy, latte-scented haven amid the woolen hat and weed sellers on Telegraph and the yoga and meditation peddlers on Shattuck. I had wandered in one day early in my time in the Bay, and although there were no sofas or cushion-backed chairs, although you could hear everybody's conversations and interviews and poorly connected Skype calls, although the lighting in the bathroom was terrible and the door didn't lock properly, People's—for a few months—became my place. It was the beginning of feeling local, of planting my feet down, of becoming *of* this place. A local with a café—how much more grounded could it get?

It is a jarring feeling to learn that People's is now across the street, now completely revamped inside and out. I am looking to recall that era, my era of People's. I want to be able to sit back down in my early twenties self, drink what she drank, see what she saw, feel the same scratches on the table as she read yet another Audre Lorde poem aloud under her breath. I am looking to reinhabit myself by rein-habiting the places I knew and loved and frequented. But People's has changed. It seems, in fact, to exist in name only. Nothing else bears resemblance to the café that housed my early Berkeley dreams. If a café is stripped of its location, its tables and chairs, its decor, its baristas, and then reinvented anew, can it really be considered the same café?

From People's I had watched the Occupy movement set up tents and signs. I had joined an ambling, shuffling march to city hall and found my way next to Kyle. Of course, he wasn't yet Kyle when we marched together that warm September afternoon. He was a red-headed, curly-haired, lean runner's body with a sign I've since forgotten. I walk along the route of that march again on one of my weekend walks, remembering how Kyle and I kept bumping into each other, how I'd felt that warm, prickly feeling of the beginning of something, of sex hovering just under the surface, of one more drink and let's keep talking all night. Strange to connect that feeling with years of doing laundry together, of watching the dishes pile up, of rolling over in bed after he touched my hip to signal *not tonight*; with that comfortable, sweatpants feeling, when I was grading papers on the couch and he put a cup of tea down next to me, and I felt how loved I was, how seen; with the way that comfort eventually devolved into silence, into judgment, into breaking up over the phone, standing barefoot at the edge of the ocean.

There are still things even now, both little and big, that make me reach for my phone to text or call Kyle. When I see a pokeberry bush growing amid a neighbor's tomato patch; when a coworker tells me about some amazing hot springs in the Sierras she has just discovered; when, for a moment, I was pregnant and alone and curled up on my bathroom floor. But I haven't heard from him since the fires of last fall, since he texted to tell me he was going back East. Back home. Backward.

I walk to the apartment I shared with Monica that first year living in the Bay. There is a foreclosure notice tacked up on the door and the building looks older, sadder, sagging slightly. The paint is chipping. An old Bernie sign from the 2016 primary is still posted in the window. I snap a selfie in front of the house and text it to Monica and Rae as I try to peer over the gate to the backyard to see the lemon tree. I think about knocking on the door, to see if I can go up to the orange-painted apartment where Kyle and I had sex for the first time, where Monica fell for Rae, where we arranged a dozen mason jars filled with dried beans and lentils on an open shelf in the kitchen, only to realize that realistically, we were only ever going to cook with canned. At some point during the year, Monica came home with a microwave. We never spoke about it, didn't ever acknowledge it, but we both started nuking Trader Joe's ninety-second rice and Amy's enchiladas in the evenings, while our cast-iron pans lay unused on the stove.

Each home I have lived in out here has felt like a different era. The apartment with Monica felt of beginnings and falling in love and learning how to teach and how to cook and how to *be* in my new city. Of still being more connected to college than adulthood, of those fights particular to roommates—silly things about not flushing the toilet or leaving the dirty dishes until the next day or using her mascara and razor. Of also those late-night conversations on one of our beds—after first dates and first days, after a shitty conversation with my mom or her brother, about what to wear to an interview and borrowing each other's shoes and sweaters and earrings without asking. And then how it ended, how we shifted our focus to our romantic partners, exchanging roommates for lovers. Some of the same fights still occurred, as we were tying up our logistical lives with another person in ever more intricate ways. The thing is, though, I didn't expect my trajectory to be from roommate to boyfriend to just me in a studio.

The summer has taken on a strange glow. I barely make it into the city these days, not being able to stomach the conversations about ever-increasing benefits and perks, or the minutiae of scanning functionality. The gray skies of July have settled in, and I bundle up as though it were fall on the East Coast on my afternoon and weekend walks. I circle the two-mile radius in which I have lived these past seven years. Each of my apartments has been within walking distance of Ashby BART, as though Ashby were a magnet or an anchor weighing me down, pulling me to shore, keeping me oriented in one direction. Seven years I've been here. Almost twice college. A week in years. The length of time it takes for all the cells in the body to regenerate. Or so I've heard. In which case, am I even the same person who arrived here seven years ago? Or have I reformed anew? In any event, aren't I due a sabbatical?

This weekend I go farther afield, to the loop hike in Tilden I used to do with Kyle on Sunday mornings. I pause in front of the rocky stream that runs alongside the trail, where once, on a particularly foggy day, we stripped our clothes and waded in, giggling at the cold and the impropriety. The next day I go to Lake Merritt, where Jesse and Paula and I used to walk and brunch. I stand in front of a little bistro with outdoor seating and watch as customers sip their orange juice from champagne flutes and spear marinated tomatoes. I have the sensation that I am watching myself from a couple of years ago, and I cannot shake the feeling that things are starting to come apart at the seams. I can still feel the reverberations of the suction tube from the D&C rattling around inside me, only now it also seems as though the air around me is pulsing in tiny waves, the way it had done when Kyle and I did shrooms together at Sykes Hot Springs—except then the pulsing was like a heartbeat filled with love and light and breath, and now the pulsing feels like a migraine, like the air around me is pounding my head against a wall and I am standing in the middle of a deep valley, trying not to scream.

Chapter 42

My grandfather died this morning. August 23, 2018. My mother calls at 5:00 a.m. to tell me. Peacefully, she says. He passed away peacefully at home; my grandmother held his hand. She says he sort of coughed, and a tear rolled down his cheek, and then his face changed, went rigid and slack all in an instant. *Peacefully.* Why do we take comfort in that? He went without complaint, without a fight, submissively. But what if I wanted him to fight? To rise up in protest? To rage? I hope he was telling stories to the angel of death. Story after story after story, regaling the afterlife with his never-ending trove of random facts and tidbits and bizarre obsessions and long-winded explanations to questions he was never asked.

Then again, maybe he was tired of all that. Tired of his insatiable curiosity, tired of his mind that would not let him rest, the mind that kept seeking, reading, learning, writing, explaining, unraveling the mysteries of the universe, trying to come closer to an understanding of the whole, not just the tiny part he could see. Maybe his body needed to take matters into its own hands, shut the system down, force the mind to cease, so that rest would come, unbidden but not unwelcome.

I just want to talk to him, to hear from him the story of his dying, of his death. Did you go singing? Arias from Mozart or the Yiddish lullaby your mother used to sing? The one that drew you to Grandma in the displacement camp. The one you would hum to yourself on walks around the Brooklyn neighborhood where you built your new life, that you would sing to my mother as she fell asleep. The one that my mother then sang to me when, as a baby, I would not sleep, and she would tuck me under her arm and curl her body around me on the bed and whisper-sing into my ears, willing me to close my eyes and rest.

"What was it like, Grandpa?" I want to ask. "Your passing, what was it like?"

"Ah, Elenoosh," I hear him say, "it was really something!"

Chapter 43

I take a red-eye to New York and my mom picks me up at the airport in a rental car. She just missed him, she says to me. She's been back and forth all summer, has spent countless days sitting in the armchair next to his bed, reading aloud translations of French existentialism. At times, she told me on the rainy drive—the world as bleary-eyed as I felt—he would interrupt to ask her to read it in the original. He didn't speak French, he just wanted to hear certain thoughts in the language in which they were conceived. But in the end, she had missed him. She was at home, preparing for the start of the semester, throwing out uneaten food from her refrigerator and surviving on the bags of day-old bagels she'd brought home from Brooklyn the week before.

"How's Grandma?" I say, rubbing the sleep from my eyes.

"She's wandering," my mom says.

"Wandering?"

"She keeps getting up and wandering into another room in the house. She starts talking and then trails off."

"She's looking for him."

"Yeah. Listen, I should also tell you—"

"What?"

"She's going to sell the house."

"What?!"

"She's been thinking about it for a long time. Ever since the heart attack in the spring."

"But what do you mean? Where will she live?"

"She's going to come home with me for a few months, until we figure it out."

"But the house, Mom, that house."

"I know."

"That's home."

"I know."

At the funeral I am distracted; my black dress is scratchy, uncomfortable in the summer heat. The rabbi-for-hire intones the Kaddish and my mother and I stumble along; the words are heavy and unfamiliar in my mouth. My grandmother seems serene, resigned, and also as if she has shrunk five inches since the last time I saw her. My mom and I shovel dirt into the open grave, and I keep wondering, *Is this what he would have wanted?* I remember sitting at the table with my grandparents, flipping through stacks of *National Geographic* magazines; my grandfather quizzed me on the flags and capitals of all the countries in the world while my grandmother played record after record of string quartets and piano concertos. In the summers we went to petting zoos and art museums and ate whole balls of mozzarella cheese straight from the brine, popping them into our mouths like popcorn. Only in those fights with my mother, or on Friday nights when the mood struck, did my grandfather reveal his Jewish soul, his roots tangled and woven and stretching out across time and the sea and half of Europe to the little patch of dirt where God was a fellow neighbor, one who was regularly drunk and had overdue bills.

Is this, then, what he wanted? The rituals of death lifted straight out of the shtetl, out of the dusty roots, like an old prayer book found in the back of a desk drawer, pages stuck together and spine broken, the Hebrew smudged from fingers running across the words? Maybe. Maybe this is exactly what he would have wanted. Returned to the earth in the way he came into it. Shrouded in the religion of his fathers. Is this how I'll go too? Or once my grandmother dies, will I feel free from the last remnants that tie me to something I cannot name, that I do not feel is wholly mine? I've heard you can be cremated and buried in the roots of a tree; I think this is what I would want. Associations with the Holocaust—and gas chambers—aside, of course.

"Come home after the shiva," my mom says to me as we walk back to the car. The ground is damp, clumps of dirt peering through the grass. We wind our way between headstones, some cracked and crooked, others so old and weatherworn that the name is no longer visible, others adorned with piles of pebbles. Jews do not place flowers on gravestones—flowers are ephemeral, temporary; they die. Instead, we place stones, which do not die. An offer of eternity to the dead. Walking through the cemetery, I feel as though I am on a remote hiking trail, where trekkers who have gone before me have marked the path with stones.

"For how long?" I ask.

"Just come," she says. "Work from home. Grandma is coming; she needs us."

"Okay," I say, "I'll come."

There are logistics to deal with when someone dies. The logistics of a funeral, a burial, yes, but also others. To remove a person from the bureaucratic record of the living, there are forms to fill out, people to call, taxes to file. I haven't told my team at CloseR; I just took a few personal days and rushed off to the airport. I barely remembered my toothbrush. I emailed Sandy from the plane before we took off. I wonder if she'll give me a discount on the rent.

Back at my grandparents' house, I hug my grandmother for a long time. I can feel her shoulder blades jutting out of her back, feel the softness of her upper arms encircling me. She seems to get smaller each time I see her. In my arms, my grandmother feels diminished, inconsequential.

"How are you, Grandma?"

My grandmother shrugs. Her skin looks yellow, leathery. Battered by wind and cold.

"People keep bringing us food," she says.

It's true. All available countertop space has been filled with platters piled high with chewy bagels; bowls covered in tinfoil holding all manner of salads: creamy potato, oily pasta, leafy greens, dry, acidic tabouleh; tins of cookies and muffins; plastic containers of unidentified casseroles and stews; a whole lasagna rests on the stove.

I pull a chocolate chip cookie out of a tin and begin to break it into tiny pieces.

"They just want to help," I say.

My grandfather's old students come swarming in two by two, three by three, over the week-long shiva. Hats in hands, they are uncomfortable with the ritual of it all, the way the mirrors have been covered and how my grandmother does not get up to greet them, stays seated. They stand in the doorways and shift from foot to foot, bodies tall and gangly. Some of them are now parents and they bring their children, who stare and touch indiscriminately. But they are soon at ease, sitting down on the sofa and chairs and pillows on the floor, eating the smoked salmon and whitefish and noodle kugel that my grandmother's neighbors have prepared, telling their own stories of my grandfather, how he never taught them from a syllabus, how they learned more from him than any other teacher they'd ever had, how he believed in them, how he'd yell and rage at them for not studying for a math test or an English test, and they'd apologize to him as though he were their mother.

My grandmother has made shiva into a week of purging the house, despite my protests. Everyone who comes leaves with something: a vase, a piece of art that once hung on the wall, the record player, a mismatched china tea set. She is giddy in giving away. I see her visibly lightening as the house is emptied, piece by piece, as though she herself is emptying out, releasing her body from its own cluttered burdens.

I am beginning to understand what my mom meant when she said my grandmother was "wandering." It is hard to sit still. I pick at my plate of food, and then jump up to get a glass of water for my grandmother. I've barely checked my phone all week and Slack seems like it's about to explode. The app icon shakes on the screen, notifications popping up uncontrollably; a little red circle alerts me to the hundreds of unread messages I have waiting for me. But it doesn't feel real. The Bay has receded in the wake of my grandfather's death. I am bored and sad and have heard the same stories of my grandfather repeated over and over again, so that it feels as though he is being reduced to just a few representative memories, and I am not ready for his large, complicated self to be confined to slivers of story. Anecdotes. My grandfather was not an anecdote.

I do not want her to sell the house. In some ways more than my own house, my grandparents' house feels like home. It is like a memorial to past selves. Layers of drawings I completed throughout my elementary school years are still tacked to the fridge with heavy-duty magnets. In the dining room I see the familiar piles of magazines, newspapers, and paper bills littering the table. Stacks and stacks of my grandfather's magazines stand on the floor along the edges of the room. Magazines about gadgets. The latest technologies. They date back years. Most are still in their plastic coverings, never opened, never read. Alongside the magazines are piles of the *New York Times*, the *Herald Tribune*, or the *Forward*, pages marked down to stories he would never read, recipes my grandparents would never make.

I wander into my grandfather's study; my grandmother has not yet started to purge this room. The room is lit only by a few lamps scattered among the books; I sit in the well-worn chair behind the mahogany desk. In the half-dark, half-light, it seems as though the shadows have wills of their own and come and go as they please. I love the smell of this place, dust and heavy velvet curtains and the bottle of Scotch my grandfather kept in the bottom drawer. I take out a glass, pour some of the amber liquid, and listen to the voices in the living room.

Towers of books stretch out along the walls of the study. They spill out of the shelves onto the floor, onto the desk piled high with pens and paper clips and scraps of paper scribbled with notes, onto the chairs. Books lie open to certain pages, marking the moments where my grandfather had stopped reading in a particular one. As long as the books stay open, I feel as though my grandfather is not wholly gone, that he is still in the middle of reading, studying. Time would like to scuttle mercilessly over the open pages, closing the books and scattering their memories. I want to bar Time from this room. Inside the study, I wait for the ghost of my grandfather to visit me, to return to the questions that propelled him forward, the questions that had yet to be answered at the time of his death.

On the wall hang two old photographs, each in a large oval frame. One is of a young boy in a dark suit, a blue-and-white prayer shawl draped over his shoulders, a raised black hat perched on his head. The other is of a young girl, maybe six or seven. She is sitting on a velvet chair and her feet dangle above the floor. She is wearing a white dress that extends just below her knees, and long white stockings. Her hair is short and dark, and somebody has clipped a bow into it. This is my great-grandmother. She did not make it through the war. My grandfather came to America with these pictures stuffed in his shoes.

Once when I was a child, I stole my grandfather's inkwell. I used to come into his study during our visits, enchanted by his desk. The desk stands in front of three windows, overlooking the little patch of green that stands in as a front garden, the gray trickle of streets and cars, the brown brick houses, the church steeples spiking up into the overcast sky. It was on the desk, underneath the maps that outlined the battles of World War I and the books written in various languages, that I found the inkwell. Small and curved, cut out of clear glass, it was filled halfway with a black, viscous liquid that reflected the light in such a way as to give the impression of being bottomless. I knew this was the source of the black scrawls on the scraps of paper scattered all over the desk, and I wanted it.

I took the inkwell and hid it on my bookshelf. I slipped it behind the books, shoved it against the wall. Sometimes I would take it out and smell the dark, inky smell; I would set it beside a clean white sheet of paper. There were moments of almost putting ink to paper—I was desperate both to throw the whole viscous mess over the white sheet, and also to keep the ink from ever touching the paper, from marking it, from ruining it.

When my mother came looking for the inkwell, I was ashamed.

My bedroom was short and narrow, and I felt squeezed between the walls, in the bed that had been my mother's when she was a child. When I was sure he was not in his room, I took the inkwell and tip-toed back inside the study. Underneath the maps, underneath the world wars and the history of the Catholic Church and the treatise on existentialism, I slipped the inkwell back into its place, inside the black ring stained onto the mahogany desk.

I look now for the inkwell, moving papers and books and black-and-white photographs with fraying edges aside; I can't find it. It's not here. But the black ring is here; the stain still stands out prominently amid the scratches and nicks. I run my fingers around and around the stain until I hear my mother calling for me.

Chapter 44

I am going home, back to the tiny town in New England where I grew up, to be one of those millennials who takes Zoom calls from their childhood bedroom. It is not even a charming village with an overly quaint downtown. It is just a small, unremarkable American town, dropped somewhere in the wooded north. There are a few collections of stores and strip malls clustered in various points, loosely gathered under one official boundary. And then the roads sort of spider their way outward, trickling like rivers and streams into the open countryside, past cows and horses and thickets of evergreens. It feels a little bit out of time, out of place. In the winter, it is like living inside a snow globe.

Earlier this year, the newspapers reported that last December, Moscow saw only six minutes of sunlight. Six minutes of direct light. The image in the paper made it seem very romantic—hazy and dark, with the ornate buildings at the center of the city lit up, emanating a warm, golden light. But I know what it is for darkness to descend earlier and earlier each day. To actually feel as though the world is spinning farther and farther away from the sun. For the cold to slip in through the cracks between the windowpanes and the walls. There is nothing romantic about it. Stultifying, perhaps. The way the body turns in on itself to keep warm, and the mind seems to turn in as well.

Alongside the article about Moscow, there was a short announcement that Britain had appointed a minister for loneliness to combat the "serious health problems associated with isolation." I can't help but imagine how Borges might story that moment, that occasion. Perhaps he would send us into a labyrinthine world, in which this unnamed minister, in order to fight loneliness, must become intimately acquainted with it. Will this minister, to become truly expert in loneliness—ostensibly for the sake of eradicating it—necessarily become, herself, the loneliest person in her country?

We drive home together, my mom, my grandmother, and me. The car speeds past former marshlands that now host Target and Walmart, along concrete roads rippled with potholes that sink deeper each winter, past the wooden slats of New England homes, roofs sloping to make sure the snow does not accumulate, porches decorated with cobwebby rocking chairs, red-faced men and women who in the winter will be scraping car windshields, shoveling snow out of driveways and sprinkling coarse salt along the roads. We drive up and down the familiar hills, winding alongside the street corner where I once waited for the school bus, beside the pink house where I was terrified at a Halloween party as a child, past the smaller, brown house where my mother's best friend lives, along the side streets named for types of trees and long since vanished Native American tribes, until we reach the tall, pale-green house where I spent my childhood.

I have always thought it was strange that a house built here—even one as old as ours—should not have been built to properly greet the winter. To properly protect against the cold. My mom took out the great wood-burning fireplace when we moved in, afraid of the smoke and what she assumed to be the inefficiency of such a heating method. Yet after years of gas and propane and a switch-on fireplace and attempts at central heating, we have both begun to doubt that decision. Perhaps a hearth is exactly what this old, rickety home has needed all along.

I start to remember how to slip into the soft banter, the gentle way that consonants are articulated up here in New England. A place imprints itself in tiny, intimate details. I know this place. I know, for example, that the best place to get high is late at night on the golf course behind the airport, because you can lie down on the grass and stare up at the planes flying low overhead. I know about the $5.99 buffet lunch specials at the Chinese restaurant downtown. I can remember when the bookstore on the corner was a cell phone shop, and a boho clothing boutique before that. There's a way in which I belong to this place simply by my knowledge of it.

In the grocery store, I bump into an old, quirky high school English teacher of mine—Mr. James. He is wearing a red cardigan with large buttons that I could swear he used to wear when he was my teacher fifteen years ago. Mr. James used to leave me notes on my essays and response papers recommending additional books, poems, and articles I should read. Once he suggested I connect with a boy in one of his other Honors English sections because our essays had touched on similar themes. That boy and I spent the next two years flirting over AIM, sending lines of poetry back and forth throughout the evenings. Sometimes, he would drive over to my neighborhood at 9:00 or 10:00 p.m. and we'd go on long, chaste walks around the playground at the top of the hill. The summer before we left for college, we kissed beneath the orange glow of a streetlamp and gave each other books of poetry— Billy Collins for me, Yehuda Amichai for him—as goodbye presents. I've never been able to read Billy Collins without thinking of him and the swing at the park and the streetlamp and the awkward summer evening kisses, and regretting that we hadn't spent more evenings kissing and fewer constructing our romance over a screen.

Mr. James has filled his basket with a take-and-bake garlic bread, frozen chicken, a head of lettuce, and some overpriced bars of fair-trade chocolate. I find him in front of the cheese, and even though it has been years, I have that old, embarrassed feeling of coming across my teacher in his regular life, of seeing him as a mere mortal like the rest of us.

So many teachers are impatient. They throw up their hands and snatch the essay or the book or the analysis out of the student's hands to do it themselves. They don't have the language to break the action down into its teachable parts. I think many are afraid that if they unpack the mechanics, they will somehow do an injustice to the magic. That it will be as though there is none. But Mr. James always believed that the mechanics and the magic were not at odds with each other; they were not enemies. A teacher can model magic, can believe in magic, but a teacher must teach mechanics. The building blocks. Then the student will do what she will with them.

When Mr. James would recommend those extra articles and poems and books, I would hurry to read them over the weekends. I often spent my free period in his office arguing about whether Anna Karenina was a sympathetic heroine or not and offering up my own attempts at poetry. Once, after reading one of these attempts, he looked up at me, blue eyes blazing out from his white-bearded face, and said, "The world will be hearing from you soon enough." It was because of Mr. James that I first thought I might like to be a teacher myself.

"Mr. James," I say.

"Yes? Hi—"

"Elena, Elena Berg."

"Well, well, Elena! Look at you. You're home? Visiting your mom?"

"Yes, well, my grandfather died."

"Oh, I'm sorry."

"I came back for the funeral."

"You're living in California, still?"

"Yes."

"How is it? The California dream still going strong?"

"Um—"

"And are you teaching?"

"No. I mean, I was, but—"

"Ah, yes. Not for everyone, the teaching life! Tell me, what are you doing, then?"

"I work in tech."

"Good for you! That's exciting. That's the future. What do you do? What does your company do? Are you saving the world?"

"Probably not anytime soon."

We walk to the checkout aisle together, Mr. James quizzing me on what I am reading, much as he used to when I was fifteen years old. I stumble at his questions, tripping over unformed ideas and clumsy arguments. I remember how Mr. James wanted us all to stop looking at him—or anyone else—to discover what we thought. He demanded that we arrive to class with our own vision, our own ideas about the book or the poem or the short story we had read. He wanted us to become our own teachers, to figure out our own metrics for what we were trying to create or say or do in the world. At the checkout, Mr. James points to me and says to the cashier, "This was one of my best students in my entire career of teaching."

In the parking lot he asks, "How long are you home?"

"I don't know," I say, shading my eyes, the shopping bag cutting into my shoulder. "Maybe a while."

"Done with California?"

"Done? No," I say, caught off guard by his question, "but—"

"Say no more," he said. "Sometimes a spell of being home is just what you need."

"Yeah," I say, "I guess so."

"Say hi to your mom for me," Mr. James says, "and if you're still home once school has gotten going, come by and talk to my class about your tech job. It's the future! They would love to hear about it."

"Thanks," I say. "Okay, yeah."

I walk home and the neighbors wave, each of them older and with more wrinkles than the last time I was home for this long. The shopping bag bounces against my leg, and I pull my sweater close around me, the summer already starting to turn toward fall and the beginning of the school year. Soon there will be bags and bags of leaves piled up at the edges of the street, ready to be picked up by the city. The boys from down the road will come by on weekends with their rakes, offering to clear yards and make piles for $10 an hour. In Berkeley, the flowers are still blooming and the fruit trees are ripening. I didn't even bring a fleece—I'll have to take one out from the mudroom closet before long, if I'm still here, if I stay. *Done with California?* It hadn't crossed my mind. But Mr. James always did have a way of seeing what I couldn't.

Chapter 45

The last summer I was home, we painted the walls of the basement. My mom and I spent the days in ratty old pairs of blue jeans and oversized T-shirts we'd gotten for free from the state fair. We would get up early that summer and try to catch the end of the morning sunrise. Those glorious streaks of pink and orange haze that sat on the horizon like cotton candy. I would wander into the tomato patch and linger there among the twisted, knotted vines. I loved lifting up the leaves and the stalks to find the little plump red tomatoes growing. I remember the way the colors changed each day, yellow turning to orange turning to red, as though each tomato had caught the sunset in its skin.

The basement is both the laundry room and a storage closet. Dryer sheets and detergent pile up on top of the boxes of books and old journals and little tchotchkes that neither of us could throw out. My old bike leans against the wall, rusted yellow with tattered handlebar ribbons and flat tires. It still has a woven basket hanging from the handlebars. Underneath, a little bell. I think my mom enjoyed painting the basement that summer. That it was a welcome break from the hours and hours spent poring over student papers and preparing next semester's lectures. That it was a relief to work with her hands rather than her mind, to fall into a kind of meditative, rhythmic motion with the brush and the paint and the wall.

I do laundry religiously every few days. I do my laundry and my grandmother's and my mother's. I do my sheets and towels. In Berkeley I dragged myself out to the coin-operated laundry machine once a week, maybe every ten days. At home I can't seem to stop doing laundry. It gives a certain sense of order to the week, to my day. When I need a break from Slack or spreadsheets, I go down into the basement and move the laundry to the dryer. I take greater care than I ever have before—I separate my whites from colors; I make sure to clean the lint off the dryer sheet; I hang my delicates to dry.

At dinner, my mom and grandmother psychoanalyze me.

"You're developing OCD," my mom says. "You're trying to regain control."

"I'm just doing the laundry," I say.

"It's more than that," my grandmother says. "You're avoiding something."

"You guys are being ridiculous," I say. "What is this, a therapy session?"

"Since when do you fold your laundry and put it away?" my mom says.

"I'm not sixteen anymore," I say, "I'm an adult now. I take care of my stuff."

"What would Grandpa have to say about all this?"

"He'd tell me the history of laundry machines," I say. "He'd tell me about his mother scrubbing clothes outside in the cold, in a bucket of soapy water."

"Maybe," says my grandmother, "or maybe he'd tell you to stop doing laundry and instead figure out what you want to do with your life."

"What?"

My mom and grandmother look at each other.

"Come on, Elena," my mom said.

"What are you talking about?"

My grandmother squeezes my face in her hand.

"Oh dear," she says, "you'll figure it out."

Being home brings out my family self; the self I was in Berkeley—
friend dates and long walks and sitting at a café on a Saturday afternoon, book in hand—starts to recede to the background. At home, in
the quiet suburban north, I bake apple cake with my grandmother
in between Zoom meetings and crawl into bed at 9:00 p.m. There is
something about eating at the same dining room table, off the same
plates and bowls as I did growing up, about stretching out on the
same blue couches and staring at the same weird abstract art on my
mom's walls, that sends me into a kind of time warp. Where has the
last decade gone? I am eighteen again, filling the dishwasher after
dinner, walking up and down the wooded street listening to the
crickets and the leaf blowers.

My grandmother sits in an armchair and plays operas on the
radio all day long. Sometimes she knits, making a gentle *clack-clack*
sound in time with the music. Other times she is still, silent, barely
breathing. She sees me watching her from the doorway.

"That's how you know," she says.

"Know what?"

"Know that the performer has you. When the whole concert hall
sits holding its breath. No shuffling even between movements. Absolute
stillness. When an audience is still, is quiet, does not even cough out of
turn, then you know that the soprano or the violinist or whoever has

you. Bodies held up as though by marionette strings, hearts beating in time with the conductor. An audience, just like an orchestra, tries to get in sync, to align. To disappear into the music itself, to—in a way—vanish; this is what an audience can do on behalf of the music."

"Do you want tea?" I ask.

"Yes," she says, "with milk."

Sandy has started sending me emails asking when I'm coming back; I ignore her, my inbox filled with unread messages, and drink cup after cup of tea on the porch, wrapped in a woolen blanket, watching the leaves tumble down in slow spirals.

I have conversations with my grandfather in my head.

"Elenoosh, how are you doing?"

"I don't know, Grandpa," I say, "I feel a little lost."

"You know, Elenoosh, I read once that the concept of god in pre-monotheistic religions often contained a belief that by speaking the god's name, an individual could gain some kind of power over the god. That the name could be intoned as a type of summons, a magic of speech that enabled people to call their gods to them, to demand, request, plead from them."

"What are you trying to tell me?"

"There is a kind of power-sharing in this worldview. The god has a certain power, a certain domain that it has influence over—the sea, perhaps, or the rains, or the quality of the crop. But all power is not concentrated in that god. People have power too. Power to invoke the god's presence. Through a name, through an incantation."

"You think I should speak the name of an ancient god?"

"Don't be so literal, Elenoosh."

"I miss you, Grandpa."

"Remember, Elenoosh, there are things that can invoke that which is not ordinarily here. Can make that which is usually otherworldly enter this world. The invisible becomes visible. The hidden made manifest."

Tonight, I crawl into my mother's bed again, unable to sleep. She puts her hand on my back without fully waking and I curl into her, holding my stomach.

"Mom," I say.

"Hmm?"

"I had an abortion." It is the first time I have said it out loud.

She wakes and wraps her arms tight around me. I am crying now, and she holds me while I shake and rubs my back and whispers, "Shh, shh," again and again. When I am calm, she smooths my hair back and I start to drift.

"Don't go back to California," she says, before I am fully asleep. "Stay here. Stay home."

Chapter 46

On my thirteenth birthday, my mom drove me out to the high school parking lot, parked the car and handed me the key. I slid into the front seat and inched and lurched my way around the empty lot, marveling at how cool my mom was, already rehearsing the story I'd tell at school the next day. When I started high school a couple of years later, I took the bus and filed into the gray-and-red brick building along with the others too young, broke, or scared for a permit and a car. I finally started driving myself to school my junior year and felt a satisfying sense of coming full circle whenever I parked in the lot.

In my vague reminiscences about high school, I generally focus on the books I read that blew my mind—*Their Eyes Were Watching God*, *Lord of the Flies*—or the snatches of early romance I had over AIM and under the streetlamps in my neighborhood, or my prom night with the high school tennis star, eating pancakes at 2:00 a.m. and hiking up a mountain to watch the sunrise, wrapped in a woolen blanket to keep the mosquitos at bay; we didn't even kiss when he dropped me off at home. I don't usually dwell on the acne breakouts or year-long fight with my middle school best friend or the nights when I didn't sleep because I was finishing an English paper and math problems and studying for my chemistry quiz and trying to read the twenty-page history assignment about Lucy, our earliest human ancestor. But when I walk through the halls today, on my way to speak to Mr. James's senior English class, it all comes flooding back.

It is smaller than I remember it being, a little less shiny, a little more drab. There are the ramps that lead to the freshman lockers and up to the history wing; the library on the top floor, lined with windows overlooking the tennis courts and the track. The football team played at the middle school field. There is the round auditorium just opposite the cafeteria. Circling the auditorium is a hallway of practice rooms, tiny little lockboxes hosting an upright piano, some rusty music stands, and a bunch of theater and music students who spend every study hall in this wing. In the cafeteria they still sell the sticky, sweet peanut butter cookies I used to live on in high school. I am tempted to get one now as I walk through the green and white halls, past the girls in skinny jeans and oversized sweaters, past the art wing, with charcoal self-portraits tacked up on the walls, past every giggling secret, each new attempt at identity formation, all the ways in which adulthood is grasped at but not quite attained.

Mr. James's class is in the same English classroom I sat in my senior year, writing timed essays to practice for the AP exam. It has been a long time since I stood in front of a classroom—not since that spring when Paula and I trekked around the Bay trying out our prototype close-reading program on unsuspecting middle school students; back when CloseR was CloseReader and I could still draw a straight line connecting the dots of my move to California, my time in TFA, and my pivot to the tech world. For a moment when I walk into the room, I am both student and teacher, each a version of my past self. I call up the high school student in me who sat in these same chairs, itching to get out of this Podunk town, who was sure that college would lead me to great love, great adventure, and great literature. I am the newly minted TFA teacher, standing in the cafeteria as Jay told me I had no classroom for the year, trying to memorize my students' names and bribing them to read with Jolly Ranchers and Starbursts. It is disorienting; I don't quite know where to stand, or where to put my hands.

There is a girl sitting in the middle of the classroom, winding her hair around her fingers and staring dreamily out the window, who reminds me of Anna—bespectacled, unabashed Anna from my second year of teaching at BSA—and suddenly I realize that she would be a senior in high school now, assuming she made it this far. While Mr. James beckons me to the front of the room, ready to introduce me to the wary and slightly bored-looking students, I am back in my classroom at BSA, Anna skipping in late to the first day, announcing in our circle—our restorative justice–inspired circle, throwing around Roam the Buffalo—that that summer she had discovered this amazing poem by Robert Frost. *Two roads diverged within a wood . . .* and I think I took the wrong one.

"Now then," says Mr. James, calling his sleepy-eyed students to attention, "we have a special visitor today, one of our very own. Elena Berg once sat where you sit. She was literally in your shoes, in your chairs, and she's here to tell us there is, in fact, life after high school. She hails from California, the Golden State, land of Steinbeck and Hollywood and Silicon Valley and really tremendous oranges and avocados. But remember, she grew up here in the frozen north, just like you all, so don't write her off just yet. Lend her your ear—she's going to tell you the real truth about things—and then ask her your actual questions about life on the other side. I'll even leave the room if you want."

I'd forgotten just how much Mr. James likes to ham things up, and I both want to roll my eyes and feel my cheeks flush with embarrassment. I haven't really prepared anything; I don't have a SWBAT or a set of objectives. What was it he said? *She's going to tell you the real truth about things.* This was all I had to go on.

"Hi," I said, shifting awkwardly from foot to foot at the front of the classroom. I clear my throat. The students slump in their chairs and look somewhere over my shoulder.

"I'm Elena," I say, starting again, "I just turned thirty; I'm single; I hate my job; and I recently had an abortion."

That gets their attention. Mr. James's mouth falls open ever so slightly, but as the students perk up in their chairs, he closes it, nods to me, and quietly walks out of the classroom.

"I graduated from this high school and went to college, pretty much obsessed with reading novels and poetry. So, I majored in English, and when I graduated from college, I was clear that all I wanted to do was teach. Teach high school maybe, or even middle school. TFA—Teach for America—recruited me pretty hardcore and I fell into place, moving out to the Bay Area to teach seventh-grade English language arts. I thought I was going to change the lives of various twelve- and thirteen-year-olds by reciting my favorite poems to them. But it didn't quite turn out like that."

I pause and look up at the class. The students are staring at me; nobody is chewing gum or twisting their hair or texting under their desks. They're with me. I'd forgotten how much I love this feeling.

"Anyway," I say, "I didn't last long as a teacher—barely made it through the two-year TFA contract."

"Why?" asks a redheaded boy in the back. "What happened?"

"Well," I say, "it turned out I wasn't a very good teacher."

"Why not?"

"I guess," I say, "I guess it's partly because I was too caught up in my own story, in my own idea of what I thought teaching should be, of what I thought I could do. I had all these dreams, but when the dreams didn't jibe with reality, I didn't know what to do. I got scared; I got disheartened; the truth is, I ran."

"Where did you run to?" asks the girl who reminds me of Anna.

"I went to work in tech," I say. "To be fair, edtech . . . I mean, education technology. With another ex-TFAer. I still felt like I was sort of doing what I'd come out to California to do, you know? Not in the classroom, sure, but that was the gist of my work."

"So, what happened?" another student says.

"The company pivoted."

"Pivoted?"

"Yeah. We started out as one thing, doing this education-based thing, but shifted to something else based on user feedback. Meaning, what our customers were telling us they wanted."

"What does it do now?"

"Now? It's a scanner app. I've worked there now for about five years, and every day I feel slightly more bored, slightly more depressed, and generally like I'm doing nothing of value."

"So, why do you stay?"

"Yeah; why don't you quit?"

I sigh. I don't really know how to answer this question. Laziness? Inertia? For a while I was fooling around with Jesse and so it was fun to go to the office?

"Wait, wait," says another, "what about the abortion? You had an abortion? What happened? Can we ask?"

"Honestly," I say, "it was such a weird time. I mean, I had this serious boyfriend for the first few years I lived in the Bay. As in, I kind of thought we'd get married, that he was 'the one.' But like everything else, relationships in my twenties don't seem to have worked out the way I imagined."

"So, he's not the dad?"

"Kyle? No, no not at all. We broke up a long time ago, after my tech company pivoted. We were on different trajectories, couldn't seem to get past the ways in which we kept disappointing each other."

"Then, who?"

"This guy at work. We weren't even really dating, just . . . something more than hooking up but less than dating, if that makes sense. We started out as really good friends."

"But you didn't want the baby?"

"No," I say. "No, I didn't. My mom was a single mom, and I mean, I just saw . . . I saw how hard it was."

A few of the kids shift in their seats, nod their heads. I rush on.

"But just because I knew I didn't want to have a baby—at least not right now—that's not to say getting the abortion was easy or anything. The whole thing felt . . . violating. Even though it was my choice. It was like my body was having this whole other experience than my head, than what my brain was telling me I wanted. I didn't want to become a mom or have a baby, but that's what my body was doing, just all on its own. And then I stopped it. Which was the right call for me. But I was pretty messed up for a while afterward. I mean, maybe I still am. I haven't even told Jesse—"

I catch myself. I'm standing in a high school classroom—am I even allowed to talk about this? Aren't half of them already having sex? I don't totally know what I'm trying to say to them.

"But anyway. I've always heard that the time to have a baby is when you're ready for things not to be all about you. And, yeah. I'm definitely not at that stage. I have so much to figure out still."

"Huh," says a kid in the back, "I kind of thought by thirty people had things figured out."

I laugh. "Yeah," I say, "I thought so, too. And then I turned thirty."

The class is quiet for a moment, and I wonder if we're done, if I should go find Mr. James.

"What's Cali like?" asks a girl with dark brown curls that are scraped back into a ponytail.

Heads nod; they want stories of sun and beach and fifty-degree winters and anything that's different from this cold, sleepy town.

"It's a lot of things," I say. "Sometimes it feels like there are many Californias all loaded up into one."

"Okay, what's the moral?" asks a kid at the front.

"The moral?" I say.

"Yeah," he says. "Like, what's the moral of your story?"

"There's no moral," I reply, "I'm just telling you where I'm at right now, and what my life's been like since graduating from high school."

Mr. James opens the door to the classroom and sticks his head in cautiously, trying to assess how much talk of unprotected sex and abortion might be going on. I nod to him; the coast is clear. He comes in, jaunty-like, smiling, straightening his checkerboard waistcoat without a hint of irony.

"Right, then," says Mr. James, "how are we doing?"

"Fine," I say. "Just fine."

The class is corralled back to an analysis of last night's reading in *Everything Is Illuminated* and I slip out the back, my hands sweating from the hot air blowing into the school from every vent. I wander the hallways; I start to obsess about the things I said—wasn't I supposed to be inspiring? Encouraging? Wasn't I supposed to talk about how to make a career in tech? Had I really stood up there and created a personal little pity party? The bell rings and I don't even notice;

the hallways are flooded with high schoolers, backpacks slung over shoulders, elbowing their way to their next class, to lunch, to the bathroom. Mr. James finds me in the throng. He takes me by the arm and steers me back to the English wing, to the teacher lounge, where he pours himself a cup of coffee.

"They loved you!"

"What?"

"You were a total hit."

"Are you kidding me?"

"Of course not; they couldn't stop talking about you. How 'real' you were; you didn't bullshit them, didn't give them any platitudes. They appreciate that."

"Huh."

"Sit down," Mr. James says. "Have some coffee."

I sit and Mr. James plunks a mug of hot, weak coffee in front of me.

"Listen," he says, "what are you doing?"

"What do you mean?"

"I mean, what are you *doing*? With yourself? With your life? I heard what you said before I fled. You hate your job, eh?"

"I guess so," I say, the mug at my lips. "I don't think I fully realized it until I said it just now."

"So, what are you going to do?"

"I honestly don't know."

"I have a proposition."

"Okay?"

"Why not come and teach here? At the school?"

"Teach *here*? At my high school?"

"Sure. Why not? You clearly have a knack for getting through to the kids. We have a big freshman class this year; we're looking to create another English section next semester."

"Teach again. Wow."

"Listen, think on it, okay?"

"Okay, I will. Thank you."

"But don't think too long. I'll need an answer by Thanksgiving."

"Okay."

"Now, then," he says, sitting back in his chair, "tell me what you think about the narrator in *Everything Is Illuminated*."

When I leave the school, the air is flush with fall and the promise of winter. Leaves are piled up in crunchy brown mounds along the path to the parking lot. Once, when I was a freshman in high school, I slipped and fell on this icy path, wiping out as I hobbled to the front door in fashionable but impractical boots. A boy I was not friends with saw me stumble, and I readied myself for the smirk, the snicker. But instead, he nodded sympathetically and reached out his hand to help me up.

"Happened to me just the other day," he said, while I brushed the snow and ice crystals off my jeans.

I get into my mom's blue Subaru and turn on the seat warmer, settling into the plush seats, and then I put the car in reverse and pull out onto the street, passing Target and McDonald's and T.J.Maxx as I drive the fifteen minutes home.

Chapter 47

The summer after I graduated from high school, my friends and I used to go on long drives. One of us would be responsible for the music, the soundtrack, and inevitably at some point we'd be blasting Enya while driving past marshland destined to become part of the spreading shopping mall. So much of what we talked about that summer, as we parked atop a hill overlooking more hills, was getting out. Getting out of this town, out there, to the "real world." We were all leaving; I don't think I knew anyone who was planning to stick around, though I've heard or seen on Facebook the ones who did or who came back. The ones who got pregnant and got married and bought houses next to the middle school; the ones who sit in the bar downtown and play jazz music with their high school buddies and the band teacher. I always felt a type of pity for them and a sense of superiority that I had gotten out, and stayed out.

"Not forever," Mr. James had said to me when I left the school the other day. A "course correction," he had called it. Just to get me back in the classroom. A reset. It's a familiar story. In *The Wizard of Oz*, Dorothy wakes from her dream and finds she doesn't need to go anywhere for adventure, everything she needs is in her own backyard; in *The Alchemist*, the treasure that sparks the shepherd's journey around the world turns out to be buried under a tree in the shepherd's own pasture. Is this what's happening to me now? Am I being called home, back from my California adventure, back to the classroom, back to my own high school? Is my end in my beginning?

I remember, in the early months of my relationship with Kyle, we would kiss, and it felt like a piece of me dying. Dying to grant space so that he may be. And he was dying too. We were killing myself and himself, to make space for ourself. What part of me is dying now, I wonder? What am I trying to make space for?

I write to Amelia, hoping for clarity.

To: Amelia Carr
From: Elena Berg
Subject: Home
Ame,

I have an offer, a teaching job. It feels like an offer for a life. For the woods. For clean air. A life in which getting out of the driveway sometimes requires two hours of shoveling, and scraping windshields, and turning the car on thirty minutes before go-time. Just to make sure it's warm. A life of ironing my skirts on Sunday afternoons and making sure essays have been written and chapters read. A life of staying up to date on neighborhood gossip, of recognizing people by their dogs, of bumping into my high school teachers in Hannaford. Of teaching alongside them.

I hardly recognize myself. Tell me, what would you do?
Love,
Elena

To: Elena Berg

From: Amelia Carr

Subject: Re: Home

Elena,

Last night I went to a concert and I wondered, does music sweep through the years like a dust storm, picking up bits and pieces as it goes? Changing its shape slightly with the additional weight, the additional memories. If the Kreutzer Sonata could look at its reflection now, in some mirror, in some darkened window, would it recognize itself? Would it see laid out before it, like a prism, all the performances by young and old, master and novice, throughout the centuries? When it is performed now, is it as though every past performance lies within it?

And in the end, if the ship still sails, if the violin still plays, what does it matter if it was the same as it was when it began? Even if all its parts were intact, surely after its journey, after its performance, after our life—it could not be the same. How can we be the same as we were when we began? Why would we want to be?

You always were trying to follow in your mother's footsteps. You followed her out to California. Maybe now you are following her back home.

Besos y abrazos,

A.

My mother. Things always seem to come back to my mother. I've been chasing my mother—the vision of my mother—since the summer we drove to upstate New York and she handed me her stories, of tripping acid on Mount Tam and stuffing a chicken down her pants, of picking apples and hitchhiking to Berkeley, of Weathermen and bomb parts and multiple sex partners and wasted nights leading to wasted days filled with hazy dreams. Everything tinged with story truth, with capital-*F* Freedom and capital-*P* Purpose. I've been running after her for so long I can barely see back to my own beginnings. My mother lit my path to California. She laid the bricks with each memory, dropped bread crumb after bread crumb with each new anecdote.

The thing is, though, I'm not like her.

She kept teaching, and I did not.

She had the baby. And I did not.

Chapter 48

On LinkedIn I am prompted to congratulate Paula on her work anniversary at Asana and I am surprised that a year has passed already. A year since the fires in Napa and Sonoma; a year since Paula left CloseR; a year since Kyle left the Bay. Of late, I've been checking up on Kyle on Facebook, going down rabbit holes of what-ifs. He has a girlfriend; she works at the same farm—at least, that's what it looks like from the pictures he posts. They look good together, and I feel only the slightest hint of regret, of disappointment. I want to tell him about my job offer—there is still a part of me that seeks his approval, that wants to prove to him I am the version of myself he wanted me to be. And wouldn't taking this teaching job in some ways be the mirror image of what Kyle did in the past year? He, too, left the Bay to go back home. I want to ask, did it feel like giving up to him, too? Instead, I open my phone to text Paula. I send her a message and she replies immediately:

Paula: *Elena!!! Where on earth have u been? u fell off the face of the earth*

Me: *Haha, sry. I'm at home . . . my grandpa died.*

Paula: *omg so sorry :(:(:(*

Me: *thanks*

Paula: *I miss you! And so does Jesse btw . . . u really need to talk to him*

Me: . . .

Paula: *srsly! He's worried about u*

I am avoiding Jesse. I've been avoiding him since I first saw the positive pregnancy test, since I went to the abortion clinic alone and came home alone, since I turned thirty and my grandfather died, and I left the Bay and have yet to return. I've been telling myself that the time we spent sleeping together, that period of post-traumatic Trump disorder, of never quite crossing the line into commitment, into relationship, that it was just a fluke, just an extended hookup. A time to actualize the tension built up over years of weekend hikes and company retreats and late nights trading travel stories. Nothing more than that. If there were to have been a baby, I would have thought it would come out of my years with Kyle, out of shared laundry and petty arguments at breakfast and that unparalleled feeling of being cared for that came from watching him scrub the mold off the bathroom ceiling.

To abort. Underneath the dictionary entries that have to do with terminating a pregnancy or miscarrying, things start to expand; the meaning opens up. *To terminate prematurely. To stop in the early stages.* There has been so much stopping and starting for me in the last years, so many moments of "pivoting," of going down a new path, of creating and re-creating and dismantling. How do we know when we should pause, when we should terminate the mission, and when we should allow it to continue, to go to term, to birth whatever it has to birth?

I start to make lists. Lists upon lists. The weather has turned, and I am ransacking my mom's closet, pulling out wool sweaters with oversized buttons and long knit cardigans whose pockets hold trinkets from years past—an embroidered handkerchief, an earring without its pair. I work from my bed, the blankets pulled up to my waist. I've cleared the wall behind me of the Beatles posters I hung in high school and I hold Zoom meetings from here, propped up against my pillow. In between meetings I continue with my lists. Reasons to stay and reasons to go. I list the weather and the food. I look up apartments at home on Craigslist and I am floored by how much cheaper it is here than the Bay. I list the cost of living. I am just circling around and around the question. Where can I live out the version of myself I want to be?

I have become stuck; the Bay has wrapped its spell around me, and I am clinging to an old dream of California—my mother's dream. The one in which poets and protesters live and work and love together; the one in which People's Park is not a dumping ground or a homeless encampment; the one in which teachers can afford to live in the same community in which they work; the one in which the fires do not burn, and the sky is not filled with smoke. I am clinging to the dream of gold diggers and beatniks, of that sense of wildness along the Pacific coast, of the way the sea cuts into the craggy rock, the way persimmons and figs ripen on trees just outside my window, the way a person with a computer and an idea can unhinge the system as it is currently known.

This dream of California offers no explanation for the tent cities that have cropped up over the years under overpasses and alongside BART stations; there is no room for the priced-out artists and teachers or the hiked-up rent, for the needles or the cardboard houses or the man at West Oakland asking for money. This dream of California glosses over the millennial millionaires and their pot brownies and Vuori sweatpants, over the unaffordable yoga classes and green smoothies and gym memberships. The gold-tinged California with million-dollar homes furnished with West Elm beds and Persian rugs in gentrified neighborhoods where the lattes are small and frothy and vegan and oh so expensive. Underneath the shine, it turns out, things are a lot more tarnished.

Maybe the myth of California is just that—a myth. And maybe, after everything that's happened, after the classroom and the startup, the relationship and the hookup, the idealism and the realism, and the piecemeal way in which I have slowly stepped out of alignment with myself, it is time for me to acknowledge that I am done with California. That California is done with me.

As the first snow of the season falls, I sit down to write an email to Andy.

To: Andy Michaelson
From: Elena Berg
Subject: Notice
October 30, 2018

Dear Andy,

This letter is to give you two weeks' notice of my official resignation as a Project Manager at CloseR.

It has been a pleasure working with you and the team, first at CloseReader, and then at CloseR. Thank you for the opportunity to learn and grow along with you all.

If there is anything I can do to ease the transition, please let me know.

Warmly,
Elena Berg

I click "send," then pick up the phone and call Jesse.

Chapter 49

It is fire season again in California, and even though I am in New England, where the air is clear and there is frost on the windows, I check the air quality index for Berkeley religiously, watching the map go from green to yellow to orange to red to purple, a color-coded representation of toxicity. The fires have been burning all fall, since the late summer when I came back East for the funeral, and they haven't really stopped since then. They were in the north, up by Redding and Lassen, winding up into the border with Oregon, and in the south, sending out columns of smoke and fire at the top and bottom of the state.

But now a fire has started in Paradise, just north of the Bay. They say it spread so quickly that there was hardly any time for evacuation orders. The community has been pulverized; people are hunkering down in Walmart parking lots, posting the names of missing loved ones on social media and in front of shelters. And in Berkeley, the air has turned black and gray with soot and ash. Schools are closed; families are fleeing. There are lines and lines of people trying to buy masks.

"I'm so glad you're not there," my mom says to me at dinner.

"Yes," I say, looking down at the table, pushing the little fragments of Brussels sprout leaves to the edge of my plate.

"Have you talked with Mr. James yet?" she asks.

"No," I say, "not yet."

"Well, don't make him wait too long," she says, "now that you've given notice."

In the week since I gave notice, I have been spending my days working on handoff documents, dumping my knowledge of CloseR onto spreadsheets and Dropbox Paper docs lined with comments from Andy. My mom has been clearing space in the attic.

"You'll need it," she says, "for all your stuff."

"My stuff?"

"Yes," she says, "when you ship all your stuff home from Berkeley. Are you going to go back to pack up? Or just hire movers?"

"Oh," I say, "I don't—"

"You don't have to decide just yet," she says, "but it does seem silly to keep paying rent, don't you think?"

I feel a type of haze settling over me, as though I am walking through smoky air in the early morning. Giving notice to CloseR had felt euphoric for a moment, a burst of certainty, of taking action, of getting unstuck. My mom and grandmother took it as given that it meant I had decided to say yes to Mr. James, to say yes to leaving California and coming back home. Clarity, though, is elusive. Each time I pick up the phone to call Mr. James, I can't seem to dial the number. I spend hours in bed each day, computer on my lap, extricating myself from the myriad online systems and calendars and messaging apps that have threaded my life, in the last few years, to a bunch of engineers and sales reps, to an edtech turned just-tech, to Paula, to Jesse, to karaoke nights and Thursday afternoon happy hours, to weekends in Tahoe and Yosemite and Joshua Tree, to the Enneagram, and even to Kyle, since we were together when I started, since we ended when I continued. Soon, I will no longer be accosted

by Slack messages or calendar reminders or Zoom invites. My phone
will go quiet; my inbox will consist solely of skincare ads and Planned
Parenthood updates. The tech apparatus that dictates my days, that
dings me to sleep and rings me awake, will shut down, turn off, go on
silent mode indefinitely. Maybe then I'll be able to hear myself think.

Tomorrow is my last day at CloseR. It is snowing again, and I am
standing at the window watching for the plows to come up the street.
I know they will come, and then they will send great mounds of snow
up and over the fence into the yard and my mom will call one of
the neighborhood boys to come up and shovel a path. But for now,
the snow is just falling. Big, soft clumps of it falling as though in
slow motion out of the white sky. It will be dark soon and the orange
streetlight will catch the snowflakes in its glow.

Thinking about the end of my time at CloseR—perhaps the end
of my time in California—I feel that lurch in my stomach, that feeling that lies somewhere between fear and euphoria. It's like the way
I felt when I bungee jumped one summer during college. Terrified
and elated. Falling and rising. And even then, I knew that everything,
every moment, every thought, every feeling, contains within it all
the similar moments that have come before. The way that when I see
the ocean now, or a mountain, I also see every other mountain and
ocean I've ever stood in front of. And it's not just that I see those past
images; I also see—I also become, for an instant—the person I was
when I saw that other ocean, or that other mountain, or that other
snowstorm. Sometimes I feel that the specters of a thousand previous
selves hover around me at all times. And which self will I become
tomorrow? When I sign off for the last time? When, perhaps, I send
Sandy my last rent check?

I suppose I am standing here almost hoping that the snow will carry on through the night, that it will create a kind of pause, such that everything grinds to a halt. To still time, to pause the endless current for a night. The roads won't be drivable. The post office will be closed. Tomorrow, the basement will smell of freshly fallen snow, damp socks on feet slipped from muddy boots, and the warm, dry scent of laundry. I think I am hoping that the snow will stretch out this night for me. And that the end will not come for just a little while longer.

Chapter 50

It is Thanksgiving, and as my grandmother makes pumpkin pie and stuffing, my mom and I argue while clearing the table of piled-up bills and unread magazines, spreading a crimson red tablecloth over the gnarled and knotted wooden farm table.

"This is a good move you're making," she says. "It's high time you got out of the ballerina phase."

"The what?"

"The ballerina phase. You know, the phase in which you don't quite exist within reality. You're still living in the vision, the imagined possibility."

"'I dwell in Possibility . . .'"

"Hmm?"

"Emily Dickinson. And I haven't actually made a decision, you know. I mean, I left CloseR, but I haven't accepted Mr. James's offer yet."

"You will, though. You need to look out for yourself, be realistic."

"I don't know that I want to teach in my old high school, though, Mom. It feels like going backward."

"It's a job, Elena. And you can't just sit around waiting for the perfect opportunity to come and knock on your door."

"It's not that."

"What is it then?"

"It's just. Leaving California feels like giving up, like calling quits on my dreams. Didn't you feel that way, too? When you left?"

"I was so strung out I can't even remember."

We are quiet for a while; the winter sky is gray, with bursts of bright light streaming through the clouds. My grandmother hums that old Yiddish lullaby in the kitchen. We fold napkins, place wineglasses next to water glasses.

"Are you following the results of the midterms?" I ask. "It's a huge sweep. We've got the House. So many women won; so many progressives."

"I'm not sure that's something to celebrate."

"Are you kidding?"

"We need to get Trump out in two years; I don't think radical politics is the way to go."

"Since when did you get so jaded? You were the one telling me to go trip acid on a mountain overlooking the ocean. What about all your stories of marching down Telegraph Avenue?"

"I grew up, Elena. Did anything actually come from all that noise we were making in Weathermen? Did anything actually change?"

"What? Of course it did—I mean, progress doesn't happen overnight."

"We ran around thinking we were making a difference, too, and in the end, we still all had to take care of what was ours. No one was going to do that for us."

"So, what? Nothing really matters?"

"Don't be dramatic."

"I honestly didn't know you felt this way."

"You thought I was still my twenty-five-year-old self, wandering around Berkeley, lost and high?"

"I don't know."

"Look, it's an old story. You can't get it all. You've got to take what you can and look out for your own needs."

Later, after a hastily eaten and stilted Thanksgiving dinner, I am in my room, watching the light fade from the sky. My grandmother knocks softly on my door and comes to sit beside me on the bed. She takes my hand.

"I don't understand her," I say.

"Things repeat themselves," my grandmother says.

"What do you mean?"

"I was listening to you two."

"I'm sorry—"

"No, no. I was listening, and it was like it was fifty years ago in Brooklyn, listening to your mom fight it out with your grandfather."

"Geez."

"Different details, but same idea. The younger generation berates the older; the parent tries to keep the child close, safe."

"What's the point then?"

"What do you mean?"

"Seriously, what's the point? If we're all just going to repeat the same argument on and on through the generations, what's the point?"

My grandmother squeezes my hand; she smooths the covers on my bed.

"Your grandpa would probably say that's the wrong question," she says.

"Well, what's the right one?"

She kisses me on the cheek and stands up.

"I'll ask him," she says, "when I see him again. In the meantime, Elenoosh, you just need to figure out what you're going to do next."

She closes the door behind her; I can hear her and my mom

cleaning up downstairs, the light noise of their conversation falling like rain.

Rain.

It is raining in California, raining in the Bay. My social media feed is lighting up with the news. It is raining and the smoke has cleared; the fire has been contained. It is raining and things are washing clean; the air is sweet and wet, the ash no longer hanging in the atmosphere like an unbidden storm cloud. It is raining and the reservoirs are filling; the almond trees are soaking up water from the earth; the redwoods are scraping their needles against the sky, the fog, replenishing themselves. It is raining and Sandy and John will be sitting on the porch drinking chai, a third cup next to them, ready for me.

I get up from the bed, the bed I got in middle school, when I was done with bunk beds. The comforter is the same one that's been on the bed since then, a dark green corduroy with big wooden buttons. I feel as if I have never really looked at it until now. I remember when I tried—and failed—to teach my first-year students Elizabeth Bishop's poem "The Fish." I had wanted to talk about what it is to really look at something or someone. How when we really look, we move beyond our initial prejudices and biases, we move past our expectations and our fixed mindsets, and begin to see things as they are, see people for themselves and not the images we have of them. I wanted them to experience—through poetry—the way we can transform our vision, our relationships, moving to the ecstasy of everything becoming "rainbow, rainbow, rainbow."

I get up from the bed and take down a book of poems from the bookshelf. I flip to Adrienne Rich's "Diving into the Wreck." "I came to explore the wreck," she writes, "the thing I came for: / the wreck and not the story of the wreck / the thing itself and not the myth . . ."

The lines are heavily underlined and circled; I have read this before. I wonder, now, if I have been looking at everything all wrong, have been looking only at the myths and not the things themselves . . . I am the dreamer in search of a dream, and I have been running after a dream of my mother, a dream of teaching, a dream of California, and a dream of myself. At each turn I have found myself confronted with the way my story of the thing does not fully align with the thing itself. And what choices have I made then? To quit? To pivot? To abort? To leave?

Is there not a way to look, to see things as they are, and to stay? To stare and stare, as Bishop did at the great, ugly fish stuck on her hook, until she came to admire it? To find its wisdom and its beauty?

And have I not learned this before, thought this before? In a yoga class long ago, when the teacher asked us to stay in chair pose, and I felt, as I squatted with knees bent, as my thighs began to shake, that I simply could not stay one second longer.

But then, I did. For one more inhale. For one more exhale.

I reach up and take down the suitcase in my closet. I start to pack.

It is raining, and I am not yet done with California. California itself, and not the myth.

It is raining and I need to go and see it for what it is, to see myself for what I am. Myself and not my reflection; myself and not the myth. To look and then to ask: can I stay? Can I stay with whatever it is that I find?

It is raining, and I am going home.

California, I'm coming home.

Acknowledgments

Some profound gratitude:

To my editor, Melissa K. Wrapp, who understood the voice and vision of this book and brought it forth with grace and finesse, I am beyond grateful.

To the whole team at She Writes Press, for helping to fulfill a lifelong dream—thank you! I'm honored to be a part of this visionary women's publishing project.

Thank you to my earliest readers, Joel Abramovitz, Nikki Lev, Noah Hoch, Zvika Krieger, and Crystal Sands, for your generosity, time, attentive reading, notes, and words of encouragement. You helped bring this project from shitty first draft to actual book, and you lifted me up when I felt discouraged.

Thank you to all those who told me stories of their own TFA experience—especially Hanna Sufrin, for insight you offered into the role of poetry in the classroom.

To the teachers "who asked questions I still [turn] over in my mind late at night, who gave me books and poems and essays to read that spun my brain into fire," this book owes much to you. Thank you especially to my high school teachers Mrs. Jones, Ms. Thibedeau, and Mr. Ames, who started me on this journey; to my college poetry professor, Peter Sacks, who introduced me to many of the poems in this book; and to my MFA advisor, Chanan Tigay, whose writing wisdom and belief in me continues to buoy me to this day.

To my beloved Bay Area chosen family—Adina Allen, Jeff Kasowitz, Joel Abramovitz, Beth Midanik-Blum, Andrew Gordon-Kirsch, and Talia Cooper—thank you, thank you for celebrating, supporting, loving, holding, and being with me along this whole crazy journey! You are my California dream.

To all my wonderful siblings, siblings-in-law, nieces, and nephews, thank you for the big love! Thank you particularly to Danny Cohen, for all the ways we have grown up together; to Max Cohen and Tsipe Angelson, for the many Berkeley walks and chats while this book came into being; and to Ilana Silver, for being, at times, the "one reader" for whom I was writing.

To my sister-friends Hannah Kapnik Ashar and Nikki Lev, thank you, thank you. To Hannah, for the gift of a lifelong *chevruta* and for loving me all along the way to here. And to Nikki: has ever there been a marriage of truer minds? For a long-ago conversation about *Anna Karenina*, and all the ones before and after; above all, thank you for walking this life with me.

To my parents-in-law, Tammy and Andy Cohen, thank you so much for giving me a home in which to finish the first draft, and for all the ways you have taken care of us over the years.

Thank you to my grandfather Thomas Fitzpatrick (*z"l*) for the endless stories, the endless cups of tea, for endlessly believing in me.

To my parents, Noreen and Phillip Silver. This is in your honor. Thank you for showing me that this is possible.

To my magical daughters, Alma and Leila Cohen-Silver. The gift of each of you takes my breath away time and time again. Thank you for all the ways you bring me back to presence. And thank you, too, for the naps you took as babies (both on and off me), during which I wrote and then edited this book.

Finally, to you, Jack. For the gift of a typewriter many years ago, and everything every day since.

Permissions

"The Summer Day" by Mary Oliver
Reprinted by the permission of The Charlotte Sheedy Literary Agency as agent for the author.
Copyright © 1990, 2006, 2008, 2017 by Mary Oliver with permission of Bill Reichblum

Excerpts from "The Fish" from POEMS by Elizabeth Bishop. Copyright © 2011 by The Alice H. Methfessel Trust. Publisher's Note and compilation copyright © 2011 by Farrar, Straus and Giroux. Reprinted by permission of Farrar, Straus and Giroux. All Rights Reserved.

Excerpts from Poems by Elizabeth Bishop published by Chatto & Windus. Copyright © The Alice H. Methfessel Trust, 2011. Reprinted by permission of The Random House Group Limited.

Excerpt from "A Blessing" from The Branch Will Not Break ©1963 by James Wright. Published by Wesleyan University Press. Used by permission.

Wendell Berry, excerpts from ["It is hard to have hope. It is harder

About the Author

photo credit: Nicole Lev

Noa Silver was born in Jerusalem and raised between Scotland and Maine. After receiving her BA in English and American literature and language from Harvard University, Noa lived and taught English as a Second Language on Namdrik—part of the Republic of the Marshall Islands and the smallest inhabited atoll in the world. She later completed her MFA in creative writing from San Francisco State University and then worked as an editor on various oral history projects, ranging from an archive documenting the Partition of India and Pakistan to a cancer researcher telling the stories of trauma experienced by cancer survivors. Noa lives in Berkeley, California, with her husband, Jack, and their two daughters, Alma and Leila.

SELECTED TITLES FROM SHE WRITES PRESS

She Writes Press is an independent publishing company founded to serve women writers everywhere. Visit us at www.shewritespress.com.

Andrea Hoffman Goes All In by Diane Cohen Schneider
$17.95, 978-1-64742-099-4
Written for everyone who's had a love/hate relationship with their job, this smart, funny novel by a former Wall Street sales pro reveals what it was like for a woman to build a successful career and a satisfying personal life in the macho world of 1980s stock trading.

My Thirty-First Year: (And Other Calamities) by Emily Wolf
$17.95, 978-1-64742-082-6
In this funny, unfiltered coming-of-age story, Zoe Greene approaches her 30th birthday grappling with abortion, divorce, family drama, and the modern dating pool—and discovers hope and resilience along the way.

Unreasonable Doubts by Reyna Marder Gentin. $16.95, 978-1-63152-413-4
Approaching thirty and questioning both her career path and her future with her long-time boyfriend, jaded New York City Public Defender Liana Cohen gets a new client—magnetic, articulate, earnest Danny Shea. When she finds herself slipping beyond the professional with him, she is forced to confront fundamental questions about truth, faith, and love.

After Perfect by Maan Gabriel. $16.95, 978-1-64742-203-5
When the only man thirty-six-year-old Gabriella Stevens has ever loved walks out on her, she feels like her world is ending—but as she begins to forge her own way forward for the first time in her life, she discovers an inner resilience and strength that she never knew she possessed.

In a Silent Way by Mary Jo Hetzel. $16.95, 978-1-63152-135-5
When Jeanna Kendall—a young white teacher at a progressive urban school—becomes involved with a community activist group, she finds herself grappling with issues of racism, sexism, and oppression of various shades in both her professional and personal life.